EPICENTER

OTHER BOOKS AND AUDIO BOOKS
BY SONIA O'BRIEN:

Perfect Shot

The Raging Sea

EPICENTER

a novel by

SONIA O'BRIEN

Covenant Communications, Inc.

Covenant

Cover image: *Composite Image of a Chart and a Richter Scale,* photography by Jason Reed ©
Photodisc/Getty Images. www.gettyimages.com

Cover design copyrighted 2008 by Covenant Communications, Inc.

Published by Covenant Communications, Inc.
American Fork, Utah

Printed in Canada
First Printing: September 2008

14 13 12 11 10 09 08   10 9 8 7 6 5 4 3 2 1

ISBN 13: 978-1-59811-598-7
ISBN 10: 1-59811-598-4

ACKNOWLEDGMENTS

I would like to express my gratitude to the firefighters of the Conway, Arkansas, Central Fire Department, with special recognition extended to Captain Danny Shock. The information they provided was extremely helpful. To my readers' group—Kyler, Vickie, Buffie, Jesse, Haley, and Emily—as well as to my family, I love you all and appreciate the gifts you are in my life. Thanks also to Pam Sheperd for her helpful tidbits. Finally, I would like to express my love and gratitude to my Heavenly Father, whose hand is evident in everything around us.

CHAPTER ONE

Thursday, April 17 / New York City

"But he's guilty!" McKenna Bradford exclaimed, her green eyes flashing and her cheeks instantly competing with the hue of her long auburn hair.

"It doesn't matter," Lawrence countered as he sat down heavily in the black leather chair behind his large mahogany desk. "The officer neglected to read him his Miranda rights."

"So because of some technicality this lunatic is going to walk?" McKenna snapped as she began pacing back and forth in her father's spacious office. "If anyone deserves to spend the rest of his life behind bars—if not worse—it's that monster!"

"You know as well as I do that our judicial system is one of law and order."

"What about right and wrong?" McKenna spouted, all semblance of professionalism overcome by her passion. "Do we sacrifice all decency on the altar of bureaucracy?"

"McKenna," Lawrence Bradford replied testily, the fatigue of the last few hours weighing heavily on his features, "as defense attorneys we have a job to do. Right or wrong, guilty or innocent, our job is to see that the governing laws are enforced. If we forsake these laws, *these rules*, what will differentiate us from the lawless?"

McKenna began to shake her head. It was the same lecture she'd been spoon-fed as a child. But she was unable to override the mental image of their client smiling cruelly at the husband of his victim once he had been acquitted.

"This is wrong," she said quietly.

"McKenna, it's been a long day. Go home. Take tomorrow off."

"I can't do this anymore," she said, shaking her head again. She walked toward the window, her insides churning until she thought she might be sick. "I can't!"

When her father remained silent, she turned back to face him. He was riffling through a stack of paperwork on his desk, his face impassive. "Did you hear what I said?" she asked.

"I heard you," he said, his tone even and calm as he lifted his gaze to meet hers. "Now go home."

McKenna stalked to her Lexus, unable to smother the bitterness that seemed to heighten with each step. It was the same old story. Though her father had heard her, he hadn't *heard* her. McKenna shook her head in frustration. She'd completed four years of college, then four more years of law school, for what? For *whom?* She had known from the start that she didn't share her father's passion for law, but she had tried to convince herself otherwise through the years. Why did she want—*need*—his approval so badly? Was she willing to surrender who she was to attain it? The fact that she was twenty-eight years old and asking that very question was answer enough. She let her breath out in an explosion of self-deprecation, then climbed into her car and slammed the door.

The thirty-minute drive to her New York City apartment did little to improve her mood. After kicking off her expensive high heels at the door and checking her answering machine, she plopped down on her overstuffed couch. Her eyes went immediately to the manuscript pages scattered across her coffee table. With a tired sigh, she began to carefully organize the stack, chiding herself for a dream she knew would never be fulfilled. She was a defense attorney, not a writer. She accepted this, and even found a degree of satisfaction in vindicating the innocent. The enigma that remained, however, the part that she couldn't quite come to terms with, lay in forgiving herself when the opposite was true.

Her eyes lifted to the view of the city provided by the large, full-length windows before her. She frowned, knowing that the view, which had cost her father a pretty penny, was just one more anchor that held her to a life she didn't want. Not only that, but it showed how very little her father really knew about her. McKenna was terrified of heights and had been since she was a child. She couldn't get within four feet of her living room windows without her palms instantly becoming damp and her heart racing. She let out a labored sigh before reaching for the cordless phone on her glass coffee table. The familiar baritone voice she heard seconds later brought an instant smile to her face.

"Hi, James. You wouldn't be up for some Chinese, would you?"

"*Chinese?*" he asked groggily. "McKenna, it's ten-thirty at night!"

McKenna looked down at her watch. "Okay, how about a late-night snack? I think I still have a little rocky road in the freezer."

"Not anymore," he said, and McKenna heard him yawn. "I finished that two nights ago, but you were too preoccupied with your briefs to notice."

"Sorry, I guess I have been a little distracted lately. It's this case."

"Just the McKenna girl I know and love," he teased. "By the way, how *did* you do in court today?"

"I got an acquittal," she offered, her voice lacking any trace of triumph.

"And that's a bad thing?"

"It is in this case," she said soberly. "Anyway, how did your date go last night?" she asked, anxious to change the subject.

"Same old, same old. I do real well until I mention the part where I'm a starving artist whose paintings probably won't sell for any real money until long after I'm dead."

"You mean she didn't fall for your we-can-just-live-on-love-and-ramen-noodles speech?"

"Okay, so maybe I need a different approach . . . especially on a first date."

McKenna laughed, reminded again why she adored him. "Maybe. And maybe I should take my father's advice and learn to celebrate a win without analyzing every moral detail."

"Tell you what—I'll be over in fifteen minutes with emergency junk food for both of us."

"Make it chocolate and it's a date."

When McKenna opened the door twenty minutes later, James was standing in the doorway wearing a white T-shirt speckled with multicolored paint from his latest project, and a pair of faded blue jeans. His whole face lit up with a smile as he held out a chocolate bar and a half gallon of rocky road.

"I love you!" McKenna grinned.

"Me or the chocolate?" James asked, cocking his head to the side accusingly, though his blue eyes danced with pleasure.

"Both," she said, taking a step forward and kissing his cheek. When she stepped back, her eyes went to a few wayward strands of his sandy-brown hair, still ruffled from sleep. "I'm sorry I woke you. I owe you big time for this."

"Remember when I cut off a handful of your hair in third grade?" He paused, waiting for her to react, then smiled when she did. "Now we're even."

"*Even?* You scalped me!" she protested, poking him in the chest. "It took me three years to grow my hair back out. Not to mention the fact that all the boys started calling me *Ralph.*"

"Want to know the worst part?" he asked with a grimace.

"What?" she asked, her green eyes narrowing accusingly.

"I'm the one who started the nickname."

"*You?*" McKenna exploded, swatting at him playfully. "I thought you said you had a crush on me back then!"

"I did," he said with a laugh as he dodged her blows.

"Well, I'm glad you got over it before I was completely bald," she said, snatching the chocolate bar and ice cream from his hands before turning toward the kitchen.

"Who says I did?"

"Your steady stream of girlfriends," McKenna countered.

James walked over to the couch and sat down. "So, what happened today?"

"Turn on the television and see for yourself," McKenna said, poking her head around the wall that separated the kitchen from the living room.

James reached for the remote on the coffee table, clicked on the flat-screen TV on the wall adjacent to the windows, then scanned through the channels until he came to a twenty-four-hour news station. A reporter was broadcasting live from Sacramento, California, where a string of minor earthquakes had recently occurred. A few of the country's most noted seismologists were predicting that a substantial quake along the San Andreas Fault was not only probable but imminent.

"So, whatever happened with the woman you were dating a few weeks ago?" McKenna called out from the kitchen.

"Not much," James mumbled to himself.

"The one you introduced me to at the art exhibit," McKenna continued, not hearing James's comment. "You know . . . the tall blond with features the rest of the female population—including yours truly—can only sit back and envy."

"Why would *you* envy anyone?"

McKenna entered the living room carrying two bowls of ice cream. She handed James his bowl, then sat down on the couch next to him, tucking her legs up underneath her.

"Let me see," she began thoughtfully. "For one thing, I'm about four inches too short, irreparable even with painfully steep high heels. For another," she continued, getting into it, "I have this stubborn cowlick that splits my hair right in two no matter what I do or how I fix it." She pointed up to her auburn locks in disgust. James just shook his head, a broad smile on his face. "Then there's my nose. It's sprinkled with freckles and does this little flip thing at the end, giving me a perpetually girlish look which, I might add," she continued indignantly, "is extremely counter-productive in my profession."

"Your nose is adorable."

"*Exactly!* I'm cute and sweet, while woman like your art gallery friend are stunning and sophisticated."

"I like cute and sweet. I like your cowlick and your height, *especially* because it gives you a self-proclaimed disadvantage. And with someone as smart as you, a guy needs all the advantages he can get. As far as sweet goes . . ." he paused, a smile twitching at the corners of his mouth. "I've seen you in court, and *sweet* isn't always the first word that comes to mind."

McKenna laughed out loud. "You're good, you know that? Remind me again why you're single."

Before James could answer, McKenna glanced toward the TV. Prerecorded footage of her client descending the front steps of the courthouse filled the screen. His shoulder-length black hair was pulled into a tight ponytail, contrasting sharply with the tailored suit that her father's law firm had purchased for him just days earlier. He had a cocky smile plastered on his face in response to the throng of reporters peppering him with questions.

"Is that him?" James asked.

McKenna nodded, a vile taste rising in her throat. She watched as the camera zoomed in on his face to show a grotesque tattoo of a black spider that looked as if it were crawling up his cheek. The image sent a chill down her spine. She shook her head, berating herself for believing him when he had sworn that he was innocent, insisting that his rough past was the only thing that brought any validity to the charges. He had been so compelling, so believable. It wasn't until early this morning, right before they'd entered the courtroom to hear the verdict, that she had learned the truth.

The defense had built their case around a minor infraction made by the arresting officer. As McKenna waited outside the courtroom, she felt confident that Eddy Manning would walk. Manning had extended his hand to thank McKenna. When she took it, he held it firmly, his lips lifting into a smile.

"I should thank you," he'd said, all pretense suddenly gone from his face. "It was almost too easy this time."

McKenna had stepped back, the look in his lifeless eyes stealing her breath. Then Manning had laughed coldly as he sauntered into the courtroom. McKenna had stood numbly, knowing there was nothing she could do.

She shuddered, and her mind jerked back to the present as she watched Manning on the screen.

"How do you feel walking away from a first-degree murder charge on a technicality?" one reporter shouted over the noise of the crowd.

"Grateful to my lawyer," he said, not even attempting to hide the smirk on his face.

McKenna felt her stomach churn.

"Do you feel that justice was served?" another reporter shouted as Manning began to walk away.

Her client stopped, then looked directly at the camera, his eyes ice-cold and his face slowly lighting into a smile. "Absolutely."

Without another word, he walked past the reporters and down the courthouse steps to freedom.

"He's going to kill again," McKenna whispered, shaking off a shiver as it raced across her shoulders.

James immediately picked up the remote and clicked off the television.

"Did you see the look in his eyes?" she continued, placing her ice cream on the coffee table, her appetite gone. "He has absolutely no remorse. He got away with it, and I'm the one responsible."

"This isn't your fault. You didn't make the laws."

"No. I might not have been able to stop what happened, but I didn't have to help him."

"McKenna—"

She stood, her self-deprecation quickly replaced by anger. "James, he killed an innocent woman. She had three little kids and a husband who loved her more than life itself. I watched him leave the courtroom today, and the look on his face . . ." McKenna swallowed hard, then shook her head. "I felt so horrible for him—so ashamed I was a part of it."

She turned away, overwhelmed by a flood of emotions. James stood and wrapped his arms around her.

"McKenna, it's okay," he whispered.

"No, it's not, James! This is all wrong. All of it," she said, no longer trying to stop the tears that spilled down her cheeks.

"I know," James whispered, holding her close as he stroked her hair.

He held her in his arms until her last tears were spent and she finally stepped back. "I'm sorry," she said with a halfhearted smile as she tried to regain her composure.

"Don't be," James said, his expression suddenly resolute. "Maybe it's time."

"Time for what?"

"To live your own life instead of doing what your father wants you to do."

McKenna wiped at her cheek, then picked up her bowl of ice cream and started toward the kitchen. "It's not that easy."

James followed her, unwilling to let the subject drop. "Why is the truth so hard for you to face?"

"What are you talking about? A homicidal maniac is free to prowl the streets because of me. That's the truth!" she snapped, her frustration momentarily directed at him.

"And your career?" he asked, his eyes racing across her face. "McKenna, you're a writer and a talented one at that. But instead of pursuing your own dreams, you're living the life you've allowed your father to plan for you."

"I don't want to talk about this."

"No, you don't want to face it."

"I face it," she said, feeling agitated. "I face it every day. I know I'm a puppet sitting quietly by while my father pulls the strings. I'm well aware that I'm trapped in a career I hate, helping people I would just as soon see behind bars. And I don't need a shrink to tell me that my longest relationship, besides yours and mine, lasted only three weeks because of my fear of falling short, which clearly stems from my relationship with my father. Trust me, James, I'm aware. But if there's something else you think I should face, please let me know," she snapped, angry with herself and angry with James for knowing her so well.

"McKenna—"

"Just say it, James!" she demanded, the anger, trepidation, and regret she had felt, not only today but for most of her adult life, building until it was almost unbearable. "Stop spouting platitudes about truth. If you have something to say, *say it!*" she shouted, her face within inches of his and her heart beating so fast she felt dizzy.

James's eyes raced across her face, his own expression impossible to read. Then, before she knew what was happening, he pulled her into his arms and kissed her, his intensity taking her breath away. Despite her brain telling her to stop, McKenna found herself returning the kiss, all rational thought lost in the moment. When James finally pulled back, his eyes were gentle, almost vulnerable.

McKenna stared at him, her lips still warm from his touch and her head spinning as if it were in orbit. "What just happened?" she breathed, the heat in her checks intensifying until she was sure they would burst into flames.

James took a deep breath, his eyes racing over her face. "I kissed you."

"Yes," she admitted, fighting the urge to reach out and grab hold of her marble countertop for support. She took a quick breath, not exactly sure what to say—or think, for that matter. "But *why?*" she finally managed.

The vulnerability in his light blue eyes was immediately replaced by disappointment. "Why do you think? Probably the same reason I got out of bed and rushed over to your apartment at eleven o'clock at night. And the reason I care that you're spending your life fulfilling dreams that aren't your own."

"A friend would do that," McKenna said weakly.

He shook his head in frustration, then started for the door.

"James, we've got to talk about this," McKenna said, taking him by the arm.

"Apparently there's nothing *to* talk about."

"What do you mean? One minute we're eating ice cream, talking about your latest date and my latest case, and the next . . . I mean it doesn't take a Supreme Court justice to see that something's up. We can chalk it up to the heat of the moment, or a split second of insanity, or both," McKenna rattled off, "but I think we should at least talk about it."

"Okay. I plead guilty on all counts, especially the insanity part. Because after all of these years, I'd have to be insane, wouldn't I? Now can I go? Or do I have to wait around for sentencing?"

"What do you mean, after all of these years?" McKenna asked, raising her brow sharply while her elevated heart rate took another leap.

"McKenna, it's late," James said as he opened the door. "Let's just rule that it was an incredibly awkward crime of stupidity and call it a night."

"James, I'm serious," she pressed, gently taking hold of his arm so that he'd have to face her. "What did you mean?"

"I didn't mean anything," he said, avoiding eye contact.

McKenna raised her brow. "James, you and I both know you're a terrible liar."

"Good night, McKenna," he said as he closed the door.

McKenna slowly released the air in her lungs as she stared numbly at the door. On more than one occasion she had flirted with the idea of becoming more than just friends with James, but she had never pursued it. She didn't know why. James was attractive, that was obvious. In fact, if McKenna was painfully honest with herself, she knew that when the two of them entered a room together, it was James that turned heads. He had been an avid swimmer and rock climber since junior high, and he was in great shape. He had thoughtful blue eyes and soft lips. She could feel her face flush, knowing she'd confirmed that firsthand tonight. McKenna shook her head, then quickly walked to the couch and clicked on the TV, not yet ready to face the feelings that were trying to surface.

* * *

"I thought you were taking the day off," Lawrence said as he eyed McKenna over his reading glasses. His expression revealed that he was pleased she had declined his offer to stay at home.

"I had some work to do," she lied, knowing she was only there to keep her mind off James and to receive the nonverbal accolade that was now written on her father's face.

"Did Tatum get the DNA results for Mr. Cypress?" McKenna asked, trying to get her mind on her next assignment.

"You're off that case."

"What!" she exclaimed, instantly on the defensive. "Look, if this is about our conversation yesterday—"

"We took on a new client this morning," Lawrence said, his expression difficult to read. "I've assigned it to you. I want this case handled . . ." he paused as if considering his words, "discreetly."

McKenna raised an eyebrow, her curiosity instantly piqued. "Who's the client?"

"Nathan Rinehart. Judge Rinehart's son."

McKenna gave him a puzzled look. Judge Grant Rinehart was a no-nonsense authoritarian, notorious for slapping cocky defense attorneys with contempt citations at the least provocation. McKenna, of course, was no exception. She had received a citation in Rinehart's court almost six months ago, and Lawrence had purposely kept her away from Rinehart since then, giving her time to season and mature as an attorney—and giving the judge time to forget.

"What did Nathan do?" McKenna asked, feeling slightly guilty for the vindication that was itching at her lips.

"You've heard of West Link Conglomerate?"

The name was familiar, but McKenna couldn't quite place it. "I'm not sure."

"Mrs. Dillon, the woman Manning killed, was an employee at West Link."

"That's right!" McKenna exclaimed, remembering now where she had seen the name. It had been in the victim's file along with her other personal information. "It's headquartered in L.A. . . . in Lincoln Tower, if I remember correctly," she added.

Lawrence nodded, his forehead furrowed.

"So what does Nathan Rinehart have to do with West Link?" McKenna asked cautiously.

"Apparently he's one of the VPs."

"And . . . ?" McKenna prompted.

"I received a phone call from Judge Rinehart last night. Apparently after the verdict on Manning came down, the judge found a manila envelope on his desk filled with documents insinuating that there might have been some embezzlement going on at West Link."

"Do the documents incriminate his son?"

"If the documents are genuine, they could do more than incriminate Nathan for embezzlement. Mrs. Dillon was head of the accounting department."

McKenna's eyes opened wide. "Mrs. Dillon found evidence of the misappropriation, told the wrong people, and was murdered."

"It's possible."

"Maybe that's why she was in New York in the first place. Maybe she knew her life was in danger and was on the run."

"That's a big assumption," Lawrence said slowly, though McKenna could tell from his expression that he had already considered the possibility himself.

"Does Judge Rinehart have any idea who put the envelope on his desk?"

"It was probably just a hired man," Lawrence replied.

"Like Manning," McKenna offered, understanding now how her client had been able to come up with the exorbitant amount their law firm had required to take him on as a client.

"The nice little note that came with the documents promised that if Judge Rinehart wired one million dollars to an offshore account, all hard copies of the supposed evidence would cease to exist."

McKenna blew the air out of her cheeks while her father pushed his chair back from his desk and stood, slowly walking to the window. "I'll handle the case in court if it comes to that, but I want you to do the ground work. If this is handled without the boy's name being dragged through the mud, it could mean good things for your career, not to mention the fact that it would mend a few fences with the judge."

McKenna stared at her father in disbelief. "So you want me to find a loophole for Judge Rinehart's son in order to to further my career?"

Lawrence turned back around, his eyes flashing. "I want you to do your job," he snapped, his steady gaze cutting right through her. Then he shook his head in irritation and walked to his desk. "Tatum has already made arrangements for you to fly to California on the twenty-eighth to talk to Nathan, and Alan Sutherland, president of West Link."

McKenna was unable to form a single intelligible word. Though she had struggled her entire life with her father's lack of approval, she had always revered and respected him. Now she found her emotions swirling inside her head in a nauseating blur. It was at times like these that she missed having a mother, someone she could talk to, someone who wasn't as infuriatingly stubborn as her father.

"In the meantime, I want you to see if you can find any connection between Manning and Nathan Rinehart," Lawrence said, ending the conversation before she could regain her wits.

McKenna left her father's office without another word and walked to the office manager's desk. Tatum, who was in her early twenties and pretty in an eccentric kind of way, was talking into the Bluetooth connected to her ear while painting her long nails a bright shade of red. She flashed McKenna a broad smile and immediately reached for a file on her desk, being careful not to smudge the fresh nail polish, all the while carrying on a conversation with whomever was on the other end of the line.

"Mr. Rinehart's file?" McKenna asked.

Tatum nodded, her elaborate earrings jingling. "I've got everything in there from his junior-high prom date to his favorite brand of aftershave."

"Thanks," McKenna said, looking down at the file as she turned to leave.

"He killed her," Tatum said frankly.

McKenna's eyes widened in surprise as she turned back around. "How do you know?"

Tatum smiled, then pointed to the phone connected to her ear. "Sorry, wrong conversation."

McKenna shook her head as she turned to go. Tatum was quirky in both appearance and personality, leaving most people wondering why she held a position at Lawrence Bradford's New York City law office. But Tatum was a master at collecting information. McKenna had personally seen her dig up details that made the difference between conviction and total acquittal, using nothing more than a laptop and the Bluetooth that seemed permanently attached to her ear.

"By the way," Tatum began as McKenna moved toward the door, "James called. He said to tell you that he's going to be gone all next week doing some rappelling in the Adirondacks." She paused. "The man has no heart."

McKenna's eyes opened wide. "Excuse me?"

Tatum shook her head, then pointed to the phone again. "Not James," she mouthed as she began applying a second coat of polish to her nails.

McKenna shook her head, wondering if the information Tatum gleaned was worth the exasperation. As she walked to her car, she realized that despite the nature of her approaching trip to L.A., she was anxious to put a few miles between herself, this office, and the two most important men in her life.

CHAPTER TWO

Friday, April 18 / Just outside of Los Angeles

Droplets of perspiration streamed down Chad Harrison's face, stinging his already bloodshot eyes and temporarily blurring his vision as he aimed his fire hose at the blue-tipped flames that crawled unrestrained toward him across the ceiling of the high-rise office complex.

"We need to get out of here!" Brian Lindstrom, a rookie with the department, screamed as the flames intensified, consuming everything they touched.

"If we lose this floor, we lose the building," Chad shouted, holding his position despite the intense heat.

"You're crazy! Stick around and get yourself killed if you want, but I'm out of here," Brian spat out in exasperation before turning to leave.

Chad glanced at the fireman's retreating form as he weaved through the smoke-filled cubicles of the accounting firm that occupied the whole of the eighth floor. He thought about calling the rookie back but quickly changed his mind. Instead, he turned his attention back to the fire, aimed his hose at the base of the blaze, and attempted unsuccessfully to ignore the gnawing feeling in the pit of his stomach that the rookie was right. It *was* time to get out. The other firefighters were two flights below him in a day-care center trying to evacuate the children before this floor crashed down on top of them. Chad had been sent to buy them some time, and despite the risk, that was exactly what he intended to do. So here he was, a wall of fire roaring wickedly before him, the floor below him partially in flames, and his backup man on his way out of the building, like everyone else who had any brains.

"You want some help?"

Chad jerked around as someone slapped him on the shoulder.

"*Justice!*" Chad exclaimed, clearly relieved.

"Do you always have to be the last man out?" Captain Justice Stevens shouted. "Come on. Let's get out of here."

"What about the kids?"

"They're out," he said, grabbing Chad by the arm. "Come on. This place is going to go any second now."

Chad shot one last look at the inferno. As the youngest son of the former fire chief, and with five years of firefighting experience with the L.A. fire department, he was acquainted enough with fires to know that if they didn't get out now, they would be dragged out sometime tomorrow morning in a couple of body bags.

"I'll lead the way," Chad shouted, turning his hose toward the exit. "Stay close."

As they both turned and started for the stairwell, a loud explosion rocked the building, violently shaking the floor beneath them and tossing them both like rag dolls. After a moment of flight, Chad collided with a large oak desk. It caught him in the midsection, and the force of impact knocked the wind out of him. He crumpled to the floor, gasping in the air provided by the tank strapped to his back. Once he had enough air to breathe, he rolled over to one side and, despite the throbbing in his rib cage, frantically began searching the smoke-filled room for Justice. The captain was sprawled out on the floor several feet away from him, his body motionless.

Fear temporarily numbing the pain, Chad struggled to his feet and started toward his friend. He was only a few feet from Justice when he began to feel a violent rumbling beneath his feet. Chad stopped mid-stride, his heart speeding to match the rate of the increasing vibration. He turned his head toward the stairwell, almost as if in slow motion, and then watched in horror as a stream of fire exploded from its depths with the same terrifying exhibition as a volcanic eruption, the intense heat singeing his skin through his heat-resistant suit. Chad dove for the ground, then rolled behind an overturned desk, using it as a shield from the heat. Knowing that Justice would die if he didn't get him behind the desk, Chad reached out as far as he could, barely grasping the captain's arm, then dragged him behind the desk. Though still breathing, Justice's body was limp, and his eyes rolled back into his head. Despite his desperate attempt to remain calm, Chad could hear his own sporadic breathing quicken, the amplified sound filling his air mask, while his heart thundered against the walls of his heaving chest. If he didn't do something quick, neither one of them would make it out alive.

With the stairwell no longer an option, Chad's eyes went to the only other way out—a window about ten feet from their position. He glanced behind him at the fire hose that was strewn on the floor several feet from him, but the area was already engulfed in flames. Then he reluctantly turned back to the window that had shattered from the intense heat. Waiting several seconds until the blaze in the stairwell abated enough that it was safe to stand; he hoisted up the captain's limp body and started across the floor. With deadly flames licking the ceiling and devouring the walls, Chad dragged Justice toward the window, knowing that it would only be a matter of minutes before the fire around them consumed the entire room. As soon as they reached the window and Chad set the captain down, a section of the ceiling not five feet from where they had just been sitting crashed to the floor, sending a spray of red-hot debris in every direction. Chad watched in horror as another section of the ceiling caved in, feeding the flames that were steadily turning everything around them into a fiery tomb.

Feeling his body begin to buckle under the intense heat, Chad climbed up onto the ledge and leaned out the window, being careful to avoid the few protruding pieces of glass around the frame. He strained to see through the billowing smoke and illuminating fire that seemed to permeate the entire high-rise. Within seconds, Chad spotted a fire truck, the extension ladder raised to the fifth floor, just to the left of where he stood. He quickly began to speak into the microphone inside his face mask.

"Ground control, I need emergency assistance *now!*"

"Chad, is that you?" a voice barked over the speaker.

Before Chad could answer, a window two floors below him shattered in a shock of sound and heat, sending a stream of fire raging into the air. Chad jumped back as the tips of the flames licked the ledge in front of him, threatening to steal his only escape. Fear pulsed through him. "We're on the east side of the building. Eighth floor. A window just shot out two floors below us. We need the ladder *now!*" he shouted hoarsely.

"We'll get you down, Chad," Captain Loggins assured him. "Hold on. We're sending the ladder up." But Chad could hear the anxiety in the captain's voice.

"We're not going to make it."

Chad jerked around, surprised to see Justice struggling to sit up. The captain's face was drained of color.

"Are you all right?" Chad asked, immediately climbing down from the ledge and going to his friend.

"Promise you'll watch over Anna," Justice mumbled, his words slurred. "With the baby coming—"

"You die on me now," Chad barked, "and I'll do more than watch over her. I'll marry the girl! In three months she won't even remember your name."

The captain lifted his head to look at Chad, his eyes struggling to focus. "Over my dead body," he muttered defiantly.

"Alright then, let's get out of here," Chad said, helping Justice to his feet, then on to the ledge where the extension ladder was being raised. The flames shooting up from the floor two flights down had lessened some after the initial explosion, but they were still only a few feet below the ledge. "We're going to have to make this quick."

"I don't know if I—"

"You can!" Chad shouted, his face devoid of its usual levity.

They both whipped around as another section of the ceiling caved in with a thunderous crash.

"Go!" Chad demanded, helping Justice climb safely out onto the ladder before shooting a terrified glance at what was left of the room.

As Chad turned back to the window, another explosion shook the building. He lost his balance and stumbled backward, his head slamming hard into the side of a desk as he crumpled to the floor. For a moment he lay still, his senses temporarily knocked from him and his eyes struggling just to focus.

"*Get up!*" his mind screamed to a body that was fighting the overpowering, numbing pull of oblivion. Almost without realizing he was doing so, he staggered to his feet, his eyes locked on the flames that now raged unrestrained in front of the ledge, totally blocking his escape.

"The ladder's got to be out there," he breathed. Panic welled up inside of him, threatening to paralyze him.

He glanced back at the room, fear tingling up his spine in a rush that he had never before experienced. Within seconds, the entire eighth floor would be completely engulfed with him in it. He turned back to the window, his decision made. With a much needed surge of adrenaline exploding within him, he took a deep breath and started to run. As soon as his feet touched the ledge, he jumped, hurtling his body into the air and into a wall of fire. For a split second the heat was almost unbearable, and then he was through it, his body slamming hard into the top rungs of the metal ladder while his legs swung wildly below. His hands groped for a good grip, though once he got it, he found that he lacked the strength to pull himself up.

"Hold on!" came a voice from somewhere within the billowing black smoke.

"I can't," Chad breathed, not sure if he had just thought the words or if he had actually said them.

Within seconds he felt someone grabbing his arms and pulling him up and over the top rung of the ladder.

"You've got more lives than an alley cat."

Chad glanced up, recognizing the bulky man before him instantly. "What about Justice?"

"He made it," Thomas Porterman said, pointing through the dark smoke toward a figure making his way down the ladder two flights below them. "Come on. Let's get you down."

Chad let all the air escape out of his lungs as relief washed over him, then slowly began making his way down.

"I still can't believe you just did a cannonball out that window like some crazy circus clown," Thomas called out. "The boys are going to be talkin' about this one for months." He looked down at the crowd forming at the base of the blaze. "Hey, maybe those news reporters got some footage. We might get an instant replay on the ten o'clock news."

"Hopefully by ten o'clock I'll be in bed."

"You'll be in the ER if Captains Stevens or Loggins have anything to say about it."

"I'm fine. At least nothing that a few days of R & R can't cure."

Thomas laughed as they both descended the ladder. "Rest and relaxation? Right. What's your idea of that? Bungee jumping off Mt. Everest or skydiving over the Grand Canyon?"

"After today, that would be cake."

* * *

As Anna Stevens entered her small but cozy family room holding a serving tray with three tall glasses of milk and a plate of Double Stuf Oreos, she paused briefly in the entryway to observe the two men in the room. Her husband was reclining in his favorite La-Z-Boy, his gray eyes glued on his latest toy, a thirty-six-inch flat-screen television that she had surprised him with for their sixth wedding anniversary two months ago. He had on a white T-shirt that fit snug around his biceps, and a pair of blue jeans. The ball cap that read LAFD, which was usually perched over his sandy blond hair, had been placed on the end table next to him; instead, a white bandage encircled his head. Anna shook her own head, not wanting to think about how close she had just come to losing him. Her eyes then went to the glass of beer in his hand. She let her breath out in an almost imperceptible sigh. Two months ago she wouldn't have even noticed the beer, but then again, two months ago she hadn't been the same person. At least, it felt that way. Anna smiled, her mind going instantly to a bashful Idaho farmer in a new black suit and striped green tie (she later learned he was fresh from the MTC) and his lanky Canadian companion. If someone had told her back then that those two young men would change her life forever, she would have laughed them right out of town. But that's exactly what had happened. Anna shook her head. She would be forever grateful that she had invited them in when they'd shown up on her doorstep. Justice, on the other hand, had had an entirely different opinion. Religion, in any shape or form, had never been of interest to him. It wasn't that he didn't care or that he wasn't a good person. He just felt that a person's relationship with God was personal, and so he didn't see a need to dress up on a beautiful Sunday morning just to sit in a stuffy church, especially when he could be home eating potato chips and watching whatever sporting event was in season. Anna let out a slow, sad sigh, wishing that her husband could share just a portion of the contentment she had found.

Anna's attention then went to the other man in the room—Chad Harrison. He was about three inches shorter than her husband, with an equally toned but slighter build. His thick eyebrows were slightly darker than his milk-chocolate hair, and he had hazel eyes.

She offered a glass of milk to both men.

Chad smiled and accepted his glass. "Thanks, Anna."

Anna awkwardly took a seat on the couch next to Chad, rubbing her round belly absently as she took a sip of her own drink. "So what did your doctor say?" she asked him, her eyes going to the white bandages that encircled both his forearms, covering nasty second-degree burns.

"His doctor said . . ." Justice began, turning from the TV to lift a brow at Chad, "to take a couple of weeks off, change the bandages often, and to chill out on the crazy kamikaze stunts."

"Hey, I saved *your* life," Chad protested with a grin.

"Oh, really? And just why was I up on the eighth floor in the first place?"

"I don't know . . . maybe fighting a fire," Chad said as he plunged an Oreo into his glass of milk.

"Did you happen to notice the two gold braids on my dress uniform? They're my little insurance that I get to fight fires from the *ground*—not the middle of the inferno, where you always manage to end up."

"I'm a firefighter. That's my job," Chad said before taking a bite of his soggy cookie.

"You've been in the ER three times in the last two months," Justice began, any previous flippancy in his tone quickly dissipating. "That's not doing your job. That's being reckless. One of these days, you're going to get yourself killed."

"You worry too much."

"And you don't worry enough. Brian Lindstrom is refusing to go anywhere near a fire with you now."

"That kid is afraid of his own shadow," Chad shot back. "He shouldn't be fighting fires in the first place."

"That could be true. But after watching you the last few months, I'm starting to wonder if maybe he's not the only one."

Chad abruptly set his glass down on the coffee table in front of him, then leaned forward on the couch. "So I should have just left those kids to fry in that mobile home last month? Or that older couple trapped in their condo? And what about those preschoolers last night in the day care? Come on, Justice, taking chances to save lives is what we do."

"Reasonable chances, yes. Crazy, irresponsible chances, no! Killing yourself isn't going to bring him back," Justice blurted out.

Chad suddenly went rigid. He looked away.

"I think it's time to eat," Anna quickly interrupted, struggling to get up off of the couch with her round belly sticking out over her lap.

"Look, Chad," Justice continued, his tone noticeably tempered, "you did everything you could."

"I let him die," Chad said bluntly, his jaw flexed with tension.

"You would have died with him if you'd gone in there."

"Maybe," Chad said, slowly getting to his feet, his face suddenly showing the effects of the previous night. "And maybe he'd still be here." He turned his eyes to Anna and then forced a smile. "I'm sorry to leave before dinner, but I really do feel like a locomotive plowed into me."

"You look it too," Justice interjected, breaking through the tension in the room.

Chad shook his head and smiled, then glanced down at the roundness of Anna's midsection. "Let's hope that baby of yours ends up with his mom's good looks and not his old man's mug."

Anna smiled, glad that Chad wasn't leaving angry, though she wished she could erase the pain in his eyes. "Let me get you a plate to take with you."

Chad reached down and grabbed a handful of Oreos. "Hey, what could be better for dinner than cookies?" Then he motioned for Anna to sit back down. "You take it easy. I know the way out."

"Take care of yourself," Justice called out as Chad headed for the entryway.

"Don't I always?" Chad said, turning and shooting a smirk at his friend. Then he opened the front door and closed it quietly behind him.

Anna eased herself back onto the couch and then turned to her husband, who already had his eyes back on the TV.

"I'm worried about him."

Justice looked up at her, though he didn't comment. Instead, he got up and took a seat on the couch next to her. "Come here."

Anna snuggled against her husband as he wrapped his arm around her.

"How are *you* feeling?" he whispered as he kissed the top of her head, then gently pulled out the elastic that held her soft blond hair in a ponytail so he could run his fingers through it.

"Like the Pillsbury Doughboy," she replied, repositioning herself even though she knew it probably wouldn't make her more comfortable.

"You look beautiful," he said, and she knew he was sincere.

"Well, I don't feel it," she admitted frankly. "I go to the doctor a week from Monday for what I'm hoping will be my final checkup."

"I wish I could go with you, but I have meetings all day on the twenty-eighth."

"Don't worry about it. So, what *are* you going to do about Chad?" Anna asked, redirecting the conversation.

"What can I do besides keep an eye on him and hope that he comes to grips with this soon?"

"And if he doesn't?" Anna whispered, laying her head on his shoulder.

She waited for Justice to comment, and when he didn't, she lifted her head and looked curiously up at his face. She was about to repeat her question, but her husband's expression stopped her.

"What is it, Jus?" she asked.

"Did you feel that?"

"Feel what?"

Justice remained silent, the muscles along his jaw flexed, his face drawn in a scowl.

"Is something wrong?" she asked, her tone elevated.

Justice looked down at her, his expression immediately softening. Finally he shrugged and rubbed at his bloodshot eyes. "I thought I felt a little tremor, but . . ." He rubbed at his eyes again and then let his breath out. "I think I'm just tired."

Anna laid her head back against his shoulder, her eyes focused on the drink in his hand. Though his hand was perfectly still, the liquid in the glass was sloshing back and forth.

CHAPTER THREE

Friday, April 18 / Provo, Utah

Payson Griggs sat near the back of his geology class with his arm propped up on his half-desk, his chin resting in his palm. Though he knew he should be taking notes for finals, he found his attention drawn to the scene outside the window. Barren trees were bursting with new buds while the dormant grass below promised to blanket the entire BYU campus with plush velvety green by the end of the month. Migrant birds that had returned after a long hard winter dipped and soared amid the clouds in search of a place to build their nests, their presence signaling that winter had finally surrendered to spring. The scene was inviting and serene, and as far as Payson was concerned, much more appealing than a drawn-out lecture on plate tectonics.

Payson's gaze fell on two girls who were sitting on a wooden bench next to a tree. The girl closest to him ran her fingers through her long blond hair, the gentle breeze tousling it before she let it fall down her back, but it was the brunette who instantly seized his attention, causing him to lurch forward in recognition. He watched as her lips lifted into a smile that quickly turned to a laugh. Though she was far enough away that he knew it was impossible, Payson was sure he could hear the melodic tone of her laughter, a sound that had been seared into his brain and now made his heart both race and ache at the same time.

At that moment, a guy Payson didn't recognize approached the two girls. Gwendolyn's face instantly lit up like a blue spruce on Christmas Day. To Payson's complete horror, the guy took her beaming smile as an invitation and stepped toward her, his arms opening wide as she fell into them. Payson instantly jerked forward in his seat, his heart in his throat. As he did, he knocked his geology book off his desk and onto the floor with an echoing thud. After a collective gasp, everyone in the room whirled around to face him— including Professor Tanner, his eyebrows arched in mild irritation. Payson could feel his cheeks burning and knew they were probably a nice shade of crimson. He mumbled a quick apology, and then, with all eyes still on him, he leaned down to pick up his book. Once he had it in hand, the professor cleared his throat to regain everyone's attention and then continued on with his lecture.

After waiting a discreet thirty seconds, Payson once again flashed an anxious glance out the window, but there was no sign of Gwen or the guy who had been the recipient of one of her knee-weakening smiles. Payson felt a torrent of jealousy rush through him, though he knew it was completely unwarranted. He and Gwen were no longer together. He shifted restlessly in his seat, not liking the feelings that were quickly resurfacing. Three weeks ago he had been ready to buy a ring, pledge his love, and eternally seal the most important decision of his life. Then, for some reason that she could not or *would not* explain, Gwen had broken off their relationship. Now Payson found himself struggling unsuccessfully to salvage what was left of his trampled heart.

Desperate to get his mind off Gwen, he picked up his pencil, slouched down in his chair, and turned his attention back to the professor who was addressing the class as he made his way across the room to an overhead projector.

"An epicenter is the body of land directly above the origination point of an earthquake. It usually sustains the heaviest devastation and unfortunately, in many cases, the greatest loss of life. In other words, it's ground zero," the professor stated, his enthusiasm for the subject evident in his voice, despite the probability that he had been regurgitating the same information for years. To emphasize his point, he signaled his student aide to turn off the lights. Once the room was dark, he placed a picture on the overhead projector, which displayed an image across the auditorium. "*This* was the end result of the 1906 San Francisco earthquake," he said soberly.

Payson shook his head as he took in the carnage. The first thing it brought to mind was the aftermath from an atomic blast. Several city blocks lay in ruin, with enormous mounds of twisted metal and debris scattered as far as the eye could see. Once-towering buildings, designed by the most gifted architects of their time, had swayed dangerously with the initial blow before succumbing to numerous aftershocks. Cable cars and carriages, now barely recognizable, had been overturned or flattened. Asphalt streets and cement sidewalks looked as if they had been lifted and shaken like dirty throw rugs, their paths now as rippled as the waves of the sea.

Rescue workers dotted the scene like ants in search of survivors, though the enormity of the destruction must have cast an ominous feel to the daunting task. Payson had studied the San Francisco quake in detail and knew that the fatality rate had been staggering—an estimated three thousand dead, either as a direct result of the quake or of the devastating fires that followed. Many of the dead who had lain entombed in the rubble had no longer been identifiable when found. Many more had never been recovered, making this gargantuan mass of destruction their final resting place. Payson nodded his head resolutely as the passion he felt about one day designing and constructing earthquake-safe buildings resurfaced.

"We're learning from the past that we need to change the way we build, especially in high-risk zones," the professor continued, "but even with all the added codes and reinforced building materials, sometimes we're simply at the mercy of the quake."

The professor looked at the clock on the wall, gestured to his student aide to hit the lights, then flipped off the overhead.

"On Monday, be prepared to be tested on continental shifting, plate tectonics, and everything else in chapters one through twenty."

There was an audible groan from the class, but it was short-lived when they realized that Professor Tanner was dismissing them five minutes early. Payson quickly shoved his book into his backpack, then made his way as fast as he could to the front door, hoping to catch a final glimpse of Gwen. A swarm of students had already begun to pour out onto the grass and walkways, anxious to enjoy a warm Friday afternoon, but as Payson scanned the area he couldn't see any sign of Gwen.

Discouraged and frustrated, he slowly made his way down the sidewalk, stopping briefly at a drinking fountain just off the path. He shifted the overloaded backpack that was slung over his right shoulder, then bent down to get a drink. Just as the water began to arch out of the fountain, his backpack slipped down his arm. The force from his books stooped him down just enough that the water sprayed him right in the face. He jerked his dripping head back in hopes that no one had seen, but the gentle giggle behind him told him that someone had. Payson turned around, his heart instantly shifting into overdrive as he stared at the woman in front of him.

"*Gwen!*" he stammered, quickly wiping at the water dripping from his face.

"I'm sorry. I shouldn't have laughed," she apologized as she bit her lower lip, unsuccessfully attempting to suppress a smile.

Payson shrugged. "Hey, I would have laughed myself if it weren't for the water shooting up my nose."

Payson watched with pleasure as her dimples deepened with a grin, making his entire heart ache. He forced a smile as his eyes raced longingly over her face. Her eyes were a stunning light blue with long lashes a shade darker than her hair. The rest of her features were delicate, except for the oversized dimples on each cheek that always seemed to bloom when she grinned. Her hair was short, dark, and cut in a kind of messy look. It was not a hairstyle that most women could pull off, but on her it looked fun and sassy, much like the uninhibited woman who wore it. As Payson's focus slowly returned to her eyes, her gaze seemed to go right through him, stealing his breath.

"I've missed you," he said, his resolve to not open himself up for rejection lost in the unexplainable hold her smile always seemed to have on him.

Her smile instantly faded. "Payson, I've taken an internship at the Los Angeles Department of Public Works, in their air quality department."

Payson felt as though someone had just thrust a knife into his chest. "Los Angeles?" he mumbled.

Gwen nodded slowly. "I start about a month after I graduate."

Payson took a deep breath, chiding himself for letting down his guard and vowing vehemently never to do it again. "Congratulations," he forced out, hoping that his face would convey the sincerity his heart was lacking. "I know this is what you've always wanted."

Not only had Gwen served a mission in California, quickly falling in love with the people and the area, but she had always been an ardent environmental activist. Payson knew that landing this internship was the fulfillment of a lifelong dream for her.

Gwen gave Payson a weak smile, though it vanished almost as quickly as it came. "How have *you* been?"

Payson glanced over Gwen's shoulder. There, just a few feet away, apparently waiting for Gwen to get a drink, was the guy Payson had seen her with just a few minutes before. However, at the moment, he looked too preoccupied talking to Tristin, Gwen's roommate, to notice them.

Payson glanced back at Gwen. "I'm great!" he said a little too enthusiastically, knowing that if he were to have a sudden coronary, the last words out of his mouth would have been a blatant lie. On impulse he looked over at a group of girls walking their way, smiled and waved as if he knew them, then quickly turned back to her. "Listen, Gwen," he said, looking down at his watch, "I'd love to stay and talk, but I'd better go. I've got plans."

The only plans he had that night involved barricading himself in his apartment, downing a liter of root beer, and pining away for the only girl he had ever loved—her.

"I'm sorry," she said, glancing uncomfortably at the group of girls as they passed. "I just wanted to say good-bye . . . in case we didn't get to see each other again."

Payson swallowed hard, willing his features to remain impassive, though he knew that would be next to impossible. "I'm glad you did."

Gwen stood there motionless, expectantly, as her eyes explored his face. Payson wanted desperately to reach out and pull her into his arms, to tell her that he had never loved anyone the way he loved her, and to beg her to reconsider. Instead, he forced a cordial smile until she finally turned and walked away.

* * *

"Why is she doing this?" Payson asked as he ran a quick hand through his short, mocha-colored hair.

"Who knows?" Jackson Hampton said as he took another bite of the apple he was eating, sending a spatter of juice flying. "But I'll tell you what you need to do now," he continued emphatically. "Start going out with other girls. *Lots* of them! Maybe even Gwen's room-mates. Nothing sends a girl running back to you faster than the threat of another woman—especially if it's her friend. Trust me, I know."

Payson shook his head. "Where did you get this baloney? Neanderthal Dating 101? Come on, Jax. This is Gwen we're talking about."

"Hey, I'm only telling it like it is," Jax countered. "What you do with the info is your business. But I'll tell you one thing: Gwen's hot! If you don't act fast, some smoothie like me is going to make a move before you know what hit you."

Payson surveyed the man before him. Jackson Hampton, known by almost everyone as Jax, was tall and athletic with blond, curly hair. He came from a wealthy family, drove a red sports car, and had a full-ride football scholarship to the Y. And he was an expert at attracting women. Holding onto them was another matter—usually because he couldn't juggle all their names—but he had the first step of the dating game down to a science.

"Look, I'm not going to play a bunch of mind games with Gwen," Payson said, a sudden flood of guilt rushing through him for waving at the group of girls on campus earlier.

"Well, as I see it, you've got two options," Jax countered. "You can borrow my car, splash on some cologne, and tell her you're sorry for whatever it is you may or may not have done. Or you can resort to taking out her friends, which I think is the better move. It's up to you," he said as he took another huge bite of his apple.

"You've got some real issues," Payson replied with a shake of his head.

"Hey, you want a piece of me, man?" Jax baited as he tossed his apple core haphazardly toward the trash and with a broad smile gave Payson a less-than-gentle push.

At twenty-four, Payson had left most of his brawling-it-out-on-the-front-room-floor behavior behind, but with visions of Gwen and her new "friend" filling his head, he instantly began to roll up his sleeves, grateful for the opportunity to release some pent-up frustration. "Say your prayers, Hampton."

"That's Bone Crusher to you," Jax taunted.

"Just say *uncle* now and save yourself the trouble," Hunter Campbell interrupted.

Both Payson and Jax turned to face their roommate as he staggered out of his room, running a hand through his disheveled hair, temporarily subduing the wheat-colored strands at the back of his head, which popped back up the minute he removed his hand. "He about broke my ribs last week over a bag of chips."

"Hey, I got them first," Jax protested.

"Yeah! Out of my cupboard!" Hunter exclaimed as he made his way to the kitchen.

"Did you work late again last night?" Payson asked, watching Hunter yawn broadly as he opened the refrigerator and stared blankly inside.

Hunter worked in Salt Lake City from six in the evening until midnight as a telemarketer, then started classes at the Y at ten the next morning. Payson knew that a daily nap was the only way Hunter could make it through classes without falling asleep and drooling on his desk.

Hunter nodded, attempting to stifle another yawn.

"You need to do some shopping," Jax offered as he picked up his new Wii controller and pointed it at the TV screen. "You're running low on Lucky Charms and milk."

Hunter grabbed an empty jug of milk that had been left in the fridge before glancing over at Jax, the apparent culprit, who was now throwing punches toward the TV as he boxed it out with an animated player on the screen. "Do you have any special requests for food you'd like to mooch this week? I don't have a dime to my name, but I could always hawk my ten-speed or donate plasma to the Red Cross."

"Very funny." Jax threw another punch at the screen.

Hunter's eyes instantly lit up. "Hey, speaking of funny, I heard a new joke last night at work."

Jax groaned, but Hunter was already making his way to the center of the living room, a broad smile on his face. "What do you get when you cross a kleptomaniac and a Mormon?"

Jax rolled his eyes. "What?" he asked, his voice lacking any shred of enthusiasm.

"A basement full of stolen food," Hunter offered, already laughing himself.

Jax glanced from the screen to his roommate. "Hunter, that wasn't funny."

"What are you talking about? That was hilarious." Hunter looked over at Payson to gauge his reaction, but Payson was shaking his head.

"See," Jax began. "Payson doesn't think you're funny either."

"Okay, I've got another one," Hunter said.

Jax turned to Payson. "Do you want to shut him up, or should I?"

"No, come on. This is a good one," Hunter pressed.

Jax set the controller down and started toward Hunter, but Hunter was already racing toward the kitchen.

"Okay, okay," Hunter began. "But you're the one who's missing out. You would have laughed your head off at the next joke."

"If there *is* a next one, I might have to take the boxing into the kitchen," Jax said, turning his attention back to his game.

"Alright, but you can forget mooching any food this week," Hunter said as he reached for a stack of mail on the counter.

"Oh, I almost forgot. You got your tax return back today. Five hundred and twenty-two dollars and ninety-one cents," Jax offered nonchalantly as he threw a combination of punches at the screen.

Hunter's eyes widened as he turned the letter over in his hands. Then, almost as a second thought, he turned back to Jax. "Hey, how do *you* know how much money I got back?"

"I looked," Jax admitted, not appearing the least bit ashamed.

"It's a federal crime to open someone else's mail," Hunter shot back.

"I'm pretty sure it's a federal crime to have a haircut like that, too," Jax said with a cocky smirk. "Or at least it should be." His face split into a grin as he turned to face Hunter. "Now *that* was funny."

Payson smiled as he looked over at the white line that separated where Hunter's hair was now and where it use to be.

"Sweet!" Hunter exclaimed as he kissed the check in his hand, oblivious to Jax's comment. "Anyone up for Mexican? I'm starving."

Thirty minutes later, while they waited at El Acapulco for their food to arrive, Jax pounded Hunter with ideas on how to spend his newfound money. Jax's obvious first choice was workout and weight equipment.

"I'm not going to have much use for any of that. I put my mission papers in two weeks ago," Hunter explained. "If I'm lucky, I'll enter the MTC at the beginning of the summer."

"If I'm lucky, at the beginning of the summer I'll be snorkeling off the coast of Maui," Jax offered.

Payson glanced over at his roommate, very much aware that this was a sore subject for Jax. Payson had tactfully avoided it throughout the year, deciding that if Jax wanted to be an effective missionary—or a missionary at all—the decision would have to be his. Hunter, on the other hand, had an entirely different approach. Though he was never preachy or pushy, he had a way of cutting right to the chase in a way that most people couldn't get away with.

"Hey, it's never too late to turn in your scuba gear for a couple of black suits," Hunter piped in with a smile. "Maybe we could serve together. We could arm wrestle to see who got to be senior companion."

Jax laughed. "Hunter, I could bench-press two of you."

"Good. You might be useful getting us in a few doors."

Payson laughed his first real laugh in several weeks. "I think you two would make a great team."

"What do you say?" Hunter asked.

"I say if you want to team up, you'd better buy a snorkel and a good set of flippers."

Hunter smiled as if to admit his defeat, at least for now.

"So why not just save the money for your mission?" Payson asked.

"It's already paid for."

"*All* of it?" Jax exclaimed, so loudly that several people in the restaurant turned to look at them.

"I started saving when I was twelve," Hunter began. "At first it was just fifty percent of my paper route, but when I turned fifteen I started working on my uncle's rice farm during the summers. That money combined with a healthy chunk of birthday and Christmas money, and a part-time job during the school year, took care of it."

Payson shook his head with a smile. "Wow! That's impressive. I started saving at sixteen, but I still only paid for about a third of mine."

Jax raised an eyebrow but remained silent.

"So, there's never been any doubt in your mind that you'd serve?" Payson asked curiously.

Hunter shook his head. "When I was twelve my parents were on the verge of divorce. My dad was drinking a lot and coming home late. My mom was working twenty-four/seven and coming home just long enough to argue with my dad. Then one day, two guys in white shirts came knocking on our door." Hunter shrugged. "Now, almost seven years later, my dad is the high priest group leader, and my mom is serving in compassionate service." He glanced over at Jax, who had turned twenty just a little over three weeks ago. He was shredding his paper napkin uncomfortably. Hunter turned back to Payson. "When all the other kids my age were looking up to people like Scotty Pippin, my hero was any guy in a white shirt and tie that showed up in Jacksonville, Arkansas, ready to share the gospel. Those guys changed my life."

As Jax looked up, his face showing his discomfort, their waitress arrived carrying three steaming plates of spicy Mexican food.

"You're just in time," Jax said with a wink and a grateful smile that, from the look on the girl's face, was not lost on her.

For the next few minutes the three of them ate in silence. Payson's thoughts remained focused on Gwen. How could he have been so wrong about her? Everything inside him screamed that she was the one. He had retraced every minute of the last few months in detail, desperate to figure out what had happened, but other than her being a little more reserved the last couple of weeks before they broke up, everything had been perfect.

"So, what *are* you going to do with the money?" Jax asked Hunter before taking a big bite of his enchilada.

"The three of us are going to California after finals," Hunter said, trying unsuccessfully to suppress a big grin. "This money is screaming to be used on a road trip."

"*Yes!*" Jax exclaimed. "Count me in. I'll have my dad wire us some real cash so we can do this trip right."

Payson began shaking his head, but before he could speak, his attention was drawn to a couple being seated two tables over. He stopped cold, his breath suddenly snatched from him. Seeing his expression, Hunter and Jax followed his gaze. Gwen had just taken a seat facing them. The guy she was with was straight across from her, his back to them. Though Payson couldn't see his face, he could tell by his clothes that it was the same guy she had been with earlier.

"Let's go," Hunter said as he lifted his hand, signaling their waitress to bring them their check.

As he did, Gwen's eyes lifted to them. The smile on her face instantly vanished as her eyes locked on Payson. Payson could feel a torrent of different emotions erupt at once, leaving his stomach a firestorm of acid. He held his breath as his eyes locked on hers. After an awkward moment of silence, Gwen stood and started for the lobby. Payson immediately stood to go after her.

"Don't do it," Jax warned. "Your pride's at stake."

"I hear humble pie isn't too bad if you're eating it with a beautiful girl," Hunter countered, lifting his brow at Payson.

Payson took one last look at Jax, then turned and started after Gwen.

"Gwen!" Payson called out once he had reached the lobby. Gwen stopped, though she didn't turn to face him.

Payson took a quick breath. "Gwen, I'm not sure what happened between us, but I—"

"Payson, please. Don't—"

Before she could finish, her date entered the lobby, his face showing both concern and confusion.

"Is something wrong?" he asked, walking to Gwen's side, then shooting a quick glance toward Payson, whose face was quickly turning red.

Gwen shook her head as she turned to face her date. "No, I'm fine. I just needed to get an eyelash out of my eye."

"*Gwen!*"

They all turned as Hunter entered, one of his trademark grins lighting his face.

Relief instantly flashed across Gwen's face. "Hunter. How are you?"

Hunter walked over and gave her a hug. "Couldn't be better," he said as he stepped back. "Just counting down the days 'til I can leave on my mission."

Payson watched with envy as Gwen reached out and squeezed Hunter's arm. "I'm so excited for you, Hunter. You're going to make a fabulous missionary."

"And what about you? I heard you landed some great job in Los Angeles. When do you start?"

"In about a month." Gwen reached her hand out toward the guy next to her, taking him by the arm. "Hunter, I'd like you to meet Sam."

More like Samson, Payson thought, eyeing Gwen's small hand on the guy's giant bicep.

Hunter stuck his hand out to Sam. "Nice to meet you."

Sam smiled, showing off a set of teeth that looked like they had come straight out of an orthodontic brochure. "You too," Sam offered before turning a questioning glance toward Payson, who remained silent.

"And this is Payson," Gwen offered, her eyes finally making contact with his.

"Hi," Payson said simply, forcing a cordial smile as he accepted the man's firm handshake.

"So, how do you all know each other?" Sam asked, taking a step closer to Gwen.

Payson's eyes went straight to Gwen. She opened her mouth to speak, but it seemed she couldn't quite find the words. Her cheeks deepened in hue. Again, Hunter came to the rescue.

"We're friends," he said, with a bold smile that immediately lessened the tension.

Sam smiled. "You're lucky guys then, because Gwen is pretty amazing."

Payson could feel all the muscles across his shoulders and up his neck pull taut, while somewhere inside his head it felt like a vein had exploded. "Living in Provo, I guess we're all pretty lucky," Payson began, his mouth leading the way before his brain could catch up, "because there are lots of amazing girls . . . like Gwen."

Everyone stopped, their eyes glued on Payson. Hunter just shook his head, but it was the hurt in Gwen's eyes that held his attention.

"Wait a minute," Sam began as if he had just been struck with an epiphany. "You're *Payson?*" Sam stole a quick look over at Gwen, who nodded to confirm this.

"That's right," Payson said, sure that now this guy would see just how calloused Gwen was being, flaunting this new relationship right in front of her ex-almost–fiancé.

Instead the guy looked at Payson as if he had just stepped in something unpleasant. "Well," Sam began, turning back to Gwen, "should we go back in?"

Gwen nodded and reached for Sam's arm, moving in close to him. Payson almost rolled his eyes at the gesture. Maybe Jax was right. Maybe it was time to give this girl a taste of her own medicine.

"Hey, you wouldn't happen to have Tristin's phone number would you?"

Gwen slowly turned back around, but instead of the jealousy that Payson expected to see on her face, there was only despondency. "She just got a new cell phone this week. I'm sorry, but I can't remember the number."

Sure you don't, Payson wanted to blurt out, though he decided against digging himself a bigger hole. "That's okay. I'll just have to stop by and see her."

Payson could hear Hunter groan. Sam shook his head, the veins running up the sides of his neck fit to burst, though he didn't say a word. Instead he wrapped an arm around Gwen's slender waist, and the two walked back into the restaurant.

"Well? How did that go?" Jax asked a few minutes later, a look of *I told you so* plastered on his face as Payson climbed into the backseat of his Mazda RX-8.

"If keeping your pride means acting like a total jerk, mine's still intact," Payson replied, then looked over at Hunter. "Maybe that road trip of yours isn't such a bad idea after all."

CHAPTER FOUR

Saturday, April 26 / Los Angeles

Payson sat on the bed staring down at the cell phone next to him, willing it to ring. After driving through the night and arriving at a hotel early that morning, both Jax and Hunter had changed into their swimming trunks and immediately headed for the hot tub. Though his own back ached from spending the later part of the drive in the cramped backseat of Jax's Mazda, Payson had remained in the room, intent on getting ahold of Gwen so he could apologize. When he had seen her a week ago with another man, he had felt like his heart had been sucked from his chest. But knowing he had acted just like the Neanderthal he had accused Jax of being had made him feel even worse. If anything, it had probably only reconfirmed to Gwen that her decision to end their relationship had been for the best.

Payson shook his head, wishing he could forget the look of disappointment on her face, though he knew that wouldn't happen until he had set things right. He had tried for days to get ahold of her, but she wouldn't answer his calls. Payson let out a discouraged breath, then reached out and picked up his cell phone to try again, but before he could push redial, it rang.

"Hello," Payson said, his heart racing.

"You've got a lot of nerve," Tristin Hendly snapped, skipping all formalities.

When Payson had been unable to reach Gwen the night before, in desperation he had called one of her roommates to get Tristin's new cell phone number. Finding that she wasn't home, he had left a message telling her that he was with Jax and Hunter in L.A. but needed to talk to her ASAP. Apparently, from Tristin's tone of voice, Gwen had already filled her in on the incident at El Acapulco.

"Tell me you *did not* ask Gwen for my number!"

Payson opened his mouth to speak, but Tristin cut him off. "I thought you were one of the good guys. I even came to your defense, telling Gwen that she was making a big mistake. Boy was *I* wrong," Tristin railed, her volume rising sharply with each word. "You're just like that sorry excuse for a man you call a roommate."

"Look, Tristin," Payson began, not at all comfortable with the comparison, "I was wrong. I admit it. And I've tried for days to call and tell Gwen just that."

Payson waited for Tristin to comment. When she didn't, he let his breath out hard and shook his head in defeat, his thoughts suddenly reflective. "I just don't get it. I mean, one day we're talking about our future together, and the next she's calling it quits. I could understand if something had happened, or if she just changed her mind about us, but I think I at least deserve some kind of explanation."

"I agree," Tristin said, taking Payson by complete surprise.

"You *do?*"

"Look, I'm going to forget the fact that you behaved like a complete primate at El Acapulco, though that's going to be hard to do. And I'm going to assume that the real you is still there, hidden behind your infantile urge to act like a buffoon to protect your precious ego. But if I'm wrong . . ." Tristin blew her breath out in an explosion of frustration. "I can't believe I'm doing this," she mumbled.

Just then the hotel door opened, and Hunter and Jax walked in. Payson glanced up, then immediately turned his attention back to the phone.

"Doing what?" Payson asked, shaking his head in confusion. "Tristin, I'm not following you."

Jax shook his head. "Wrong move, man," he mumbled as he headed for the shower.

Payson shot him a dirty look, then stood up and walked to the window, his back to the room.

"Do you love Gwen?" Tristin asked point blank.

Payson shrugged his shoulders. "At this point, what does it matter?"

"Just answer the question!" Tristin demanded.

"Yes!" Payson blurted out, tired of the game she seemed to be playing.

Payson expected her to snap back with a facetious retort, but instead she was silent. Payson shook his head then sighed in defeat. "Look, forget it. Maybe it's time to accept the obvious. Gwen apparently doesn't love me, so it really doesn't matter what my feelings are for—"

"Payson, Gwen's in L.A.," Tristin blurted out. "We both are."

"*What?* I thought Gwen wasn't leaving until next month."

"We'll be downtown at Lincoln Tower on Monday at eleven o'clock. I'm not sure which office, but it's on the eighth floor. If you want to talk to her, be there."

"Hold on. Let me get a pen," Payson said, feeling a sudden flood of hope rush through him as he grabbed a pen off the nightstand and quickly jotted the name of the building on a nearby pad of paper. "Listen, Tristin, thanks. I owe you big time."

"No," Tristin began solemnly, "she owes you . . . the truth."

Payson clicked off his phone and looked down at the paper in his hand, his mind racing.

"You okay?" Hunter asked, sitting down in a chair, his white towel draped over his damp shoulders.

"Gwen's here in L.A.," Payson began anxiously. "Tristin said to meet them both at some building called Lincoln Tower on Monday at eleven."

"What's she doing here already?" Hunter asked, using one corner of the towel to dry his face.

"I don't know, but it probably has something to do with her internship," Payson guessed.

"So, are you going?"

Payson shrugged. "I've got to give it one more try."

Hunter nodded before a grin began to spread across his face. "So, did Tristin say anything about you asking for her number?"

Payson arched one eyebrow in reply. Hunter grinned and said, "I like that girl. She definitely calls it likes she sees it."

"Well, I believe what she called me was a buffoon," Payson admitted.

"Hey, that's not too bad. I've heard her call Jax a lot worse."

Payson cocked his head to the side, eyeing Hunter curiously. "How come she's so nice to you?"

Hunter lifted his hands up and shrugged, his face flooding with a generous dose of boyish innocence. "Because *I'm* a nice guy. Plus I'm funny. Women like that."

"Hunter, you're not funny."

"Oh, yeah? Okay, so there's these three Mormons and a chicken—"

Payson reached over and grabbed a pillow off the bed and threw it at Hunter, clipping him in the head. "One more word and you're going to be entering the MTC via airmail, no postage needed."

"What? No good-byes for my girlfriend?"

Payson lifted a brow. "You got one?"

"No, but I thought I could borrow one from Jax. He's got enough to spare."

* * *

Monday, April 28, 11:30 A.M. / Downtown Los Angeles

McKenna Bradford climbed from the silver Lexus she had rented for the duration of her stay in L.A., then scanned the length of the building before her. Lincoln Tower was at least forty stories high, its face consisting mainly of large windows and decorative white rock. The top floors, where West Link Conglomerate was located, seemed to narrow as they rose endlessly toward the clouds. At the very top of the building perched The View, an expensive Italian restaurant. It was there that McKenna was scheduled to meet with Nathan Rinehart.

While on the plane early that morning, McKenna had reread the entire file Tatum had put together on Nathan. Nathan Rinehart had graduated from Yale, then quickly entered the business world, undoubtedly after a few well-placed calls from Judge Rinehart. Each new job came with a promotion and a lengthy title. Two years ago, he had landed the senior vice-president position at West Link. The salary he'd received from that promotion could easily have fed a third-world country for three months. In addition to this information, McKenna also knew that Nathan was single, ambidextrous (one of Tatum's random tidbits), and that if the documents she held were factual, he was possibly a killer, or at least an accessory to one. McKenna shook her head in disgust, thinking back to the contempt citation Judge Rinehart had slapped *her* with. Something about a judge who was sworn to uphold the law but found ways around it for his own family didn't sit well with her.

McKenna grabbed her leather briefcase before heading for the entrance of the building. Once inside, she quickly surveyed her surroundings. There was a coffee shop just to the left of the front doors, a small gift shop next to that, and three elevators to her right, directly across from the coffee shop. Sandwiched in the middle was a security station. The security guard behind the counter began to yawn but quickly caught himself and pretended to clear his throat when he saw McKenna watching him.

"Long night?" McKenna asked with a smile.

The guard, who didn't look a day over twenty-two, smiled sheepishly. He looked down at his watch and then lifted his bloodshot eyes back to her.

"It's almost over," he said with open relief. "Can I help you find something?"

McKenna shook her head. "No. I'm just meeting someone at The View."

"Well, I hope you enjoy your lunch," he said amiably.

"Not likely, though I doubt it will have anything to do with the food," McKenna admitted.

The security guard tilted his head and looked at her curiously, but McKenna didn't elaborate. Instead, she turned and started toward the elevators. She glanced absently at an OUT OF ORDER sign on one of the three elevators, chose one that was empty, then stepped inside and pushed the button. As the elevator made its way up to the top floor of Lincoln Tower, McKenna took a deep breath. Though she knew she should be focusing on Nathan Rinehart, her mind kept going back to James and her father. She loved both of them, though the two were as different as night and day. Her father was driven to succeed and saw everything in black-and-white, leaving no room for shades of gray— especially when it came to his daughter—while James seemed to avoid anything that wasn't gray. Though extremely talented, his artwork lacked the passion to be masterful. His personal life was the same. He was surrounded by beautiful women, but he couldn't seem to make any relationship work long enough for McKenna to remember their names.

McKenna shook her head, then stepped forward as the elevator doors opened at the top floor. One look at the sight before her and

McKenna knew exactly how the restaurant had gotten its name. The view of the city was impressive, though McKenna could already feel her palms beginning to sweat. Nathan had requested they meet here, and she was beginning to wish she'd suggested an alternate venue. She quickly diverted her eyes to the maitre d' who stood in the foyer, impeccably dressed in a black suit.

"Welcome, madame. Do you have a reservation?" he asked, his tone very formal.

"I'm dining with Nathan Rinehart."

"Ah, Mr. Rinehart," the man replied, obviously impressed. "He's at his regular table. Please, follow me."

McKenna followed as he made his way toward an elegantly spread table positioned directly in front of one of the full-length windows. Two men turned to face them as they approached. McKenna recognized the first man from a photo that had been included in the file Tatum had put together, but she didn't recognize the second man, nor had she expected him to be there. He appeared to be in his late forties, though she wondered if his athletic build made him look younger than he really was. He had striking hazel eyes and dark brown hair that was just starting to gray at the sides.

"Miss Bradford," the second man began with a broad smile as he stood and extended his hand. "I'm Alan Sutherland, president of West Link."

McKenna accepted his hand with a cordial smile. "Mr. Sutherland, it's a pleasure."

"I apologize for imposing on your lunch today."

"Actually, you just saved me a few steps. I had planned to meet with you anyway while I was in L.A."

His smile broadened. "Good, then I won't feel so bad."

McKenna's eyes then fell on Nathan Rinehart. She begrudgingly allowed that he was more attractive than his picture had portrayed. He had thick, dark hair with a slight wave, and pensive dark blue eyes. He wore a tailored pin-striped gray suit that was draped nicely over his broad shoulders, and he wore a blue silk tie that set off his eyes.

"Miss Bradford," he said simply, his tone not as affable as Mr. Sutherland's.

"Mr. Rinehart," she offered tightly as she accepted his hand in greeting.

Mr. Sutherland gestured for McKenna to take a seat, then he and Rinehart did the same. "How was your flight, Miss . . . ?"

"Please, call me McKenna."

Mr. Sutherland's smile broadened. "As long as you call me Alan."

McKenna nodded, then answered his question. "I prefer to drive, but unfortunately my career doesn't allot the time necessary for that option." She didn't add the fact that she had taken Dramamine as usual so she would sleep through the entire flight.

They all glanced up as their waiter approached carrying three menus.

"That won't be necessary," Alan Sutherland began, holding up his hand. He smiled broadly over at McKenna. "Will you allow me?"

McKenna eyed him curiously. "Be my guest."

"Mr. Rinehart and I will have the usual. The lady will have the chicken alfredo, extra sauce, a small green salad with a lite ranch dressing on the side, and a glass of mineral water," he concluded as he turned his attention to McKenna for her reaction.

"How did you—"

"I hope you don't mind, but I took the liberty of calling your office. Your office manager was kind enough to supply the information I needed," he stated, obviously pleased with himself.

McKenna smiled, though she took a mental note to have a little chat with Tatum as soon as she got home.

"So, what do you think of the view?" Sutherland asked, turning in his seat to look out the window next to him.

McKenna could feel her body tense as she glanced out the window. "It's beautiful," she said, accustomed to hiding her fear. Then she glanced over at Nathan. He looked like he hadn't slept in days. For a second, McKenna almost felt sorry for him, then the image of Mrs. Dillon's family flooded her mind. "Well, Mr. Rinehart, as pleasant as all of this is, I think for your sake we'd better get down to business." She reached for her leather briefcase next to her chair.

"I did it!" Nathan blurted out, his Adam's apple bobbing up and down.

McKenna's head jerked up as she stared at the man before her. *"What?"* she asked, not certain she had heard correctly.

"I did it," he repeated, his voice unsteady. Every muscle in his body seemed to be tensed. "I needed the money. I had some gambling debts. They were going to kill me."

"What are you talking about?" Mr. Sutherland interrupted, clearly shocked.

"I fixed the books. I didn't think anyone would notice."

McKenna could feel the burning in her stomach rising in her throat. "But Mrs. Dillon did?"

Nathan nodded. "I was desperate."

It took every ounce of self-control McKenna could muster to keep her face impassive. The man before her had killed a young mother with no other motive than greed, and the only reason he was confessing now was because of the overwhelming evidence that she had in the files safely tucked away in her briefcase. "So you hired Manning to kill her?"

Nathan nodded again, then took a sip of water. His hands were shaking so severely that he spilled a little on the tablecloth.

Sutherland exhaled slowly. "Why didn't you tell me, Nathan? I would have given you the money."

Unable to meet Sutherland's gaze, Nathan lowered his eyes.

"We're going to have to get a formal confession at the police station," McKenna said, suddenly feeling uneasy. She knew that this situation could turn volatile, especially with the look of wild desperation on Nathan's face.

McKenna glanced over at Sutherland, not at all comfortable with the idea of driving Nathan to the police station alone.

"I'll go with you," Sutherland said, shaking his head, obviously still in a state of shock over what Nathan had just confessed.

McKenna immediately scooted her chair out, but as she did, she felt a slight tremble beneath her feet. It was so slight that she wasn't sure if it had happened or if she had just imagined it. "Did you feel that?" she asked Sutherland, her eyes widening.

"You're in California. We get little tremors from time to time," Sutherland said.

As Sutherland motioned to their waiter that they would not be dining after all, McKenna glanced up at the chandelier. Each of the tiny crystals was quivering, sending a shiver down her spine.

* * *

"We're late," Payson protested as he jumped from the passenger side of the car, pulling his jacket over his shoulders as he made his way through the dimly lit underground parking lot of Lincoln Tower.

"Hey, it's not my fault we hit construction," Jax said as he pulled the keys from the ignition and started after Payson, heading to the elevators.

"Do you want me to stay here?" Hunter called out to Payson. "Just in case you miss her and she comes down here?"

Payson skidded to a stop in front of the elevators, noting that one of them was marked OUT OF ORDER with a sign and two strips of bright yellow tape forming an *X.* "Do you mind?" he called out, glancing over his shoulder at Hunter.

"No problem," Hunter said, slowing his step as Payson and Jax stepped into one of the elevators. "Good luck!"

"Thanks," Payson said as the doors closed.

After stopping at the second underground parking level to allow two people to enter, the elevator brought them to the ground floor, where the doors automatically slid open.

"Maybe we should make sure she's not in the lobby," Jax suggested.

"Good idea," Payson said as Jax quickly hopped out of the elevator and started toward the center of the busy lobby, hastily scanning the faces of the people he passed.

"Is she there?" Payson called out, stepping aside as some people got out of the elevator and others got in.

Jax turned back toward the elevator and shook his head. "I don't see her."

"Thanks," Payson said, letting the elevator doors slide shut.

"Hey, don't worry about me," Jax mumbled sarcastically as he watched the doors pinch closed with Payson still inside. He glanced over at the security guard who was stationed at the center of the lobby behind a large wraparound counter. "Hey, is there anywhere decent to eat around here?"

The security guard yawned as he pointed toward the coffee shop. "The turkey sandwich isn't half bad, but I'd stay away from the egg salad if I were you."

"Thanks," Jax said as he made his way through the crowd.

* * *

Payson glanced down at his watch. It was 11:45. He grimaced, then glanced impatiently at the numbers above the elevator doors that lit up as the elevator began to rise.

"Come on," Payson mumbled under his breath, looking once again at his watch, though he knew the time would be the same.

When the elevator doors opened at the next floor, Payson took a quick step back to make room for a middle-aged man in a business suit who had just entered. As he did, he bumped into someone directly behind him. Payson quickly turned, his eyes going first to the woman's face before falling to her round midsection.

"I'm sorry," Payson stammered anxiously. "Are you all right? Did I hurt you?"

The woman smiled, her hand going instinctively to her belly, which from its size looked like she was due any minute. "I'm fine."

Payson's shoulders fell slack with relief, though his face continued to flood with warmth. "Are you sure?"

Her smile widened. "I'm positive."

Payson slowly turned back around. He fought the urge to look at his watch and instead waited impatiently as the elevator rose to the eighth floor. By the time it did, there were only three other people left in the elevator—the pregnant woman, the man in the suit, and a middle-aged Hispanic man. Payson glanced briefly back at the pregnant woman as the elevator doors began to open.

"Good luck with the baby," he said, still feeling guilty for bumping into her.

"Thank you," she said with a smile.

Payson turned, but as he started forward, the three people standing in the hall ready to enter the elevator stopped him midstride.

"*Payson?*" Gwen said, her face revealing her confusion. "What are *you* doing here?"

Payson stood numbly, the words he had rehearsed the night before suddenly elusive. He almost did a double take when his eyes fell on Sam. Payson wanted to ask him the same question that Gwen had just asked him. Payson glanced briefly at Tristin, who gave him a helpless shrug. Sam folded his arms, sizing Payson up with a glare. Payson felt the same jealousy he had felt at El Acapulco surge through him, but this time he bit his tongue, intent on doing what he had come here to do.

"Why are you here?" Gwen repeated, her face drawn in disbelief.

"Can we go somewhere private . . . to talk?" Payson stammered, glancing uncomfortably at all the eyes that were now on him.

Before Gwen could speak, the doors began to close. Payson hastily stuck his hands out to stop them.

"Listen, buddy, either you get out or they get in," the man in the suit snapped, glancing in annoyance at his watch.

Payson started to walk forward, since Gwen was obviously not budging, but Gwen put her hand out to stop him.

"Payson, go home."

"I can't," he said, no longer caring about the stares they were receiving. "Not until I've set things right."

Sam huffed sarcastically, but Payson ignored him, his eyes remaining on Gwen. "I'm sorry, Gwen. I'm sorry I hurt you."

"Come on!" the man in the suit persisted. "I have a business lunch in five minutes."

Payson nodded impatiently, his grip still firm on the elevator doors.

"It's okay," Gwen said, though her eyes seemed to be telling another story. "There's nothing to forgive. Now go home and get on with your life."

Payson glanced hesitantly at Sam, then quickly back at Gwen, not wanting to ask the question but having to know. "Are you in love?"

Gwen held Payson's gaze for several seconds before slowly nodding. "I'm sorry, Payson. I never wanted to hurt you."

Payson's lungs felt like they were suddenly unable to expand. "It's okay," he began once he could breathe. "You told me it was over. I just didn't know why." He glanced at Sam, feeling suddenly empty. "Now I do." With that, he slowly lowered his hands, allowing the elevator doors to close.

"Don't worry. There will be other girls," the man in the suit offered as soon as the elevator started to rise. "There's probably one out there right now just waiting for the prospect of your future alimony checks."

CHAPTER FIVE

11:50 A.M. / Los Angeles; Top floor, Lincoln Tower

As McKenna walked through the restaurant, she was keenly aware of the man beside her. The anxiety inside Nathan seemed to be building at a rate McKenna was not comfortable with. Though there was not a security guard on the top floor, McKenna had already determined that as soon as they were on the ground floor she would ask the security guard at the front desk to call the police and tell them that they were in need of transport. She would have called from the restaurant herself, but given Rinehart's condition, she was afraid he would panic and change his mind about confessing. With so many other patrons in the restaurant and no security readily available, McKenna had chosen to wait. Now, as she eyed the elevator just a few feet from them, knowing that she and Sutherland—as well as anyone else who got on with them—would be temporarily confined in an enclosed space with a self-confessed killer, she questioned her decision. Clutching her briefcase, she took a deep breath, trying to convince herself that everything was going to be all right, though a nagging feeling in the back of her mind screamed that just the opposite was true.

Finally determining that the risk was simply too great, McKenna stopped directly under the intricately carved entryway that separated the restaurant from the elevators and reached in her purse for her cell phone. Sutherland lifted a questioning brow, but before he could speak, an unnatural groan resounded from somewhere deep within the infrastructure of the building. The noise thundered up through the elevator shaft, and McKenna heard what sounded like metal beams protesting as they were twisted and bent.

"What was that?" McKenna asked, her eyes wide as she gaped in horror at the elevator in front of her.

But before anyone could speak, the whole building began to tremble. McKenna reached out to grab hold of the wooden entryway beside her but instead was tossed directly into it, the floor beneath her seemingly ripped out from under her. Her left shoulder took the brunt of the blow, sending shooting pain up her arm, though she still managed to hold on and remain standing. McKenna glanced behind her as the chandelier crashed to the floor, sending a thousand crystals flying in every direction and just missing a young woman by a fraction of an inch. The woman screamed, though the sound was muted by the shattering of glass, the cracking of cement, and what seemed to be the groaning of the very earth itself. Holding onto the frame of the entryway, McKenna watched helplessly as one man stumbled toward the windows. He caught hold of a long, flower-patterned curtain as he tumbled through the glass, shattering it to pieces. McKenna screamed, sure that the man was now plummeting to the base of Lincoln Tower. A large man dove for the other end of the curtain just as it tore free from the rod mounted to the wall. Two other men, seeing what was happening, dove for the big man's feet as he began to slide toward the window ledge from the weight of the first man, who was now precariously dangling forty stories above the ground. McKenna could see the strain in the men's faces as they fought to pull the man up to safety and to maintain their grip as the building continued to crumble around them.

McKenna tightened her hold on the wooden frame, praying with everything in her that the man would live—that *she* would live. Then her eyes fell on a white pillar just feet away from the men who were struggling by the shattered window. The ceiling above the pillar was crumbling, causing the pillar to wobble. McKenna's eyes flashed back to the men, who now had the first man pulled up to the window ledge, then back to the pillar that was now completely severed from the ceiling. She screamed, knowing that within seconds the pillar would crash to the floor with all four men in its path. One of the men, who had grabbed hold of the first man's arm and was dragging him into the room, glanced up and spotted the pillar. McKenna could see him screaming at the other men, though she couldn't hear his words over all the noise in the room. Instead she watched in horror as the pillar began to fall, thundering to the floor with a loud crash. McKenna closed her eyes, not wanting to see whether the men had gotten out of the way in time.

"McKenna . . . *McKenna!*"

McKenna jerked around to see Alan Sutherland struggling to hold on to the other side of the entryway. His forehead was bleeding, and streams of blood coursed down both sides of his face.

"Hold on!" she screamed, unable to do anything else.

Although McKenna closed her eyes again, not wanting to watch the death and destruction taking place all around her, she was unable to block out the sounds. Somewhere off to her left she could hear the chilling scream of a woman in pain. She leaned her forehead onto the wooden frame, praying out loud over and over again for it all to end.

After what seemed like hours, though in actuality was only moments, the shaking lessened and then stopped completely. At first, everything was eerily silent. The only sound was the unnatural groaning of the building as it repositioned itself. McKenna had to pry her stiffened fingers from the wooden frame of the entryway, her whole body still trembling. For a moment, she just stood in a blank stupor as she scanned the scene before her, the noises and images assaulting her senses. The dust from falling debris left a light haze in the air, which mingled with the moans and cries of the wounded and the guttural groans of the dying, lending an unnerving, almost surreal, feel to the room. Tables were overturned and chairs scattered, and broken pieces of china and shattered crystal were strewn everywhere. Electrical wires sparked as they dangled from the ceiling where the chandelier had been, while the other remaining lights flickered several times before going out completely. McKenna could feel the palpitations of her heart throbbing in her temples as she took in the scene before her. She had been scared before, but the feeling of horror that now coursed through her veins was like nothing she had ever felt.

"McKenna!"

McKenna glanced blankly over at Alan Sutherland, his presence and the look on his face instantly snapping her out of her daze. She took a deep breath to steady her shaking knees before making her way over to him.

"Are you okay?" she asked, her voice shaky.

He nodded, though he looked like he was in shock.

McKenna glanced up as the backup generator kicked on and the lights flickered slowly back to life, though their strength was considerably weaker. She breathed a slow sigh of relief, but her respite was short-lived as another thought struck her cold. "Where's Nathan?" she asked urgently.

Sutherland had taken a handkerchief from his pocket and was pressing it to his head. "Well, after he did this," he began, temporarily lifting the blood-soaked hanky to expose a gash, "he took off." He glanced around at the destruction surrounding them. "Not that he's going to get far."

McKenna quickly glanced around the room, though she knew it was unlikely that she would spot him in all the debris. Then she looked over her shoulder at the stairs next to the elevators. He could be anywhere, really.

"We need some help over here!" someone from across the room shouted.

McKenna quickly turned, immediately recognizing the man who had shouted. It was one of the men who'd helped the guy who had fallen out the window. The guy that he had rescued, as well as one of the other men who had helped, were standing next to him, while the big man who had initially grabbed the curtain lay on the floor, his arm pinned under the enormous pillar. He was screaming in pain, while the men around him worked to set him free. McKenna watched as an older man made his way over to the pillar. He looked like he was barely able to carry his own weight, let alone lift a thousand-pound pillar.

"We need to get out of here before one of the aftershocks takes down the whole building." McKenna whirled around to face Sutherland. "Aftershocks?" she asked anxiously.

"With a quake as big as this one, you can expect several aftershocks. Some of them might be even more deadly than the first quake, especially considering the building's weakened structural state." Using the wall for support, Sutherland stood and pointed toward an EXIT sign near the stairs. "Come on."

McKenna glanced back at the men who were trying unsuccessfully to pry the pillar off the man trapped beneath. "What about them?"

Before Sutherland could speak, an explosion of sound caused McKenna to freeze, her breath suddenly stolen from her. She and everyone else in the restaurant slowly turned in the direction the noise was coming from. It sounded like solid metal beams being manipulated under immense pressure and then finally snapping in two as if they were toothpicks. While they watched in stunned silence, the east corner of the restaurant, where the kitchen was located, broke free from the rest of the building and plunged to the ground. McKenna stood with her mouth open wide, her brain temporarily unable to decipher the message her eyes were sending.

The sound of the massive remains of the entire eastern corner of Lincoln Tower plummeting to the ground was earth-shattering, sparking instant pandemonium. McKenna grabbed Alan Sutherland's hand and yanked him away from the restaurant's entryway, narrowly avoiding being trampled as several people in a state of sheer panic bullied their way toward the elevators and stairs, heedless of the wounded and dying who were calling out to them. One man pounded on the panel of buttons next to the elevators while two others attempted to pry open the doors, one of them almost falling into the vacant space once they did. McKenna quickly glanced back toward the man who was pinned under the pillar, relieved to see that several men were still frantically attempting to free him.

"We've got to help them," McKenna said, turning to Sutherland.

They both turned as someone else cried out for help. McKenna's head whipped around, looking for the source of the plea. After only a moment, Sutherland pointed toward an older woman not far from them, who lay on the floor next to a baby grand piano.

"You go help her, and I'll go help them lift the pillar," Sutherland suggested.

McKenna nodded and rushed over to the woman, quickly bending down to face her. The woman immediately reached for McKenna's hand, her own hand cold and clammy.

"Help me," she begged, her eyes round with fear.

McKenna glanced down at the front of the woman's dress. It was saturated with blood.

"We need help," McKenna shouted over her shoulder before turning her attention back to the woman.

"Am I going to die?" the woman asked, her voice trembling as much as her body.

McKenna began to shake her head. "No, you're not going to die," she said, tears running freely down her cheeks.

The woman flinched in pain. McKenna tightened her grip on the woman's hand as the woman's eyes grew even wider, her gaze directed over McKenna's shoulder. McKenna turned around to see what the woman was looking at, but there was nothing there. With her own brow pinched in confusion, McKenna turned back around. Looking intently at the woman's expression, she watched in awe as all the fear that had been written across the elderly woman's face slowly dissipated like fog lifting off a lake with the approach of the sun, leaving in its place only warmth and light. Then it was over. The woman's hand fell limp, and her eyes stared vacantly off into space. For a moment, McKenna just sat there, holding her hand, unable to process what had just happened.

McKenna jumped as part of the ceiling behind her caved in. She held her breath, anticipating that the rest of the roof would follow. When it didn't, she slowly exhaled, then gently placed the older woman's hand over her heart and closed her eyelids. As McKenna stood, someone placed a hand on her shoulder. She jerked around to face Sutherland.

"Let's get out of this death trap."

McKenna's eyes flashed toward the pillar, but the section of ceiling that had caved in blocked her view.

"Did you get him out?" McKenna asked anxiously.

Sutherland grabbed her hand. "Yes. Now *we* need to get out."

McKenna wiped at her damp cheeks as she followed Sutherland to the stairs, knowing that at any minute the rest of the building could crumble down around them.

* * *

Payson struggled to open his eyes, his head throbbing with the effort. It took a moment to focus and another moment to realize what had just happened. When it did, it felt like a linebacker for the 49ers had plowed into him, leaving his lungs struggling to expand.

"Are you okay?"

Payson looked up into the strained face of the woman beside him.

"I think so," Payson began, his hand going immediately to his aching head. When he pulled it back, it was sticky with blood.

"Hold still," the woman urged as she gently lifted his head and began wrapping something around his forehead. "You're lucky. I went shopping for the baby just before I came here, and receiving blankets were on my list."

Payson's eyes went immediately to the woman's round abdomen. "Are *you* okay?" he asked anxiously, absolutely positive that he did not want to deliver a baby in an elevator.

"A little banged up, but the baby's still moving," she said, her face clearly showing relief as she tied a knot in the blanket at the back of Payson's head.

"Thank you . . ."

"Anna," the woman offered. "Anna Stevens."

"I'm Payson," he said, flinching as he reached up and touched the tender place on his head.

"I am Manuel Gonzales."

Payson glanced over at the middle-aged Hispanic man. He was sitting in the corner cradling his mangled left arm with his right.

"What happened?" Payson asked them both as he attempted to sit up.

"It is either an earthquake or *explosión,*" Manuel offered, his accent thick. "We are not sure."

"We'll know soon," another voice added gloomily.

Payson turned his eyes to the man in the business suit who was sitting on the floor with his back up against the wall, his elbows on his bent knees, and his head bowed and resting in his hands.

"What do you mean?" Payson asked hesitantly.

The man slowly lifted his head to face Payson. "There'll be after-shocks if it was an earthquake. Fire if it was an explosion."

"Then we've got to get her out of here!" Payson exclaimed, not liking the implications of either scenario.

"How?" the business man snapped in frustration, gesturing over at the closed metal doors. "I've already tried to get them open. They won't budge."

In a sudden flash of horror, Payson's mind reeled back to the last few minutes before he had been knocked out. "Gwen," he breathed, his insides feeling as though they were being squeezed in a massive vise. Payson jumped to his feet, instantly woozy. He reached for the wall to steady himself, then stood still for a minute, hoping that everything would quit spinning. He could feel the wrap around his head flooding with warmth.

"You need to sit down," Anna urged, looking at him with concern.

Wanting to disagree but knowing that if he didn't sit down he would probably fall down, he reluctantly obeyed. He wouldn't be any help to Gwen if he passed out, or worse, if the bleeding continued.

"Put some pressure on it," Anna instructed, reaching over and placing his hand on top of the bandage. "That'll help stop the bleeding."

The man in the suit rolled his eyes. "That way you won't bleed to death. You'll just plummet to the ground in a sealed metal coffin or starve to death while waiting to be rescued," he said as he glanced around the tiny enclosed box that, with his morbid description, now *felt* like a coffin.

"Thanks for the visual," Payson said, still holding firmly to the blanket wrapped around his head.

Anna shook her head, but when she glanced back at Payson, her eyes widened. "You're a Mormon?"

Payson looked at her in confusion, but she only smiled and pointed to the hand still raised to his head. "You're wearing a CTR ring," she offered, seeing his confusion.

He nodded his head and then lifted his brow curiously. "Are you?"

She returned his smile. "I joined the Church a few months ago."

"That's great," Payson said.

"Yeah, just great!" the man in the suit mumbled sarcastically. "I'm stuck here with an illegal, a Mormon, and a pregnant woman who also happens to be a Mormon."

"I am not illegal. I am American citizen like you," Manuel said, his jaw tight.

Payson could feel the tension building and knew it was time to change the subject. "So, what's your name?" he asked the businessman.

"Richard," the man replied wearily.

"Well, Richard," Payson began, forcing his tone to remain civil, "you got any ideas on how to get us out of here?"

"If I did, do you think I'd still be in here with the three of you?"

Manuel said something in Spanish, his eyes racing over Richard in disgust. Though Payson didn't understand a word, he was positive that it matched his own sentiments. Payson exhaled, then lifted his eyes to Anna as she got up, took another receiving blanket from her bag, and began tying it to make a sling for Manuel.

"Gracias, señora," he said with a grateful smile, which she warmly reciprocated.

Payson looked over at Richard, who was scowling at them both. Payson shook his head and leaned back against the wall, his eyes rising to the ceiling. As he stared up, an idea struck him, causing his heart rate to jump.

"The ceiling!" he exclaimed, immediately earning everyone's attention. He slowly got to his feet, temporarily forgetting to apply pressure to the gash on his head. "There's got to be a way out through the top."

Manuel nodded as a broad smile spread across his face. *"Si, señor.* You are right, I think."

Even Richard got to his feet, his frown-creased face showing a glimmer of hope.

"Richard could give me a boost up," Payson began, talking out loud as he worked the problem out in his head. "I could pop the top and climb through . . . see if there's a way out through the shaft. The rest of you could follow."

"So you can pass out up there and leave us stranded? No way," Richard spat out sarcastically. "You give *me* a boost up."

Payson could already feel a streak of blood running down the side of his face. "Okay," he agreed hesitantly, not liking the idea of their lives being in the hands of the man before him but having no other options.

"What about me?"

They all turned to look at Anna, who had gotten to her feet, her stomach sticking out from her otherwise slim body like a bowling ball.

Payson could hear Richard mumble something under his breath, but he kept his own eyes on Anna. "You have my word. We won't leave you." Then he immediately turned to Richard, his eyes filled with warning. "Will we?"

Richard returned the glare but slowly shook his head.

Anna swallowed hard, her thoughtful eyes showing relief.

"Alright, let's do it," Richard urged impatiently as he took off his suit coat, then wiped his sweaty palms on his pin-striped slacks.

Payson crouched slightly, bending his legs and locking his fingers together to make a stepping stool for Richard. Manuel stood next to Payson to help balance Richard with his good arm. After a quick boost up, Richard pressed on the drop ceiling, lifting it up like a trapdoor.

"A little higher," Richard urged as he tried to pull himself up through the opening.

Payson strained to lift Richard's legs higher, his head pounding so hard he was sure it would explode.

"Okay, I've got it," Richard finally called out, pulling himself up through the hole.

Payson staggered toward the wall, lifting his hand to the saturated cloth around his head before glancing down at the blood-speckled floor.

"You've got to sit down," Anna insisted, taking him by one arm as Manuel took the other.

Once Payson was sitting on the floor of the elevator, Anna placed her hand over the wound and again began applying pressure while Payson lifted his eyes to the hole in the ceiling.

"Is there a way out?"

"Just a minute," Richard called out, his voice echoing through the shaft.

Manuel turned to Payson, his eyes skeptical. "He will leave us, no?"

Payson let his breath out hard, hoping Manuel was wrong but knowing deep down that he was probably right.

"Richard! What do you see?" Payson called out.

For a minute there was no sound. Payson glanced first at the pregnant woman next to him, and then at Manuel, who was still clutching his left arm, his face showing the same dread that was quickly spreading through Payson.

"There's a drop-off on either side of us, just wide enough for the other two elevators that share the shaft. But on each wall there are metal stairs running the length of the shaft," Richard called out, eliciting a collective sigh of relief from everyone in the elevator. "There's a floor a few feet up. I'm going to use the stairs just to the right of this elevator to go check it out."

"Be careful," Payson called out, knowing that his warning was not just for Richard's well-being, but for theirs as well.

Payson closed his eyes, his thoughts suddenly on Hunter and Jax. Jax was in the lobby on the bottom floor, so as long as he hadn't been hurt in the earthquake he should've been able to get out easily. But Hunter was in the parking garage, two floors underground. Payson suddenly felt sick. He forced his mind away from any thoughts of Hunter, assuring himself that he was all right, but that only brought his thoughts back to Gwen. *Where was she? Did she get on the other elevator? Was she*—Payson stopped, his eyes wide. "Richard, can you see the other elevator?"

There was silence for a moment as they all waited for Richard to respond. Finally, when Payson was sure that a vein somewhere in his cranium would rupture, he heard a loud thud as Richard jumped back down onto the top of the elevator.

"I can't get the door to the next floor open. I need a bar or something to pry it with," he called down through the hole.

"Richard," Payson began, unable to think about anything else until he was sure that Gwen was all right. "Can you see the other elevator?"

Richard hesitated. "Yeah, it's about four floors below us."

Payson sighed with relief. "Thank you," he breathed as he cast his eyes heavenward.

"It may be that there is someone in the other elevator with something we can use to open the doors," Manuel suggested, his dark eyes on Payson.

Payson nodded. "Richard, can you make it down to the other elevator? Maybe they'll have something we can use as leverage to open the door."

This time Richard stuck his head partially through the hole. "And just how do you expect me to get down there? The metal stairs that I just used are on the opposite side of this elevator. So to get down to the other elevator, I'd have to jump across the shaft to the stairs on the other side."

"If you fell, you'd land on the other elevator," Payson offered.

"Yeah, four floors down!" Richard exclaimed, his face reminding Payson of a hot chili pepper. "Are you crazy?"

"Hey, you're the one who wanted to go up," Payson snapped.

In desperation, Payson turned his eyes to Manuel and Anna. "I've got to get up there."

"Payson, until you stop bleeding you're not going anywhere," Anna warned him.

Payson covered his face with his hands. *Think, Payson, think,* he berated himself. After several seconds, he lifted his head, his eyes falling on a purse that lay on the floor in the corner. Payson immediately reached out and grabbed it. He had it halfway open before he hesitantly looked at Anna. "Do you mind?"

"Go ahead," she said, her brow lifted in curiosity.

"You wouldn't happen to have a crowbar stashed in here, would you?" Payson asked, lightening the mood.

Anna smiled halfheartedly. "I wish."

Payson dumped the contents of the purse onto the floor and began rummaging through them to see if there was anything that could help them. There was a pack of gum, a tube of lipstick, a checkbook and pen, a brush, and a Snickers bar.

"It was my last doctor's appointment," Anna said, gesturing to the candy bar. "I thought, what the heck."

Payson smiled, then lowered his head and continued rummaging through the items, his face pulling into a scowl.

"What are looking for?" Manuel asked.

"I don't know," Payson mumbled.

Anna instantly got to her feet, returning to Payson's side a second later with the shopping bag she had retrieved the receiving blankets from. "There are a few more things in here, though I don't know how much they'll help us," Anna offered, extending the bag to Payson.

From the bag Payson pulled three more blankets, a package of white and yellow onesies, a bottle of baby lotion, and a tube of superglue.

"Yesterday I broke the handle off a little china cup that belonged to my grandmother," Anna explained, pointing to the glue. "I got that to fix it."

"This is perfect!" Payson exclaimed, picking up the glue and ripping it from the package.

"What is used for?" Manuel asked, his face scrunched in confusion.

"To seal up the gash on my head," Payson said, smiling triumphantly.

"You've got to be kidding," Anna said, looking at him as if he had lost his mind.

Payson shook his head with a grin. "We did it once on a campout. My friends and I were up in the Uintas doing a snow camp. One of the guys whacked his head on a rock. We were miles from the nearest hospital, so he cleaned up the gash and had me pour some superglue into the wound. After that, I held it closed for a few minutes until it sealed."

"And it worked?" Anna asked in surprise.

Payson nodded. "We finished our snow cave, spent two nights nearly freezing to death, and went home planning how we were going to do exactly the same thing the next year."

"This can't be healthy," Anna said, taking the glue from Payson's outstretched hand.

"Neither is bleeding to death, no?" Manuel offered.

Payson nodded. "We can't just sit and wait for someone to rescue us. We've got to do something."

"My husband is a captain with the Los Angeles Fire Department. He knows I'm here," Anna said. "He'll come for us."

"There is no time," Manuel said, his eyes holding the same uncertainty and fear that filled Anna's.

They all froze as the elevator began to creak, the sound echoing through the shaft. Payson held his breath, knowing that at any minute the cable could break, sending them screaming down eight plus stories to a certain—though likely instant—demise. When the noise finally subsided, Payson glanced at Manuel, and then the two turned to Anna.

"We can't wait," Payson said. "I've got to get down to the other elevator."

Richard stuck his head through the hole, his eyes going immediately to Payson. "We need to get out of here. I don't know how long this cable's going to hold."

"What do you want me to do?" Anna asked, turning her attention to Payson.

"Take the bandage off," Payson began. "See if the bleeding has stopped. If it has, pour the glue along the edges of the cut, hold it closed for a few minutes, and then put more on top to make sure it stays sealed."

Anna nodded, then lifted her shaking hands to remove the small receiving blanket. Though the blood was still relatively wet around the cut, the bleeding appeared to have stopped. Anna dabbed at the two-inch gash with a dry section of the blanket, then took a deep breath, unscrewed the lid from the glue, and began applying it to the gash. Payson flinched but remained still for the next few minutes while she finished.

"If this were reality TV, I think this would be the part where someone would say, 'Don't try this at home,'" Payson said as he patiently waited for her to finish.

Anna shook her head, a slight smile playing on her lips. "Don't worry. I wasn't planning on it."

"Thanks," Payson said as Anna gently wrapped a clean blanket around his head.

"It was cut pretty deep. I'm not sure if it will hold. You better wait for a while to see."

Payson nodded. Though he wanted to get to Gwen as soon as possible, his body was still feeling the effects of the loss of blood. "I don't think I have much of a choice."

Appearing relieved that he was willing to wait for at least a time, Anna leaned her back up against the wall of the elevator. "Do you really think we'll get out of here?" she asked, slowly turning her eyes back to Payson.

Payson opened his mouth to reassure her, but the words just wouldn't come. His own thoughts instantly turned to Hunter, Jax, and Gwen. *Please help them,* he prayed before his gaze returned to Anna. *Please help us all.*

CHAPTER SIX

12:05 P.M. / Los Angeles; Ground floor, Lincoln Tower

"Hey! We need some help here!" Jax barked before turning back to the giant chunk of cement before him and the man who lay partially buried beneath it. The man was fighting a losing battle just to stay conscious, the immense weight on his chest slowly suffocating him.

"Hold on. I'm gonna get you out," Jax insisted, ignoring the persistent voice inside his head telling him that he was wasting precious time on a dead man. "Hurry!" Jax shouted over his shoulder to the security guard who was struggling to make his way over to them through the mounds of debris scattered everywhere.

Another man came up beside Jax, his own hair wet and matted with blood. "My wife," he said, his eyes wild and his pupils dilated. "You've got to help my wife," he insisted, pulling on Jax's arm.

"Calm down!" Jax urged, pulling back from the man's grasp and taking him firmly by the shoulders so he could look him in the eye. "Where's your wife?"

"I don't know," the man mumbled, his brow creased in confusion. He glanced over at a large mound of debris that stood where the sitting area of the coffee shop had been. "We were drinking coffee," he began, his eyes glassy. "I needed another sugar. I stood up and walked to the counter. Then I heard a horrible noise, like thunder." He stopped, his face contorting in sheer agony as the realization of what had happened sunk in. Jax could feel his own chest constrict as he watched the man slowly drop to his knees and begin to sob like an infant.

Unaware that anyone else was listening, Jax flinched when the security guard placed his hand on his shoulder. Jax turned to face him, knowing at a glance that the guard had been standing there long enough to see what had just happened. Jax suddenly felt numb. He glanced over at the man trapped under the cement just a few feet from them. Then, as if his body were on autopilot, he started toward him.

"You've got to help me lift this off him," Jax said as he attempted to lift the massive slab of concrete. When the guard didn't move, Jax glanced up at him, his despondency and shock quickly replaced by anger. "Don't just stand there. Help me!" he demanded.

The security guard reached over and grabbed Jax by the shoulders, his grip firm but his eyes filled with compassion. "He's gone."

For a minute, Jax just stared at him; the words wouldn't register. Then, he slowly turned and looked down at the vacant stare of the man trapped beneath the cement. Suddenly Jax felt like he couldn't breathe, like his lungs no longer knew how to function. The security guard bent down and closed the dead man's eyes while Jax turned away, finally choking in a couple of quick breaths of air thick with dust.

When the security guard was done, he stood, his eyes back on Jax. "I'm Mike Jevicky."

"Jax Hampton," Jax offered numbly.

Mike looked down at the man kneeling on the floor before the wall of rubble that had buried his wife.

"Come with us," Mike said.

The man shook his head. "I can't leave her."

Mike bent down next to him. "You've got to."

The man glanced at Mike, then hesitantly nodded, fresh tears spilling over. Jax felt a slight rush of relief.

"Let's get him to the front of the building," Mike said, wrapping his arm around one of the man's shoulders for support while Jax got the other.

Jax forced himself to concentrate on the light that flooded in through the front doors, making the particles of dust in the air dance, instead of looking at the death and destruction within the building. Once they were through the doors, Jax stopped, his mind unable to grasp the enormity of the devastation outside. The only thing he could compare it to was footage he had seen of New Orleans right after Hurricane Katrina. Jax's knees felt weak, and his stomach tightened until he thought he would retch.

"Keep toward the middle of the street," Mike instructed the man who had just lost his wife. "It'll be safer there. Then keep on walking until you find help."

Looking like a lost little boy, the man obediently walked out into the street. Mike let his breath out hard as he allowed his eyes to take in the scene. Though they could hear sirens in the far distance, with the amount of damage the city had received, combined with the stream of wrecked cars blocking the roadways, Jax knew it would be a long time until help arrived. Mike turned to Jax, a look of determination in his eyes.

"Look, I'm going back in to see if I can help a few people get out, but trust me, I wouldn't think any less of you if you stayed out here."

Jax glanced at the entryway to Lincoln Tower, knowing firsthand what awaited him if he went back inside. Then he looked at Mike, hardly believing the words that came out of his mouth. "I can't just leave them in there to die."

Jax could see obvious relief on Mike's face, though a look of warning remained in his eyes. "I can't promise that once we go in we'll get another chance to get out."

Jax's eyes were drawn back to the people who were slowly making their way out the front doors. Though some seemed to have made it through the ordeal relatively unscathed—at least physically—many others limped, their clothes ripped and stained with blood, their faces tear-streaked and dirty, and their eyes glazed over in a state of disbelief and shock. One man carefully helped an elderly woman out of the building, though he looked like he was in worse shape than she was, while another man angrily walked out the entryway, seemingly only concerned with the fact that his cell phone wouldn't work. Jax looked back at Mike and nodded, his decision made. "Let's do it."

Mike slapped Jax across the back, the respect that filled his eyes speaking volumes, then the two headed back into the building. Once inside, Mike went straight to the security desk. He grabbed two flashlights from under the counter, handed one to Jax, then pointed toward the elevators.

"There's a utility closet just to the right of the elevators. I'll go see if I can get some rope or any other supplies that might help. Why don't you go back over to the coffee shop and see if you can find us some food and water." Mike reached under the counter and pulled out a duffel bag, which he promptly handed to Jax, along with a first-aid kit. Then he glanced down at his watch. "I'll meet you back here in five minutes."

Jax agreed as he quickly placed the first-aid kit in the duffel bag and swung it over one shoulder.

Almost exactly five minutes later, Jax met Mike back at the security counter. Mike had a metal rod in his hand, and the flashlight he had pulled from under the counter was now clipped to the utility belt around his waist. "I found this," he began as he held up the rod, "but I couldn't find any rope. How'd you do?"

"I got a bag of pastries and six or seven bottles of water," Jax said, gesturing to the duffel bag.

Mike nodded as they both glanced over at a bundle of sparking wires snaking out from beneath a pile of rubble. Mike took a steady breath. "You ready?" he said, glancing back at Jax, his face anxious.

Jax swallowed hard, his thoughts not only on Hunter and Payson but also on what awaited him in the wreckage. "Ready," he said, his jaw set in determination.

The two of them started toward the stairs, but once they reached them, Jax quickly rounded the stairwell and headed down.

"Hey, where are you going?" Mike asked.

"I have a friend down in the bottom parking garage."

Mike scratched his head, clearly doubtful that anyone down there was still alive, but he didn't comment. Instead, he gestured for Jax to lead the way, and both of them took the stairs two at a time. As they rounded the stairwell leading to the first parking garage, Jax skidded to a stop. One wall and a section of the ceiling had caved in, completely blocking the doorway to the garage as well as the stairs leading down to the second garage.

"*No!*" Jax shouted, fighting the urge to punch the wall next to him.

As Mike came up beside him, Jax turned to face him, his eyes wide. "Tell me there's another way in."

Mike slowly shook his head. "This is the only set of stairs. We could go in through the outside entrance, but it's on the east side of the building, and it's—"

"Buried," Jax finished, the word barely escaping his constricting vocal cords.

Unable to bear the mental image of Hunter trapped in a dark, cement tomb, Jax began digging wildly through the debris. Mike shook his head, but then dug in alongside him. After digging for some time with little success, Mike finally took Jax by the arm.

"I've got an idea," he said as he reached down and picked up the duffel bag Jax had dropped on the floor.

Jax whirled around, his eyes searching Mike's face expectantly.

"Come on," Mike said, heading back up the stairs with Jax close behind him.

A few minutes later, Jax stared down through the elevator doors Mike had just pried open to the dimly-lit shaft below. Then he twisted his neck to look up at the top of the shaft. Though it was hard to see with just the backup generator providing light, Jax could make out two elevators several floors above them.

Jax turned as Mike scooted past him, grabbing hold of the metal ladder on the side of the shaft as he started down. Shooting one more glance up at the two elevators and trying not to think of what would happen if the elevator cables snapped, Jax hesitantly swung his own leg into the shaft and carefully descended into the narrow hole below.

* * *

Hunter coughed violently, attempting to clear his lungs of the thick dust that seemed to fill every inch of the dimly lit parking garage, making it almost impossible to see or breathe. He quickly pulled the neckline of his shirt up over his mouth so he could use it as a temporary filter, though the effect was only mildly better. When he was able to stop coughing, he slowly glanced around, his pulse rising. The car entrance was now an enormous mound of rubble, extending halfway into the garage and cutting off the drive-through exit completely. He stared numbly at the sight, praying that no one had been in the vehicles which had been devoured by what appeared to be a million tons of debris. Hunter began to cough again, clutching his chest in pain as he spit out several small pieces of gravel. He shook his head, knowing that he had probably aspirated enough dust and cement particles to cause serious long-term damage to his lungs. He quickly wiped his mouth with the back of his hand and shook his head. There was no sense in thinking about long term. Right now he needed to concentrate on getting out, or there wouldn't be a long term.

With the drive-through exit totally impassible, Hunter quickly turned toward the two remaining exits: the three elevators and a set of stairs next to them. What he saw left him suddenly light-headed. There was a large pile of debris directly in front of the door leading to the stairs, and a red SUV had been thrown sideways up against the elevator doors, its back tires stuck in the debris.

"No!" Hunter whispered, shaking his head slowly back and forth.

Suddenly sick, Hunter bent over and braced himself with his hands on his knees as he retched, his chest constricting painfully with each spasm. Once the nausea had lessened somewhat, he wiped his mouth on his sleeve and slowly stood, though it took several more seconds for his brain to jump-start. Once he felt steady enough, Hunter started carefully toward the SUV. If he could drive it off the cement blocks, he could pry open the elevator doors and climb up the shaft. With a shimmer of hope surging through him, he picked his way toward the vehicle, stumbling several times on chunks of cement and rebar. He was almost halfway there when he heard something. He stopped, his feet teetering on a small pile of cinder block, his eyes searching frantically in the dim light.

"Hello!" he shouted, his eyes scanning the area in and around the elevators. "Is anyone there?"

For several seconds there was an eerie silence broken only by the groaning of the building as it threatened to come crumbling down on top of him.

"Hello!" he called again, wondering if he had actually heard anything in the first place.

Then it came again. Hunter realized the noise was coming from behind him, back toward what was left of the car entrance. It sounded muffled. Hunter started back toward the rubble, calling out every few seconds and then waiting for some kind of reply. The closer he got to the debris, the louder the sound came, though he still couldn't make out any words. Then he heard it again, only this time it was loud enough that he could zero in on the location. The noise wasn't coming from around the debris—it was coming from within it. Hunter felt his heart accelerate. He threw himself on the pile, digging frantically through the rubble, then stopped and cupped his mouth with his hands.

"Can you hear me?" he shouted.

After an agonizing few seconds, the reply came, though again it was too muffled to make out any words.

Hunter moved a little to the side and began to dig with renewed strength. "Hold on—I'm coming!" he called out.

After lifting several sizable chunks of cement from off of the pile and depositing them behind him with a thud, Hunter spotted what looked like a metal roof. He doubled his fist and began pounding on it. "Are you in there?"

"I'm here—please hurry!" a woman shrieked. "The roof's caving in."

Hunter grabbed several more chunks of cement, tossing them out of the way as he cleared off a section of the roof. He tried to remove a few bigger slabs of cement, but they were too heavy. It would take several men to move them. Then a thought struck Hunter. *Leverage.* Maybe with a little leverage he would be able to remove or at least reposition some of the pieces. Hunter's head jerked around, scanning the poorly lit area for something to position under the cement. Off to his left, about twenty feet away, he spotted it—a broken piece of rebar on top of a pile of rubble.

"I'll be right back," Hunter called out to the woman.

"Don't leave me!" she begged, her voice shrill with panic.

"I'll only be a second," Hunter promised. "I need to get something to help me pry the cement off your car."

With the woman still begging him to stay, Hunter climbed off the pile of rubble and made his way over to the rusted metal bar. Once he had it, he turned to make his way back over to the woman. But before he was halfway there he heard the sound of metal buckling under pressure, followed by a high-pitched scream. Hunter ran to the pile of debris and threw several small chunks of cement aside before scrambling up the side, his knees feeling the jagged edges of the rocks.

"Are you okay?" he shouted, finding the place where he had been digging.

"You've got to hurry!" the woman cried, her voice weaker. "It's not going to hold much longer!"

Hunter took a deep breath, wedged the metal bar under a large slab of cement, and then, calling on God for strength beyond his own, began to push down on the bar.

* * *

McKenna stayed on Alan Sutherland's heels as he headed for the stairs, weaving his way through a crowd of people going in the same direction. Hoping she wouldn't see Nathan Rinehart, but unable to resist looking, McKenna anxiously searched the faces of those around her. The stream of blood on Sutherland's face attested to the cold-blooded killer hiding behind Nathan's upper-crust facade.

"Stay close," Sutherland called over his shoulder as they squeezed into the stairwell.

McKenna bobbed her head—she wasn't about to let him out of her sight. Holding onto the handrail, she started down the stairs. Sutherland glanced behind them several times, apparently just as paranoid about Nathan as she was. McKenna tried to force the thought from her mind, concentrating instead on making her way down to the ground floor, but the uneasiness persisted.

They had only made it down the first flight of stairs when they heard a deafening crash. A man on the other side of the stairwell called out a warning that the stairs below had just collapsed. McKenna glanced at Sutherland, her eyes wide, but he only quickened his pace, slowing only after they had rounded the bend in the stairwell. He pushed his way through the crowd with McKenna close behind him, then stopped, his lips pulled into a pensive frown. McKenna's own jaw fell slack as she too stared down at the gaping hole where the majority of the staircase had crumbled. The remains of the staircase, as well as those who had been on it, had been deposited in a heap two flights below. Feeling suddenly light-headed, as if the blood in her veins had instantaneously frozen, McKenna reached her hand out to brace herself with the wall.

"They're going to fall," Sutherland said, watching as four men in a crazed panic grabbed hold of what was left of the twisted metal handrails that were partially ripped from the wall and began to climb down. "Come on," Sutherland began, turning to McKenna and taking her firmly by the hand. "We've got to find another way."

"Where?" McKenna asked as they turned around.

"I don't know," Sutherland admitted, dragging her with him.

They both flinched as a loud crash resounded from behind them, followed by several high-pitched screams. Without turning to look, McKenna knew instantly what had happened. She shook her head, her hands flying up to cover her ears.

"What were they thinking?" she said, feeling utterly helpless.

"They weren't," Sutherland said, coming to a stop in front of the door to the thirty-ninth floor. "That's why we've got to, if we want to stay alive."

Sutherland pushed opened the door and stood back for McKenna to enter. She walked past him hesitantly, her eyes going to a man sprawled on the floor in front of the elevators. She rushed over and bent to feel for a pulse, but Sutherland reached down and pulled her up.

"We don't have time," he said, his eyes widening as the floor beneath them began to tremble. "We need to get under a door frame!" Sutherland grabbed McKenna by the hand and started up the hall to the first door.

Clinging to the frame, McKenna closed her eyes, praying that the building would be able to withstand another beating. Though the trembling was intense, the duration seemed much shorter than the initial quake. After it was over, McKenna slid to the floor, her hands still clutching the wooden frame.

"Come on," Sutherland began, pulling her to her feet. "It's over."

McKenna shook her head, but Sutherland was insistent. "I've got an idea," he said, pulling her farther into the room.

Once inside, McKenna quickly looked around what appeared to be an office. Most of the partitions that had sectioned the office into small cubicles had fallen over, leaving the room almost impossible to maneuver.

"There's no way out of here," McKenna protested, her eyes going immediately to the shattered windows on the far side of the room. "And I'm *not* going out there."

Sutherland climbed up onto a desk, his eyes glued to a large vent in the ceiling. "We'll get out through here."

Before McKenna could respond, Sutherland hopped off the desk and began rummaging through the top drawer.

"What are you looking for?" McKenna asked, taking several tentative steps toward him.

"I'm not sure," he began. Then he held up a silver letter opener. "But this will do."

Sutherland climbed back onto the desk and began using the letter opener to loosen the screws that held the metal vent in place.

"Are you serious? Can we get out through there?" McKenna asked.

Instead of answering, Sutherland gestured toward the room. "See if you can find a flashlight or a lighter. It's going to be dark."

McKenna swallowed hard, trying not to look as frightened as she felt. She yanked open a drawer and began rummaging through it, anxious to do something other than wait around to see if there would be any more aftershocks. Finding nothing in the drawer that they could use, she hurried over to another desk. In the top drawer of the next desk she found a pack of cigarettes, which she left, and a lighter, which she quickly stashed in the inside pocket of her tailored suit. She was just about to shut the drawer and continue looking for a flashlight when she spotted a makeup bag. Feeling strangely compelled to open it, she did, and immediately withdrew a mirrored makeup compact. Not sure how it could help them, but feeling strongly that it would, she placed it in her pocket next to the lighter. Next, she tried the bottom drawer of the desk, spotting both an umbrella and a flashlight. Picking up the second item and leaving the first, she held up her find for Sutherland to see.

"Good," he said, pulling the metal cover off the vent shaft and tossing it to the floor with a clang. He climbed off the desk, grabbed a chair, propped it on top of the desk, and reached his hand out for the flashlight. "Stay right behind me," he said, shooting a quick glance back at the door.

McKenna likewise turned to look anxiously at the entrance of the office, but to her relief saw no one there. When she turned back to Sutherland, all she saw were his legs disappearing up through the hole.

"You're next," he called, his voice echoing through the vent shaft.

McKenna took off her heels and reluctantly tossed them on the floor. She shot one last glance at the door before turning her eyes back to the vent. A moment later, she was in the duct work of the crumbling high-rise. Sutherland flipped on the flashlight, shining the beam down the narrow shaft. McKenna guessed that the shaft opening was no bigger than three by three feet. McKenna was suddenly relieved she was afraid of heights and not claustrophobic, though she knew she very well might be after this ordeal.

"How do we know which way will take us down?"

"We don't," Sutherland said, starting down the shaft.

Not liking his answer but having no other alternative, McKenna stayed right behind him, though her mind suddenly took her clear across the country. By now both her father and James would likely know about the earthquake. She couldn't stand imagining what the two of them were going through, not knowing if she was dead or alive. She tried to push the thought from her mind as she continued forward.

"Do you see anything?" she asked, Sutherland's form blocking almost all of the light produced by the flashlight.

"No," Sutherland snapped, his nerves clearly raw.

McKenna continued to make her way forward, glancing anxiously through the tiny slits in the metal vents at each room they passed.

"Wait a minute," Sutherland began, "I think there's a shaft going down a few feet ahead."

McKenna felt her heart race at the possibility. Then she heard a noise behind her that raised the hairs on the back of her neck. It was a low ping, like aluminum being bent—like someone climbing into the shaft behind them. McKenna froze, her heart thundering wildly in her chest and her breathing sharply amplified in the enclosed space.

"Did you hear that?" she whispered, her voice so soft she almost couldn't hear herself.

Sutherland, who apparently couldn't hear her, continued to crawl forward. McKenna glanced over her shoulder, but it was too dark to see anything. Someone could be right behind her and she wouldn't be able to see them. That thought propelled McKenna forward, but Sutherland had stopped and was trying to maneuver his body down into the descending shaft. Once he had a grip on the metal stairs that led down, he turned and shined his flashlight toward McKenna, his brow pinched.

"Are you okay?"

"I thought I heard something behind us," she said.

Sutherland's frown deepened, then seeing the look on her face, his expression softened somewhat. "It was probably just a rat."

That notion under any other circumstances would have sent an unnerving chill down McKenna's spine, but now, knowing what else could be behind her in the shaft, she would welcome a whole family of rats.

"Keep close," he said as he descended the stairs.

As soon as Sutherland was out of sight, McKenna quickly climbed into the shaft behind him, resisting the urge to strain her eyes into the darkness.

"You okay?" Sutherland asked again once they had reached the bottom.

"I'm fine. But how long do we have to stay in here?"

"Just until we get below the collapsed staircases. After that we can pop open a vent and take the stairs."

McKenna nodded, wishing she could shake the feeling that they were not alone.

CHAPTER SEVEN

12:15 P.M. / New York City

"Where's McKenna?" James blurted out as soon as Tatum answered the phone.

"James, she's in the middle of it all," Tatum said, her voice more harried than usual.

James could feel the acid in his stomach burning halfway up his esophagus. McKenna had called him late last night, but he had still been upset over their last encounter, so he had let the answering machine get it. She hadn't said much other than that she was going to be in L.A. on business for the next few days and that she would call him when she got back.

"I can't believe this is happening," Tatum spouted. "I mean, it's bad enough that half of L.A. has been destroyed with McKenna probably trapped somewhere under the rubble dead or dying, but then that body had to show up."

"What body?" James asked hesitantly, not sure he wanted to know.

"Manning, the client that McKenna helped acquit. We just got word ten minutes ago that his body was found early this morning out at the city dump."

"Maybe I'm not following," James said, wondering for the ten thousandth time how Tatum had ever landed a job at one of the most prestigious law firms in New York. "What does this have to do with McKenna and the quake in L.A.?"

Tatum let out her breath in exasperation. "Nothing, if you ignore the fact that McKenna might be trapped in Lincoln Tower with a killer."

"What are you talking about?" James asked.

"The police found a piece of paper in Manning's pocket with Nathan Rinehart's phone number on it–the *same* Nathan Rinehart that McKenna was supposed to be meeting for lunch at the time of the earthquake."

The burning in James's stomach now felt like a full-blown volcanic eruption.

"The police have already issued a warrant for Rinehart's arrest, not that that's going to do anyone any good," Tatum concluded.

"I'm going down there."

"James, there's nothing you can do. The National Guard has already been called in, and they're not letting civilians anywhere close to L.A."

"I'll find a way."

"Hold on, James. Mr. Bradford wants to—"

Lawrence Bradford's voice came on the cell phone. "You've heard?" he asked, his usual pompous demeanor replaced with alarm.

"How could I not?" James replied. "It's all over the news."

"Well, I know you sometimes lock yourself away in that studio of yours for days at a time."

James ignored the dig, too worried about McKenna's safety to care about the petty remark. "I'm flying out there in a little over an hour."

"They're not allowing any planes to land in L.A.," Lawrence said.

James grabbed the duffel bag he hadn't yet unpacked from his rappelling trip to the Adirondacks the week before, opened the front door of his studio apartment, then closed it quickly behind him, not even taking the time to lock it. There was nothing that couldn't be replaced, nothing that mattered. The only thing he cared about was finding a way to get to McKenna.

"I know. I have a friend just outside of San Bernardino who's got a couple of four-wheelers. I'll borrow one and go the rest of the way on it."

"I'm going with you," Lawrence stated flatly.

James shook his head adamantly. "I don't think that's a good idea. I know you're worried about McKenna, but to be honest, you'll just slow me down."

"My private jet can be ready for takeoff in thirty minutes. We'll land a short time later in your friend's backyard if we have to. How's that for slowing you down?"

"Look," James began. "I think—"

"I don't care what you think. I'll be at the hanger in thirty minutes. If you're going with *me*, be there!"

James let his breath out slowly. "I'll be there," he said begrudgingly to the dial tone, knowing that arguing with Lawrence was as useless as sweet-talking a charging bull.

Twenty-five minutes later, James screeched his jeep to a stop in front of the hanger that housed the Bradfords' Learjet. The jet was outside the hanger being prepped for takeoff, while Lawrence Bradford paced impatiently next to it, talking animatedly to the pilot. As soon as Lawrence spotted James, he pointed toward him and then said something to the pilot. The pilot nodded, then hurried over to James, still shaking his head.

"We're taking off in ten minutes," the pilot reported. "Just as soon as we finish fueling."

"Any idea where we'll be able to land?"

"There's a landing strip about ten miles out of San Bernardino. Mr. Bradford requests that you call your friend and have him wait for us there."

James pulled out his cell phone and then glanced back at the pilot. "Landing strip? You mean an airport, right?" he asked hesitantly.

The man glanced over his shoulder at Lawrence, then heaved an irritated sigh. "No. I mean a strip of dirt in the middle of an orange grove. The airport there has been closed down to all private and commercial planes. Just tell your friend what's going on, then hand me the phone, and I'll give him directions."

Ten minutes later, James gazed across the horizon as the New York City skyline drifted into the distance. He could hear Lawrence talking on the phone at the back of the small jet. He was attempting to get some kind of clearance into L.A., though so far he didn't seem to be having any luck. Apparently money, name, and reputation were not going to be enough for Lawrence Bradford this time. Ironically, this was the one time that James wished Lawrence *could* get everything that he wanted.

James's stomach turned as he glanced up at the television screen at the front of the jet. A news helicopter was flying over downtown L.A., while a reporter James didn't recognize pointed out the massive destruction that had taken place. Communities up and down the California coastline now lay in ruin, the estimated cost running into the billions. But nothing even remotely compared with the devastation in and around L.A. Huge skyscrapers had toppled, their remains deposited in a heap on the congested city streets, bringing traffic to a complete standstill. Fires from the broken gas lines and downed electric wires were springing up everywhere. An entire city block on the outskirts of L.A. was engulfed in flames, threatening to consume the entire downtown district if not stopped. The quake had registered 9.5 on the Richter scale and was, according to the reporter, a national disaster unprecedented in the United States.

"Please," James whispered as he shook his head in horror. "Please, let her be all right."

"That reporter, what channel does he work for?"

Startled, James looked up to face Lawrence, who was standing in the aisle next to him looking intently at the screen.

"Some local station in or around L.A., I think," James offered, watching Lawrence curiously as he took the seat across the aisle then quickly dialed his cell phone.

"Can you read the logo on his shirt?" Lawrence asked, glancing up briefly.

James looked back at the television screen. The cameraman, who had been showing a steady stream of footage from the L.A. area, had temporarily zoomed in on the reporter.

"RTL," James offered, not sure why Lawrence wanted to know. "Why?"

Lawrence held up his hand to silence James. "Tatum, get me RTL. It's one of the local news channels in L.A. I'll hold." Lawrence turned to James, his brow creased. "Maybe we can get ourselves a little footage of Lincoln Tower." Then, not waiting for James to comment, he stood and began walking up and down the aisle, his impatience evident in his expression.

James turned back to look out the window but jerked back around the second Lawrence began to speak.

"Yes, this is Lawrence Bradford of Bradford and Associates in New York City. My secretary is waiting for my order to transfer fifty thousand dollars to any account you want if you'll have your pilot fly over Lincoln Tower and get me some decent footage. No, this is not a joke," Lawrence countered after a pause. "Just the easiest money you'll ever make in your life."

James shook his head in wonder and then lifted his eyes to the screen. Within five minutes the helicopter took a sharp right, the reporter indicating that they were going to get some footage of the destruction near the center of the city. Thirty seconds later, the cameraman zoomed in on Lincoln Tower. If James's stomach had been tight before, it was now ready to split wide open. The east side of Lincoln Tower had completely collapsed, while the rest of the building looked like a slight gust could bring it down. Though there was a light haze of smoke hanging around the building, it appeared to be from the recent destruction and not from fire. James heaved a sigh, relieved by at least that fact, then glanced at Lawrence, whose expression matched his own. The helicopter continued to circle Lincoln Tower for the next minute or two, then veered off to the outskirts of town, where most of the fires were concentrated. James leaned back in his chair, praying that they would reach McKenna in time.

* * *

Sirens blared in the background as Justice ran to the back of the fire truck, his heart racing like a freight train ready to derail. The sight before him was overpowering. Flames exploded from an enormous, billowing shroud of smoke, threatening to consume what was left of the city if not quickly extinguished. Some people stood immobilized at the scene, their faces black with soot and their eyes wild with fear, while others raced to get out of the fire's path, their arms loaded with their salvageable possessions. Justice looked on in disgust as a group of men ran down the street, oblivious to the wounded as they busted the windows out of several small businesses, their arms filled with high-tech stereo and electronic equipment. Justice shook his head, then grabbed a fire hose. Though the National Guard had been called in, it would be several hours before they could establish any type of control. Until then, the looters would be able to do as they pleased, and they knew it. Right now the police and fire departments had more important things to worry about.

Justice had recently been given word that fire stations within a two-hundred-mile radius had been asked to aid in the situation, though Justice suspected that more would quickly be enlisted. The problem would be getting the men and equipment into the city. Though Justice's station was only fifteen miles from the fires, it had taken them an hour to reach the inferno. Also, because of the extent of the damage, many of his own men who had been off duty when the quake happened were unaccounted for—including Chad.

Justice shook his head, forcing those thoughts from his mind, though an even more horrifying thought remained. Anna was in downtown L.A. He had tried frantically to reach her on her cell phone, but all service was down, with no hopes of it being up anytime soon. To make matters worse, because of the lack of manpower to fight the fires, he had no choice but to leave her in the hands of rescue workers while he and his men battled the blaze. Besides, if they didn't stop these fires soon, Lincoln Tower would be among the many other buildings in the fire's path. That thought alone propelled Justice forward.

"Captain, where do you want us to start?"

Justice glanced at Thomas Porterman. The bulky man stood amongst the men of the 447. Justice could feel his throat catch. These men were not just members of his unit: They were his friends. It was impossible to place your life in another person's hands and not form a bond akin to family. Justice swallowed hard, knowing that it was likely some of these men would not survive the day.

"Right here. Most of the buildings behind us are beyond saving, but if we're lucky, we might be able to contain the fires and stop them from spreading," Justice said, pushing his emotions to the back of his mind. He glanced first at the city before them. Although devastated by the earthquake, it was still unscathed by the approaching fire. He looked back at his men. "We're all that stands between these fires and almost four million lives." Justice could feel a spark of electricity run up and down his spine. He paused for a split second as his words sank in, then he turned, his jaw tight. "They're counting on us. So let's get it done!"

Every head nodded as the men, their eyes aflame at Justice's words, moved toward the fires. As Justice started after his men, a black Harley skidded to a stop just feet from him.

"Need some help?"

"*Chad!*" Justice exclaimed, relief washing over him. "You're okay."

Chad pulled off his helmet. "I would have been here sooner, but my apartment complex took a beating. I had to help a few of my neighbors out of the building," he said. "Is Anna okay?"

Justice could feel his chest tighten. "She was at a doctor's appointment when it happened."

"Where?" Chad asked, his voice suddenly tight.

"Lincoln Tower."

Chad let his breath out, then hesitantly asked, "Is she okay?"

"I don't know," Justice began, glancing over his shoulder at the downtown area. "I don't think any crews have been able to get down there yet. I'd go, but—"

"You can't," Chad offered knowingly, his eyes going to the flames. "If you don't contain this, there'll be no need for rescue workers to go in, because there won't be anyone left to rescue."

Justice nodded.

Chad took a deep breath, his face a mask of frustration. Then his expression changed suddenly, his eyes widening in determination. "I'll go."

Justice shook his head, though his words were slow in coming. "We need you here."

"I'm on medical leave right now anyway, right?" Chad stated, holding his arms out to his sides, his black leather jacket covering the second-degree burns on his forearms. "So technically I'm not even supposed to be here."

Justice glanced at the fire, then quickly back at Chad. "Look, I don't know."

"You'll stop the fires," Chad said confidently. "Let me do this. With my bike I'll be able to get there in minutes. I'll get Anna out, and then I'll come back to help."

Justice hesitated for only a second and then bobbed his head. "Okay. I'll head that way as soon as I can."

Chad put his helmet back on and climbed on his bike, revving it to life with a quick thrust of his boot. "Good luck," he said, turning his bike to leave.

"Hey, Chad," Justice called out.

Chad glanced over his shoulder.

"Thanks," Justice said, the words feeling wholly inadequate.

Chad flashed Justice a thumbs-up, revved his engine one last time, then quickly disappeared down the street. Justice heaved a sigh of relief, knowing that if there was any way to get Anna out of Lincoln Tower alive, Chad would find it. With renewed determination, Justice tightened his grip on the fire hose, then turned and started toward the blaze.

CHAPTER EIGHT

1:00 P.M. / Los Angeles; Elevator shaft, Lincoln Tower

Payson stared down the darkened shaft, focusing on the other elevator. He was grateful the light from the backup generator, although dim, provided some visibility.

"There's no way you're going to be able to jump across this shaft," Richard protested, looking at the dried blood on the side of Payson's face.

"You watch me," Payson said, his eyes going first to the metal stairs on the wall directly across from them and then to the drop below. "I ran track and jumped hurdles in high school."

"With a glob of superglue holding your head together?" Richard spat out dubiously.

Payson didn't even turn to look at him. Instead, he backed up as far as he could to get some kind of running start, then took a deep breath. "I'll be back."

Richard snorted. "Maybe as a ghost."

Ignoring Richard's remark, Payson bent down like a runner ready for the start of a race. He could feel his heart pounding, sending a surge of blood through his body. He offered a quick, heartfelt prayer, then sprung into action. Thrusting his body forward, he took the last step, his body hurtling over the second elevator four floors below. His arms and legs were still in motion, even though there was only air beneath him. Then, with a resounding thud he slammed hard into the metal shaft on the other side, his arms grasping frantically for the ladder rungs. Grabbing hold of one with his left hand, he pulled his body onto the ladder, only then looking down at the drop below. With his legs trembling, he glanced over his shoulder at Richard, who stood shaking his head.

"You're crazy!" Richard called out.

Payson nodded, finally in agreement with the man. "Hold tight."

"Like I have a choice."

Payson started down the metal rungs, his legs quivering beneath him. About halfway down, he felt a warm streak of blood streaming down the side of his head.

Just keep going, he prodded himself. *You can make it. You're almost there.*

Three-fourths of the way down, he stopped, then tightened his grip on the ladder. The dizziness he had experienced in the elevator was returning, and beads of sweat dampened his forehead.

"What's wrong?" Richard called down. "Why'd you stop?"

"Just give me a minute," Payson mumbled, suddenly feeling light-headed as the dizziness continued and the quivering of his legs intensified. *Please, Father, let me reach her,* Payson begged, though his peripheral vision was already beginning to dim and his grip starting to weaken.

The last thing Payson heard was his name echoing up and down the darkened elevator shaft.

* * *

"Payson! *Payson!* Can you hear me?"

The muffled words, which sounded like they were resounding in a distant, hollow drum, reverberated inside Payson's pounding head.

"Payson, please wake up!"

Though he could hear the words, he couldn't quite manage the task.

"Payson, it's me . . . Gwen."

It took a moment for her words to register, but when they did, Payson instantly felt a surge of adrenaline rush through his body. He slowly opened his eyes, her face gradually coming into focus.

"Gwen?" he whispered, hardly believing that it was possible.

Gwen nodded, tears now falling from eyes that were already red and swollen.

Payson slowly reached up to touch her face to make sure that he wasn't just hallucinating.

"You've lost a lot of blood," someone to his right offered.

Payson turned to see Tristin, who shook her head with a half-hearted smile, though she, like Gwen, looked clearly relieved. "I told Gwen you'd find a way to get to her."

"Richard said you fell about twelve feet," a male voice next to Gwen said.

Payson turned to see that there were two other people besides himself, Gwen, and Tristin in the elevator. Sam shook his head. "You could have snapped the cable when you fell, killing us all."

"Oh, please don't say that!" an elderly woman who was standing next to Sam exclaimed as she clung tightly to a walker.

Tristin shot Sam a dirty look as she turned to the woman. "Mrs. Rutledge, we're all going to be fine. You'll see." Then Tristin bent down so she and Gwen could help Payson sit up.

"Are you hurt anywhere besides your head?" Gwen asked once Payson was propped up against the side of the elevator.

"No. I'm okay. I guess I just passed out." He reached up and touched his head, expecting the cloth to be saturated. Instead it was snugly wrapped around his head and dry, other than a quarter-sized spot directly over the cut.

"After we stopped the bleeding, we rebandaged your head with Mrs. Rutledge's scarf," Gwen said, handing him a half-empty can of Sprite. "Here. Take a drink."

"Thanks," he said, slowly finishing off the can before turning his attention back to Sam. "Is everyone in the other elevator okay?"

"I guess. I haven't called up to them since we got you off the top of ours."

All conversation stopped as the building began to creak and moan. No one moved, no one spoke or even breathed as they waited to see if there would be another earthquake. After several seconds the noise stopped, followed by a collective sigh of relief from everyone in the elevator.

"There's got to be a way out," Payson said, his eyes on Sam, any jealously or hard feelings forgotten.

"The door's jammed. There must be something pushed up against it," Sam explained, his broad shoulders assuring Payson that if it were humanly possible to open the elevator doors, Sam would have already done it.

"Does anyone have anything we can use to pry open one of the other doors in the shaft?" Payson asked, quickly eyeing the group.

"Look, we've already done this. We don't have anything," Sam snapped in frustration.

Payson shook his head, then glanced toward the door. As he did, his gaze fell on Mrs. Rutledge. He scanned over her walker down to her left leg, which had a metal strip that was connected to her shoe as well as to a strap that wrapped around her calf for support.

"Your brace!" Payson exclaimed, getting to his feet so fast that his head began to spin.

Gwen quickly stood up and took him by the arm. "What about her brace?" she asked in confusion.

Sam nodded his head knowingly. "I didn't even think of that," he admitted, quickly bending down next to the elderly woman so that he could examine it. "If we can wedge the metal strip between one of the doors, we might be able to pry it open," Sam concluded, eyeing Payson appreciatively.

Payson touched Mrs. Rutledge's arm. "Would you mind if we borrowed your brace for a while?"

"The dadblam thing itches like crazy anyway," Mrs. Rutledge said, winning a broad smile from Payson.

Sam and Tristin quickly helped Mrs. Rutledge to the floor so they could take off the brace. Payson glanced at Gwen. Her dark lashes partially concealed her blue eyes, though Payson could still see the fear in them.

"Are you okay?" Payson asked, reaching out and holding her arm.

She nodded, but quickly averted her eyes. Payson swallowed hard, reminded that although she seemed grateful he'd come to help them, she was in love with another man.

"I got 'em," Sam said, holding up two thin metal bars.

Payson let go of Gwen and turned to Sam. "I'll give you a boost up."

Within a few minutes, Sam was on the top of the elevator. "I'll try the floor that's one flight up," he called down into the elevator. But before he could move, the building began to shake.

Payson, Gwen, and Tristin, who had all been standing in a semi-circle in the middle of the elevator in order to see up through the hole in the ceiling, dropped to the floor next to Mrs. Rutledge. Payson held his breath, sure that at any moment the cable would snap, sending them screaming down the dark shaft. But the shaking stopped after only a few seconds.

Payson let his breath out slowly, his eyes going to the women in the elevator. "Is everyone okay?"

Gwen, who had her arms wrapped around the older woman's shoulders, nodded her head.

"I'm worried that all these little aftershocks are building up for a big one," Tristin said, her eyes wide.

Payson nodded, knowing that Tristin was probably closer to the truth than any of them wanted to believe.

"Payson!" Sam called out, his voice echoing up and down the dark shaft and causing them all to jump. "You need to get up here!"

"What's wrong?" Mrs. Rutledge asked, her voice high and her wrinkled face stressed with worry.

"Everything's fine," Payson offered reassuringly, though his eyes told a different story. He turned to Gwen and Tristin. "I'm going to need some help."

"Do you feel strong enough?" Gwen asked, her eyes locked on his.

Though the Sprite already seemed to be helping, he still felt weaker than he was willing to admit. "I'll be fine," he said, determined to do all he could to help.

Gwen nodded reluctantly. She and Tristin interlocked their hands so they could boost Payson up through the hole in the ceiling. Sam met him as soon as he was up, his face drained of all color.

"What is it?" Payson asked, his stomach tight.

Sam pointed to one of the cables connected to the elevator. It was noticeably strained, with the intertwined metal stretched almost to the breaking point.

"We've got to get them out!" Payson whispered breathlessly. "This cable's going to snap even if there's *not* another earthquake."

"What's going on down there?"

Payson looked up the shaft to the other elevator. Richard was leaning over the side.

"You need to get up here quick," Richard snapped. "Anna's having labor pains, and I am *not* delivering this kid."

Feeling worse for Anna than he did for Richard but unable to do anything about it, Payson turned to Sam, then gestured with a nod to the floor just above them. "You've got to get that door open while I get them out of the elevator."

Sam nodded as he grabbed onto the metal ladder and began climbing, both of the thin metal bars from Mrs. Rutledge's brace tucked safely in his back pocket. Payson dropped to his knees, his eyes going to each of the three women who stood staring up at him, their faces filled with terror.

"We've found a way out," Payson said, trying to keep the fear that was tingling up his back from showing on his face. "You two give Mrs. Rutledge a boost, and I'll pull her up through the hole."

Relief washing over her face, Tristin immediately obeyed, helping Mrs. Rutledge to her feet as the older woman repeated over and over again how grateful she was that she had worn pants that day instead of her paisley dress. But Gwen hesitated, giving Payson a worried glance. Payson looked nervously over at the cable before quickly wiping his sweaty palms on his shirt.

"Give me your hands," Payson urged, reaching his hands down toward Mrs. Rutledge.

"My leg," she said, her face twisting in pain as she attempted to balance herself on Gwen's and Tristin's cupped hands. "It hurts too much."

"Please!" Payson exclaimed, his voice beginning to show the strain of the situation. "Just give me your hands."

Now even Tristin eyed him nervously as she and Gwen hoisted Mrs. Rutledge up so that Payson could grab her arms. Once Payson had ahold of her, he slowly pulled her up, leaving Gwen and Tristin staring anxiously up at the hole in the ceiling.

"I've been meaning to take off a few pounds," Mrs. Rutledge said, her cheeks flushed as she awkwardly attempted to get to her feet.

"Climb onto the stairs," Payson demanded, reaching out and giving her a hand.

"But he doesn't even have the door open yet," the woman protested.

Payson glanced up at Sam. He had stabbed the metal bar between the closed doors that were about three feet away from the stairs. It looked like he was struggling just to keep his balance as he teetered sideways, his body stretched out as far as it would go.

"We don't have time!" Payson exclaimed, causing Mrs. Rutledge to furrow her wrinkled brow. "The cable's about to snap."

At Payson's declaration, the elderly woman sucked in her breath, her eyes going for the first time to the fraying cable. Then, without further prodding, she leaped onto the stairs, the pain in her leg temporarily forgotten. Payson dropped to his belly and reached his hands down through the hole. His head was pounding, but so far he couldn't feel any blood seeping out from the cut on his head.

"Hurry!" he shouted, reaching for Gwen, who was closer to him than Tristin. Gwen immediately nudged Tristin forward.

"Go!" she shouted, interlacing her fingers so Tristin could use her hands as a stirrup.

With no time to argue, Tristin pushed off from Gwen's hands and caught hold of Payson's wrists. Within seconds she was on top of the elevator, heading for the metal stairs. Payson glanced up at Sam, who had finally been able to pry open the metal doors to the next floor. Sam had made his way through the opening and was now helping Mrs. Rutledge through. Relieved, Payson got back down on his belly so he could reach for Gwen, but as he did the building began to shake. Tristin let out a shrill scream that echoed up and down the elevator shaft as she fought to keep her balance on the ladder.

"Jump!" Payson screamed, his voice muffled by the chaos around them.

"Just go!" Gwen cried to Payson, shaking her head back and forth. "There's no time."

"I'm not leaving you!" Payson shouted, his jaw tight and his eyes ablaze.

Payson knew without a doubt that he would die rather than leave her. Gwen looked up at him for a moment and then jumped, her hands just barely grasping his. With a surge of much-needed adrenaline, Payson pulled her up through the hole. Gwen's body collapsed next to his on the top of the elevator.

Payson's chest was heaving, and blood was rushing through his veins like a raging torrent as he got to his feet, dragging Gwen with him. As the building around them continued to tremble, Payson's eyes locked on the nearly unraveled fibers of the cable.

"Jump!" Payson screamed again, clutching Gwen's hand and leaping toward the stairs just as the cable snapped and the elevator began a freefall.

After a split second of flight, and with the elevator below them picking up speed as it plunged to the ground, Payson caught hold of the cold metal ladder with his right hand, his other hand clutching fervently to Gwen's as she dangled helplessly over the dark shaft.

* * *

After climbing to the bottom of the elevator shaft, Jax and Mike had gone to work prying open one of the elevator doors with the metal rod Mike had found in the utility closet. After successfully wedging it between the elevator doors leading to the parking garage, the two had been able to force them apart—only to find a large red SUV wedged against the opening. Quickly realizing that there was no way to budge the truck, they had shattered the passenger-side window, intent on climbing through. Now, with most of the protruding glass cleared off, Jax was ready to climb in.

"There's no sense in both of us going in and risking getting trapped," Jax began, glancing at Mike. "Why don't you—"

Before Jax could finish his sentence, the ground beneath them began to tremble. Jax's eyes opened wide as his gaze instinctively lifted to the elevator directly above them, its dark shape just barely visible in the dimly lit shaft.

"It's gonna fall!" Mike shouted, his eyes round with fear.

With nowhere else to go, Jax turned and leaped through the window of the SUV, his body landing hard on the broken glass sprinkled all over the seat. Not stopping to worry about the glass embedded in his skin, he immediately turned to help Mike. As he did, he heard several chilling screams echoing up and down the shaft, followed by a rush of air, as if a large object were plunging down the elevator shaft toward them. As Mike stood frozen, gaping up the shaft, Jax grabbed his hand and pulled with everything he had. Mike's legs had barely cleared the vehicle's window when they heard what sounded like a bomb detonating, the force of impact causing the side of the SUV closest to the elevator to shoot off the ground before crashing back down with a thud. Mike lay awkwardly across a bucket seat hyperventilating while Jax sat on the floor, his entire body shaking.

"Are you okay?" Jax finally managed, hardly recognizing his own choppy voice.

Mike lifted his head, his face pale. Then he glanced anxiously at all his limbs before slowly nodding. "I think so."

"I hope there wasn't anyone in there," Jax said, his stomach twisting with the thought as he eyed the remains of the elevator now blocking their way out.

Mike lifted his head but didn't speak; instead he looked past Jax into the parking garage, his eyes suddenly wide. Following Mike's gaze, Jax immediately pulled himself up to a kneeling position so he could look out the window of the SUV. Though the room was thick with dust, Jax spotted what looked like the outline of a man standing on a large pile of debris on the far side of the garage.

"Hunter," Jax breathed, praying with everything in him that he was right.

"Your friend?" Mike asked.

Jax shook his head, his hand going to the door handle. "I don't know."

Finding the door jammed, Jax repositioned himself and kicked the door open with both feet. As he did, the man called out to them.

"I need some help," he shouted before turning toward the pile of debris.

"Hunter, is that you?" Jax called out, climbing from the vehicle.

The man instantly turned back to face them. "*Jax?*" he cried, his voice immediately flooded with emotion.

Jax felt his shoulders fall slack with relief.

"You've got to hurry," Hunter called out, cutting their reunion short. "There's a woman trapped in a car, and the roof's collapsing."

Both Jax and Mike quickly made their way over to Hunter, who was now down on his hands and knees digging. "I can't get her out. I tried to pry the heavier pieces off, but I just couldn't get them to budge," Hunter said, his face drawn with fatigue.

Jax picked up the length of rebar next to Hunter and wedged it under one of the bigger pieces of cement. "You just keep talking to her."

Hunter nodded his head, appearing too tired to do much more, then bent down toward the exposed portion of the roof.

"Lakesha, I've got some help," he said, sweat streaking his dirty face.

Jax and Mike quickly positioned themselves and began to push down, their muscles flexing and their faces straining with the effort. At first nothing happened. Then, slowly, as the woman in the car screamed in terror, the cement began to lift. Hunter, seeming to find a hidden reserve of energy, placed his hands under the cement and also began to lift, the three of them gradually moving the rock enough that Hunter could finally see into the car through the shattered windshield.

"I can see her!" Hunter exclaimed as the cement toppled off the roof of the car.

A black woman who appeared to be in her early twenties was wedged between the driver's seat and the floorboard, the steering column the only thing preventing the slabs of cement protruding into the car from crashing down on top of her. Hunter reached his hand down between several pieces of rock, awkwardly taking the woman's outstretched hand.

"Are you hurt anywhere?"

"I think both my legs are broken," she said, wincing in pain as she spoke.

"You're going to be okay," Hunter promised, quickly letting go of her hand as Jax and Mike reached into the interior, attempting to remove some of the rocks around her.

"Hurry!" the woman begged.

Within a few minutes, Jax and Mike had cleared a path for one of them to climb in and help the woman out.

"I'll do it," Hunter said, looking at the men before him. "I'm a lot smaller than the two of you."

Jax nodded in agreement before glancing at the large mound of cement in front of them that, with another quake, could crush the car sealing the woman's fate. "Just be careful."

Hunter nodded, dropped both of his legs into the interior of the car, and then, almost as an afterthought, turned to Jax. "Thanks for coming after me."

Jax huffed and wiped at his face, which was streaked with sweat and dirt. "You? I came down here to find my Mazda. Now get the girl, and let's get out of here."

Hunter smiled before slowly lowering himself into the mangled interior of the car. It took several minutes just to position himself around the crumpled vehicle and the rocks that were either still in the car or outside it pressing down dangerously on top of them.

"My legs are still pinned down," Lakesha said, her face twisted with pain.

A large chunk of cement was wedged between the passenger seat and the floorboard, where Lakesha's legs were positioned.

"Hold on," Hunter said, reaching his own cut and bleeding hands around the rock. "When I lift this, I want you to try and pull your legs out."

"I don't know if I can," Lakesha said, her voice trembling.

"Hurry!" Jax called out as the building began to creek and moan, the sound echoing ominously through the garage.

"You've got to," Hunter said urgently.

She nodded her head quickly, her dark eyes wide with terror. "Okay."

"On three," Hunter said, and positioned himself closer to the rock.

On the count of three, Hunter pulled on the rock with everything he had. At first it didn't seem to budge, but then, slowly, the rock began to move. With a loud cry, Lakesha pulled her legs out from under the rock as Hunter's strength gave way and the rock crashed back down on the floor of the car. Hunter turned to Lakesha, his chest heaving.

"Take my hand," he said, his voice trembling from exertion.

Within a couple of seconds, Hunter had Lakesha positioned so that Jax and Mike could reach down and pull her up.

"Thank you," she whispered to Hunter as they began lifting her up.

Hunter bobbed his head in response. Jax looked at his friend and saw the exhaustion written across his face.

After they had pulled Lakesha up and out of the car and placed her on the ground a safe distance from the enormous pile of debris, Jax and Mike scrambled back to the car. Hunter attempted to pull himself out with shaking hands, but after a moment's struggle, he lost his balance and fell back into the interior.

"Give me your hand," Jax demanded, reaching down through the broken windshield, his arms streaked with dried blood.

"Is she okay?" Hunter asked, glancing anxiously up at Jax.

"She'll be fine. Now let's get you out of here," Jax urged.

As Hunter reached out to take Jax's hand, the entire area around them began to shake. This time the sound was almost deafening. Hunter's eyes opened wide, the fear in them making the blood in Jax's veins instantly turn cold.

"No!" Jax screamed, feeling the rocks around them beginning to shift. *"No!"*

CHAPTER NINE

"I've got to go up," Payson said, eyeing the group that stood gawking at him in the hall.

"What?" Tristin exclaimed, gaping at Payson as if he had just lost his mind.

"Tristin, that other elevator won't make it through another after-shock like the last one. I'm not going to leave those people in there to die," Payson said.

Sam nodded his head in agreement. "I'll go with you."

"You can't! You've got to get *them* out," Payson said, gesturing to Gwen, Tristin, and Mrs. Rutledge.

Gwen was already shaking her head. "I'm going too."

Payson threw his hands up in frustration. "This building's coming down. Don't you understand that?"

"I almost died in that elevator shaft with you. I think I'm aware of the risks," Gwen said, her mind obviously made up.

"What about Mrs. Rutledge?" Payson asked, glancing over at the older woman who was sitting on the floor rubbing her leg.

"Tristin can help her out," Gwen offered.

"Aren't you going to talk some sense into her?" Payson asked, turning to Sam.

"Gwen's a big girl. If she says she's coming, then I guess she's coming."

Gwen reached out and touched Sam's arm. Payson just rolled his eyes.

"You're all crazy!" Tristin exclaimed. "Can't the others just wait for the police or the fire department or whoever it is that's supposed to come?"

"There's no time," Sam said.

"It'll be okay," Gwen offered, reaching out and touching Tristin's arm.

"I'm just so scared," Tristin cried, tears beginning to streak her face.

"I know," Gwen said tenderly as she wrapped her arms around her friend. "We all are."

"Promise you'll be careful," Tristin said, her voice cracking.

Gwen nodded, looking like she was on the verge of tears as well.

"Look, do what you want. I don't have time to argue," Payson relented. "There's three people trapped in the other elevator, and one of them is about to have a baby."

"Then let's go," Gwen said, finally stepping back from Tristin and turning to lead the way.

Payson shook his head in frustration, but realizing he didn't really have an alternative, he quickly helped Tristin get Mrs. Rutledge to her feet before starting with the group toward the stairs.

"We'll have to go to the floor above the elevator and then go down the shaft," Payson said, taking the stairs two at a time.

Gwen and Sam nodded. There was an eerie silence in the stairwell that made the hair on Payson's arms and up his neck prickle. Those who were capable of getting out had already done so, leaving the stairwell deserted. Gwen threw her hands to her mouth to stifle a scream as they rounded a corner to find a man sprawled out face first on the stairs, his body motionless and bloody. Payson felt for a pulse, then shook his head and turned back toward Gwen, who was already wrapped in Sam's arms.

"Don't look," Sam said, pulling her close as they continued up the stairs.

When they reached the floor they needed, Payson raced toward the elevator with Sam and Gwen behind him. Sam put one of the metal bars from Mrs. Rutledge's brace between the doors and, with Payson's help, began to pry them apart. After only a second, the doors opened, and Payson stuck his head into the shaft.

"They're still there!" he exclaimed, relief making him feel light-headed.

"But for how long?" Sam asked, his face grim.

Payson didn't speak. Instead, his eyes continued to scan the shaft. There were four ladders running vertically up the narrow passage, one on each wall. Payson was about to reach for the one positioned in between the elevators on the side of the shaft just a few feet away from them when he spotted Richard clinging to the stairs just a few feet down.

"Hold the door!" Richard shouted, climbing the last remaining stairs before sticking his hand out to Payson.

Payson grabbed hold of his hand and swung him over to safety, just as Sam had done for the rest of them only moments before.

"What about Anna and Manuel?" Payson demanded, his face hard.

"What about them?" Richard shot right back, instantly on the defensive.

"You just left them there?" Payson snapped, the blood in his veins flooding warmly across his face.

"I'm not risking my life for anyone! Now get out of my way," Richard snapped, pushing past Payson.

Payson swallowed hard, wanting to say more but not willing to waste another second on the man. Instead, he reached for the ladder and, in one swift motion, swung his own body into the shaft.

"Stay there," Payson called out to Sam. "They'll need some help getting up."

"I'll be right here," Sam said, interlocking his bulky arms as he cast a dirty look over his shoulder at Richard, who was scurrying toward the door to the stairs.

Payson glanced quickly at Gwen, wanting to say something to her, but no words came. Instead, he turned back to Sam, his face shadowed in the dim light. "If something happens, get her out." With that, he quickly descended into the narrow shaft.

* * *

As soon as Payson stuck his head through the hole in the top of the elevator, he knew he was in trouble. Anna was on the floor, her knees bent and her face contorted in pain, while Manuel was at her feet, his face as white as a ghost.

"What are you doing?" Payson blurted out. "You can't have the baby now. We've got to get you out of here!"

Completely oblivious to anything but the pain, Anna let out a cry, her neck muscles taut as she bent forward. Payson quickly lowered himself into the interior of the elevator and immediately went to her side. As he did, Manuel hastily got up and moved to the far corner of the elevator so that Payson would have enough space to sit.

"Wait a minute," Payson stammered, his own face quickly draining of color. "I can't deliver a baby . . . I'm just a student," he added lamely, too scared to worry about how ridiculous he sounded.

Payson yelped as Anna reached out and grabbed his arm, her fingernails digging deep into his flesh.

"I don't care if you're the pizza delivery boy," she began, tightening her grip. "*I* am going to push, and *you* are going to deliver this baby."

"Okay, okay!" Payson said, knowing deep down that they were way past the point of moving her. She was in hard labor now and wouldn't be going anywhere until the baby was born. Payson turned to Manuel, reason slowly returning to him. "We need to lessen the strain on the cable. You'll have to go up."

Manuel nodded briskly, relief flooding his features.

"There'll be someone up on the next floor to help you," Payson added as he stood and interlocked his fingers to give Manuel a boost. The man attempted in vain to pull himself up using only his good arm, but unable to heave himself out, he hesitantly resorted to using both. With a loud cry and a string of Spanish expletives that needed no translation, he slowly pulled himself up through the top of the elevator. Once he was up, Payson took a much needed deep breath before bending down next to Anna.

"Okay," he began awkwardly. "What do I do?"

Anna grabbed his hand, squeezing all the blood from it until the contraction had passed and she had relaxed a little. "Get one of the receiving blankets," she said, her hair damp and matted to her head.

Payson grabbed the bag on the floor and quickly withdrew a blanket. "Now what?" he asked hesitantly, not entirely wanting to hear what was coming next.

Anna, who had sweetly bandaged his head and helped him recover after the initial earthquake, now glared at him as if to sear a hole through his thick head. "Now you deliver the baby!" she growled.

Payson nodded obediently, wiped his sweaty palms on his pant legs, and positioned himself next to her bent legs. "Okay," he offered reluctantly, his head instantly feeling woozy, though this time it had nothing to do with the gash. "I'm ready."

Clearly no longer caring if he was or not, Anna bent forward, every muscle in her face and neck straining as she gritted her teeth and pushed. The sweat that was beaded on her brow now fell in streams down her face.

"You can do it," Payson urged, his own hands shaking, a dark patch of perspiration seeping through the back of his shirt. He wanted to take off his jacket, but there wasn't time.

Anna relaxed for a split second and then bent forward again, crying out and gripping her knees until her knuckles were white. Then, with her body near exhaustion and Payson praying with everything in him that the elevator cable would hold, it was over. Payson stared down in wonder at the warm little body in his arms.

"It's a boy," he whispered, his eyes shining as he glanced with an added measure of respect at the child's mother.

"Why isn't he crying?" Anna asked, her voice rising sharply as she stared at the small bundle in his arms.

Payson's eyes immediately shot back to the baby. Though the baby's body was warm, his tiny lips were quickly turning blue.

"I don't know!" Payson cried, panic welling up inside him. "What do I do?" Then almost instantly, a thought came to him. Payson grabbed a corner of the receiving blanket, wrapped it around his index finger, and swabbed the baby's mouth. Once the sticky mucus was cleared, the baby cried out, his face quickly flooding with color.

"He's okay," Payson said, the effect of the moment still tingling through his body.

Anna's whole body relaxed, her tears falling freely onto her cheeks. Cradling the baby in one arm, Payson fished through his pocket for his pocketknife. Then, after carefully cutting the cord and clamping it off with the elastic band from Anna's blond ponytail, Payson wrapped the receiving blanket around the baby and placed him in his mother's outstretched arms.

Anna smiled through her tears as she touched one of her son's tiny fingers. "He's beautiful!" she whispered, kissing his tiny forehead.

Payson knelt next to the two of them, still in awe over what had just taken place and eternally grateful for inspiration from above.

"Thank you," Anna said, her eyes misty.

Payson smiled awkwardly, his face warm and his eyes shining. Then he quickly turned his attention to the afterbirthing, as well as helping Anna get cleaned up.

After several minutes, someone called down to them, their voice echoing through the shaft. "Hey, what's happening down there?"

Payson's eyes lifted to the hole in the ceiling, and then he reluctantly glanced at Anna. "We've got to go."

Anna nodded, brushing her baby's cheek with her lips before lifting his small body toward Payson. As Anna got herself ready, Payson glanced anxiously around the elevator, suddenly wondering how he was going to climb the stairs with a baby in his arms. His eyes reluctantly fell on Anna's shopping sack. With no other option readily available, Payson grabbed hold of the handle and pulled the sack over to him. Then, praying that the sack wouldn't rip, Payson placed the infant inside, then turned to Anna.

"I'll take the baby up and then come back for you," he said, carefully helping Anna to her feet so she could hand the baby to him once he was through the hole in the ceiling.

A moment later, Anna reluctantly handed the sack to Payson. "Take care of him," she said, the pleading in her voice causing Payson's throat to catch.

"He'll be fine," Payson said, trying to reassure her. Then, having no idea how much longer the cable would hold, he turned and started up the stairs.

* * *

"Come on. We don't have much farther," Sutherland called over his shoulder to McKenna, who had fallen several feet behind him in the narrow vent shaft.

"Can't we stop for just a minute?" McKenna called out, balancing herself so that she could keep as much pressure off her right knee as possible.

During the last aftershock, a portion of the vent shaft had buckled, pinning McKenna's right knee between the buckled metal. It had been extremely painful and had cost them valuable time, but McKenna had finally been able to yank her leg free. Though grateful to still be alive, she had a severe cut on her leg that was now leaving a trail of blood behind her.

"There's no time. We've got to get down below the collapsed staircase before there's another earthquake."

Knowing that he was right and never being one to quit, McKenna steeled herself against the pain and continued forward; however, the distance between herself and Sutherland seemed to grow with each passing minute. And the farther McKenna got from Sutherland, the darker the narrow vent shaft became.

"Wait up!" she called out as Sutherland rounded a corner, leaving her in almost total darkness.

McKenna waited for him to answer, but other than the sound of her own breathing, which was increasing rapidly, there was only silence. McKenna opened her mouth to call out to him again, but an eerie feeling that sent a chill through her entire body stopped her. She stiffened, her eyes wide and her limbs trembling. Someone *was* behind her; she could sense it. Shakily, McKenna pulled two items from her inside suit coat pocket—the lighter and the makeup compact with the mirror. She opened the compact with her thumb and placed the cigarette lighter next to the mirror, then flicked the lighter so she could see what was behind her. Nathan Rinehart's face instantly reflected in the mirror. McKenna could feel a scream rising from deep within her, but before she could give it life, Nathan spoke.

"Don't make a sound!" he warned, causing her body to tremble so intensely that she thought for a moment another quake was happening.

"I left my briefcase back at the restaurant," she began, her voice a shaky whisper. "There's no proof that you did anything. You could disappear. With the earthquake, the police will just assume you're dead." McKenna tightened in anticipation, realizing that she was the only thing standing between him and freedom. "I won't tell anyone," she lied, knowing intuitively that he would know better.

"McKenna!"

McKenna's eyes opened wide as she stared at the darkness before her. Alan Sutherland's voice still echoed through the vent shaft.

Nathan dropped his voice to a raspy whisper. "I wasn't the only person with access to West Link files. You're a smart woman—think about it. Besides, if I were a killer, wouldn't you be dead right now?"

With that said, he slowly began to back away into the darkness.

"McKenna? Are you all right?" Sutherland called out, his voice louder this time.

McKenna heard a muffled clanking and knew that Sutherland was making his way back through the vent. She quickly placed the lighter and the compact back inside her suit coat pocket. Then, despite the pain in her knee, she scrambled toward the light from the flashlight that was now playing randomly across the walls of the vent as Sutherland made his way toward her.

"Why did you stop?" Sutherland asked once he had rounded the bend.

McKenna fought to control the quivering in her lower lip.

"Are you okay?" Sutherland asked, his brow suddenly raised in concern.

McKenna opened her mouth to tell him what had just happened but abruptly stopped herself. Though she didn't believe Nathan was innocent, he had made a point. Why *hadn't* he killed her? And who else *did* have access? The answer to the last question was staring her right in the face. McKenna searched Sutherland's face, but there was no indication as to his guilt or innocence written across his features.

However, as she looked into Sutherland's eyes, seeing only apparent concern for her well-being, McKenna's skin still crawled. Although she felt she had fairly intuitive perception, McKenna knew she had been fooled in the past. Manning was a prime example of that. No longer certain whether she should be more concerned about the man somewhere in the shaft behind her or the man directly in front of her, McKenna decided it would be safer to keep quiet until she knew for certain.

"I just had to stop for a minute," McKenna said, watching Sutherland's eyes to see if he believed her.

He hesitated for a moment. "The stairs leading down are just around the bend. Once we're down to the next level, we'll be able to get out of the vents."

McKenna shrugged off a shudder. "Good. I'm ready to get out of here."

McKenna followed Sutherland as he backed his way to the stairs, since there was not enough room to turn around, and then the two quickly descended the stairs in the shaft. Reaching the vent opening on the next floor, Sutherland kicked it open and lowered himself onto a desk in a room that looked like a law office. Once he had made it down, he helped McKenna lower herself out of the shaft, off the desk, and into a chair.

"Why don't you sit for a minute. You're not going to make it far on that leg. My office is just down the hall. I'll check my receptionist's desk and see if she has something we can use to wrap your knee. I'll be right back," Sutherland said as he headed purposefully to the door.

As soon as he was gone, McKenna immediately looked down at her knee. Though the bleeding from the three-inch gash had stopped, her knee had almost doubled in size, making it extremely painful to bend. McKenna lifted her head and quickly scanned the room, looking for something to use as a crutch. Though she knew it would be difficult to make it to the ground floor of Lincoln Tower alone, an uneasy feeling was growing in the pit of her stomach, and she no longer had any intension of sticking around until Sutherland made it back.

The office she was in was decorated like an old sea harbor, with pictures of nineteenth-century fishing boats taking up the wall space not already monopolized by framed law degrees and special recognition awards. McKenna's eyes widened as she came to a full-length, rustic paddle placed on the wall next to the door. If she could get it down, it would make a perfect crutch. Desperate to leave and not wanting to depend on a man she no longer trusted, she stood, then hopped on her good leg over to the paddle, the jarring motion sending sharp, shooting pains through her swollen kneecap.

Once she had reached the paddle, McKenna's eyes went to a hat rack to her left. Quickly picking it up, she lifted it toward the paddle, knocking the rustic decoration from the wall with one swipe. Relieved, McKenna carefully bent down, attempting to keep her right leg as straight as possible as she picked up the paddle. Though it was bulky and uncomfortable as she placed it under her armpit, it took a considerable amount of pressure off her right knee. As she started toward the door, she stiffened as an almost-imperceptible sound behind her sent off alarms in her head. McKenna's eyes opened wide and her heart accelerated as she glanced at a framed picture on the wall next to the door. Through the reflection she could see a pair of legs emerging from the vent in the ceiling. McKenna could feel her body tingling with fear as she watched Nathan slowly lower himself into the room. Knowing that she would never be able to outrun him, McKenna lifted the paddle, holding it like a baseball bat as she jerked around to face him, the movement sending excruciating pain through her entire leg. Nathan froze, his eyes wide, staring not at her but at the door behind. Fighting the urge to glance toward the door herself, McKenna kept her eyes on Nathan; she gasped as he reached for a solid brass paperweight on the desk. McKenna stumbled back several feet, then turned just in time to see Sutherland duck, the weight hitting him hard in the shoulder. With Sutherland temporarily distracted, Nathan jumped onto the desk that was positioned under the vent, then scrambled back up into the shaft. At the same time, Sutherland reached inside his suit coat and, to McKenna's complete horror, pulled out a gun. He fired three rapid shots into the ceiling where the vent would lead. McKenna screamed as she covered her ears with her hands. Sutherland, who had started toward the vent, turned his eyes to her.

"Go," he shouted, still aiming his gun at the ceiling. "I'll meet you out there."

McKenna didn't hesitate. Using the paddle for a crutch, she hobbled toward the door. Once safely out in the hall, she quickly glanced around. One wall, not far from the ladies' room, had partially collapsed, knocking over a water fountain and causing its pipes to rupture, saturating the thin carpet and causing large puddles to form. McKenna looked past the fountain to the end of the hall, where the elevators and stairs were located. She shook her head, knowing that she would never make it before Sutherland came looking for her. She would have to hide. Cringing as two more shots rang out, McKenna hastily limped toward the ladies room, her decision made. But once inside the relatively small room, McKenna was already bemoaning her decision. Other than the stalls, which would be obvious hiding places to anyone searching for her, there was nowhere to hide. In addition, there was also only one way out—back through the door she had just entered. Resisting the urge to hurry back out into the hall, McKenna ducked into the third stall. Using the paddle to balance herself, she climbed up onto the toilet seat, then lifted the paddle up off of the floor so that anyone glancing inside the room wouldn't see anything.

McKenna had been standing on the toilet seat for two or three minutes when she heard the door slowly creak open. She sucked her breath in and waited. Seconds later the door closed with a gentle thud. McKenna held her breath, praying that whoever had opened it had left, though that hope was quickly dispelled. McKenna could hear footsteps starting toward her on the tile floor, followed by the sound of the door to the first stall pulling open and then closing just seconds later. McKenna fought to control her breathing. She tightened her grip on the paddle as the second stall door swung open, again swinging closed almost immediately. A moment later, McKenna saw a pair of black dress shoes standing in front of her stall. Unable to stand there and wait for it to open, she lunged at the door, plowing into the man on the other side of it and sending him flying back toward the sinks that had been ripped from the wall by the earthquake. McKenna started for the door, slowed by her knee but no longer feeling the pain. Then, just as she reached for the handle, a hand reached out and took her by the shoulder, jerking her around to face him.

"I didn't kill anyone," Nathan said, his eyes round and intense. "You've got to believe me."

"Then why did you confess?" McKenna asked, her breaths coming in shaky bursts.

Nathan was already shaking his head angrily. "Sutherland said he'd kill my father if I didn't, that Manning was just waiting for word to do it."

McKenna's eyes raced over Nathan's face, looking for any sign that he was lying. "What do you want from me?" she finally asked, the fear in his eyes causing a sudden surge of power within her.

"If Sutherland has anything to say about it, I'm not getting out of this building alive. And," Nathan continued, shooting an anxious look at the closed restroom door, "if he thinks you suspect the truth, neither are you."

Nathan's words hit her with a blunt force, but it was the look in his eyes that made her own eyes widen. *He is telling the truth.*

"Where's Sutherland?" McKenna asked, not sure she wanted to know.

"He went to the stairs. But when he realizes that you're not there, he'll come back. Sutherland's not one to leave any loose ends, and right now he has two."

"Where can we go?"

"We'll have to hide for a while until we're sure he's gone. Then we can take the stairs."

McKenna nodded slowly, suddenly feeling numb. Though she had believed Nathan a moment ago, she was already starting to question the impulse. But, not having a better plan, she took his hand as he inched the door open. Finding the hall empty, he opened it all the way. He glanced at her once, his eyes registering her lingering doubt, then started down the hall, heading back to the law office they had just been in.

"Let's hope he doesn't think to look for you back in here," Nathan said, trying to sound confident.

"And if he does?" she asked hesitantly.

Nathan took a shaky breath but didn't speak, apparently not wanting to consider that option any more than McKenna.

CHAPTER TEN

2:30 P.M. / Downtown Los Angeles

Chad's motorcycle squealed to a stop in front of the building as his eyes quickly climbed the length of it. Almost every window he could see on the face of Lincoln Tower was shattered. Pieces of glass covered the base of it, while the structure itself looked as if a small sneeze could bring it down. Chad took off his helmet to get a better look at the sight, though the effect was much the same. The front of the building was still standing, but the entire back corner had crumbled in the earthquake, forming an impenetrable wall. The other corner was likewise surrounded by a massive mountain of debris, though one small section, closer to the front of the building, had remained relatively unscathed. Chad looked up near the third-floor window and noticed a trash slide—a tool construction workers often used during a remodeling project to get excess materials down to a waiting dumpster—attached to it. Chad shook his head, knowing that with all but one of the entrances blocked, it was going to be very difficult to extract survivors. He was sure of one other thing: This building was coming down. The only questions that remained were when, and how many people would be trapped inside when it did. He had gotten there as quickly as possible, but there had been so much devastation that it had taken him an hour and a half just to get across town. Not wanting to lose another second, Chad hastily climbed off his bike, pulled his backpack over his shoulders, and started toward the building.

"Hey, buddy. Where do you think you're going?"

Chad lifted his eyes to a man in fatigues carrying an M-16 and walking purposefully toward him. Chad had spotted a few guardsmen on his way over, though nothing seemed to be very organized yet. It would take hours before enough troops made it into the area to establish any semblance of order, and by then it would be dark.

"I'm a firefighter," Chad said, pulling his identification from his wallet and holding it out to the soldier.

The soldier examined it for only a moment, then handed it back. "I'm glad you're here. I've wanted to check whether anyone's trapped inside, but I have strict instructions to stay out here, maintain order, and help with the wounded until enough troops get in here to start an organized evacuation."

Chad nodded his head in understanding, comprehending the enormity of the task at hand, but the soldier was already looking past him to a group of teenage boys trying to sneak into a jewelry store across the street. "They're going to get themselves killed," the soldier mumbled before calling out to them. "Stop right there!" he shouted, his words causing the boys to do just the opposite.

Chad watched as the soldier took off after the boys, shooting several warning shots in the air. Not waiting another moment, Chad turned his attention back to Lincoln Tower. He took a deep breath, recognizing just a hint of smoke in the breeze, then glanced toward the section of town that was on fire. Dark clouds fed by the hungry blazes below were quickly spreading. The wind that had picked up in the last twenty minutes was stoking the flames, lifting them higher and promising that a quick fix to the situation was not likely. Chad had the sinking feeling that before this was all over, he would be in the midst of a fire, the likes of which he had never experienced. He fought a wave of panic as he was reminded of another time and place, another life that had been placed in his hands. Not liking the mental images resurfacing or the emotion constricting his throat, he forced the thoughts to the back of his mind, as he had so many times before, then hoisted his gear higher on his back and started toward the front doors.

Once inside, Chad took a quick look around the lobby, spotting two people, a man in his early thirties and a woman, much younger, heading toward him, coming from the stairs.

"Hey, you didn't happen to see a pregnant woman, did you?" Chad asked, starting toward the man.

Completely ignoring the question, the man pushed past Chad roughly, almost running as he headed out the front doors. Chad turned to watch him go but then quickly turned back around, his eyes on the woman, who was shaking her head in open disgust.

"If he did see a pregnant woman, he would have pushed her down and plowed right over her," she growled.

Chad didn't comment; he had seen people panic before during fires. "Did *you* see a pregnant woman?" he asked, anxious to begin searching.

The woman shook her head. "I didn't see one, but if she was above the thirty-seventh floor it's gonna take a long time to get her down."

"Why?"

"The stairs collapsed. Two flights. A few of us tied tablecloths from the restaurant together to make a rope to rappel down, but we were the first ones to try it," she said, her eyes flashing back to the man that had preceded her. "It was supposed to be women first, but in his case, you see how that worked."

Chad could feel his heart racing. The woman standing in front of him was petite and obviously in good physical shape. Rappelling down three flights would be difficult, if not outright impossible for a pregnant woman, regardless of what kind of condition she was in.

"Thanks," Chad said.

"Good luck," the woman said as she passed Chad and continued on to the doors.

Chad hurried over to the elevators, knowing that there would be a bulletin board listing all the offices in the building. However, as his eyes fell on the elevator doors, his firefighter sense kicked in. They were open, but there was no elevator inside. Chad stuck his head into the shaft, gazing up as far as he could in the dim light. He spotted one elevator several flights above him, but there was no sign of the others. Chad dropped his focus to the bottom of the shaft. He could see particles of dust rising up from the wreckage of another elevator. Chad let his breath out slowly before pulling back from the shaft, forcing himself not to think about the people who had likely lost their lives in the fall. Instead, he turned toward the office listings on the wall. He quickly scanned the board, hoping that any OB-GYN listings would be well below the thirty-seventh floor. Chad spotted three OB-GYNs: one on the third floor, one on the tenth, and one on the thirty-eighth. He let out a tense sigh when he read the last one, then began berating himself for not asking Justice the name of Anna's doctor, or at least what floor the office was on. Now he would have to check them all—assuming of course that Anna hadn't already made it out and that he had just missed her on the road somewhere. Chad had passed so many people on the way over that it would have been easy to miss her in all the confusion. Pushing those thoughts aside, Chad opened the door to the stairs and took them two at a time. As he reached the third floor, he almost ran into another woman who was rounding the stairwell.

"Were you up above the thirty-seventh floor?" he asked, taking the woman gently by the arm.

The woman took a moment to catch her breath as she nodded her head.

"Did you see a pregnant woman up there? Shoulder-length blond hair, probably pulled back in a ponytail?"

"I didn't see one, but I wasn't looking either."

Chad acknowledged her answer with a quick nod of his head and then opened the door to the third floor, relieved by the fact that no one he had talked to had see a woman matching Anna's description above the section of staircase that had collapsed. That narrowed his search considerably. *Unless* . . . His mind went instantly back to the remains of the second elevator at the bottom of the shaft. He shook his head, dismissing the thought, even though he knew that Anna, at nine months pregnant, would never have used the stairs. Calling out her name as he went, he made his way to the first OB-GYN's office. It only took a few minutes to see that the entire floor was vacant. Relieved that at least these people had made it out of the building but growing increasingly anxious that he still hadn't found Anna, he started up to the tenth floor.

By the time Chad had reached the tenth floor, he was struggling to catch his breath, mainly because he had been taking the stairs two at a time. It reminded him of a time in high school when, after his team had lost a game, the coach—a cocky man accustomed to winning—had made them run the bleachers for an hour after they had already played an intense two-hour football game. Most of the guys had puked their guts out after the incident, but not Chad.

Growing up with a dad who was a fire chief, Chad had been taught to suck it up and get the job done, whatever the price. And that's what he had always done—until it had really mattered. Then Chad had fallen short, and it had cost him a life—his father's.

Feeling a flood of memories he had struggled for the past year to erase, Chad pushed open the door to the tenth floor, hoping that the task at hand would keep the memories at bay, at least for a time. That's what he had done day after day, pushing himself until he was too tired to think, while hoping and sometimes praying that the things he did to help others would somehow compensate for his failure. Deep down he knew that was impossible. Each life he saved offered its own reward, but it never alleviated the guilt and remorse of not saving his dad. It was something he would just have to live with.

As soon as Chad opened the door to the tenth floor, his eyes were drawn to two men and a woman standing next to the elevator shaft.

"What's going on?" Chad asked, watching with concern as one of the men stretched his arm out into the shaft, while the woman held tight to his belt loop so he wouldn't lose his balance.

"There is a woman in the elevator," said a Hispanic man standing next to the others and cradling his right arm.

Chad immediately took hold of the first man's belt loop. "I've got it," he said as the woman stepped aside. "I'm a firefighter with the Los Angeles Fire Department."

Relief washed over the face of the woman as well as the Hispanic man. The woman continued to thank him as she leaned against the wall, the reality of the situation seeming to catch up with her. Chad turned his attention back to the man, who reached his arm out into the elevator shaft and then stepped back with a shopping bag in his hands. Chad looked down at the bag in confusion, but before he could question what was going on, he heard a baby cry from inside the sack. The man turned and handed the sack to Chad, then leaned back into the shaft as someone called up to him.

"I'm going back for Anna," the voice echoed.

Chad's head jerked up from the newborn in the sack to the dark shaft. "Anna!" Chad gasped, relief hitting him with almost palpable force.

The man standing next to the shaft turned to face him. "You know her?"

Chad nodded with a smile, feeling like he might fall over from relief. "Is she okay?"

"I think so," the man said. Then he extended his hand. "I'm Sam."

"I'm Chad," Chad offered, glancing back down at the baby. Still in a state of shock, he carefully reached into the sack and withdrew the infant, holding the baby awkwardly in his arms. Then he turned to the woman, knowing that he needed to help with Anna.

"Will you hold the baby, ma'am?"

"Call me Gwen," she offered as she reached out and accepted the baby. "And this is Manuel."

Chad nodded. Once his arms were free, he stepped past Sam and looked down into the shaft. He immediately spotted the elevator below them, as well as a man climbing down a set of metal stairs not far from it. The man had what looked like a scarf wrapped around his forehead.

"Anna," Chad called down. "It's me, Chad. Are you okay?"

Though he couldn't see her, Chad could hear a little burst of emotion. "I'm okay," she finally managed, her voice noticeably strained. "Is the baby all right?"

"The baby's fine. How about you? Are you really okay?"

"I had a baby in an elevator during an earthquake—I'm just great!" she exclaimed, both crying and laughing at the same time. "Where's Justice?"

"There are fires everywhere on the other side of town. He's trying to put them out, so he sent me here to find you."

"But he's okay?" she asked, her voice laced with worry.

"I'm not with him—so you have nothing to worry about," Chad teased, hoping to alleviate her concerns.

Chad watched as the man who was now on top of the elevator climbed down through the hole. A few minutes later, Anna's hands appeared on top of the elevator, but after several attempts she still wasn't able to pull herself up, and her hands disappeared. Chad immediately grabbed hold of the ladder and swung himself into the shaft.

"Just a minute!" Chad called out. "I'm coming."

A moment later Chad stood on the top of the elevator, peering down through the opening. Anna smiled, her face showing relief, though she still looked thoroughly exhausted.

"You don't know how glad I am to see you," she said.

Chad returned the smile, then flattened himself down on his stomach and reached his hands out toward her. "You don't know how glad *I* am to see *you!* If I came back empty-handed, your old man would mop downtown L.A. with my face."

Anna smiled.

"On the count of three," Chad said, his eyes on the man in the elevator who was ready to lift Anna back up.

A moment later, Chad pulled Anna up through the hole. "It's a good thing you had that baby before I had to pull you up through this hole." Chad laughed as he helped her to her feet and then onto the metal stairs. "You might have gotten stuck."

Anna smiled halfheartedly, too exhausted to do anything else.

"Be careful climbing up," Chad said before turning his attention back to the man still standing in the elevator.

Chad quickly dropped back onto his stomach and extended his hands down through the hole. "What's your name?" Chad asked.

"Payson."

"Alright, Payson, I'm Chad. How about on the count of three you jump, I pull you up, and the two of us get out of this hole?"

They both froze as the building began to groan, the sound echoing up the narrow shaft. Chad could feel his heart thumping in his chest.

"Make it two," Chad corrected, seeing his own fear reflected in Payson's face.

On the count of two, Payson jumped, and Chad caught his hands. Chad had to strain to pull him up, but finally Payson emerged through the opening, the eerie sound still rumbling all around them, though the building remained still. Once the two were on their feet, they gripped the metal ladder and started climbing the rungs, Payson taking the lead. Chad had seen the wreckage at the bottom of the shaft and had no intention of becoming part of it. He lifted his head just as Sam reached for Anna's hand and swung her over to safety. A moment later, Sam reached his hand out to Payson, who had since reached the opening, and pulled him over. Chad quickly climbed the remaining stairs, sure that at any moment the trembling would begin. But instead, the creaking and groaning lessened, and Chad soon found himself in the hall next to the rest of them.

"Is everyone all right?" he asked, knowing they were still not in the clear.

Most of them nodded, though Anna slumped to the floor, the effort and exertion catching up to her. Chad squatted down next to her, placing his hand on her shoulder. She quickly lifted her hand and placed it over his.

"Thanks for coming," she said, her face pale but her eyes filled with gratitude.

Chad just smiled as Anna lifted her eyes to the baby in Gwen's arms.

"You're sure he's okay?" she asked, extending her hands as Gwen brought the baby to her.

"He looks healthy to me," Chad said. Then his smile broadened. "And you're in luck; he looks nothing like his old man."

Anna smiled, though it quickly faded. "How bad are the fires, Chad?"

Chad glanced at the baby, averting his eyes from Anna. "Enough to keep him busy for a while, but he'll be fine," he quickly added.

When Chad looked back he could see the hesitancy in her eyes, though she didn't press the issue. Instead, she gestured toward his arms. "How're your burns?"

"They're the least of my worries right now," he said as he turned his attention to Payson, Sam, and Manuel. "Have you checked this floor to see if anyone's still in here?"

Sam shook his head. "No. We haven't had a chance to look yet."

Chad looked back at Anna, knowing that she would need some time to rest before she could make it safely down the stairs.

"I'm going to take a look. I don't want to leave anyone trapped in here."

Payson and Sam immediately stepped to his side, indicating that they would help with the search.

"Will you stay with them?" Chad asked Manuel as he gestured toward Gwen and Anna, who were sitting on the floor.

Manuel nodded his head. "*Sí.*" Then he glanced at his arm, his expression apologetic. "I wish I could do more to help."

"Trust me, this is a help," Chad said. Then he looked at Payson and pointed down the hall. "You check the rooms that way." They all instinctively turned their heads to look at the open space at the very end of that hall where the remainder of Lincoln Tower had been. It was now ripped wide open, giving them a clear view of the building that sat parallel to it. "And Sam and I will check the other end."

Payson nodded in agreement before setting out to check the rooms that were still intact. Chad and Sam turned and started in the opposite direction.

"You check the left side of the hall, and I'll check the right," Chad said, wanting to make this quick. "Call out if you find anyone," he added as he disappeared into the first room.

He had just stepped inside when he heard someone shouting in the hall. Chad immediately turned around and ran back in the direction he had just come from. Sam met him at about the same time, and the two turned toward the far end of the hall, where the shouting had come from. Payson was motioning to them from that direction.

"I found someone!" he shouted, waiting only long enough to ensure that they had seen him before disappearing back into the room.

Chad and Sam raced down the hall, slowing once they reached the spot where Payson had been.

"In here!" Payson shouted, straining as he struggled to lift a heavy partition that had fallen over.

Chad and Sam were beside him in seconds, and the three of them easily lifted the wall divider off the woman trapped beneath. She cried out once she was free, reaching out toward a leg that was noticeably broken, though the side of her head was also badly bruised and swollen. Chad immediately bent down to pull her out, while Payson and Sam continued to hold the divider. The woman's cries intensified as Chad moved her.

"She's going into shock," Chad said, lifting his eyes to the two men above him. "I need something to keep her warm."

Sam quickly pulled off his jacket and handed it to Chad, who placed it gently over the woman.

"I need a wet rag or something," Chad said once the woman was covered.

Sam spotted a water cooler on the far side of the room that had tipped over, though the plastic container was still intact. He hurried over to it, lifted the dispenser, grabbed one of the small paper cups that was still attached to the side, and filled it with water. He then carefully made his way across the room and handed the cup to Chad. Once Chad had the cup, Sam quickly grabbed the bottom of his pullover and brought it up over his head, leaving him standing in a white undershirt.

"Use this," he said, extending the shirt.

Chad dampened the shirt with water, then placed it on the woman's head while calmly reassuring her that she was going to be all right. After a couple of minutes, a bit of color began returning to her face, though she continued to stare blankly at the men before her.

"Earthquake," she whimpered.

"What's your name?" Chad asked, bending down close to her and glancing at the bruises around her head with concern.

"Kimberly," she said, her eyes wide and unblinking.

"We're going to get you out, Kimberly," Chad assured her as he pulled the jacket that was draped over her up around her neck. "Make sure there's no one else in here," Chad said, turning his eyes to Payson and Sam.

The two began to search the rest of the room while Chad took a look at the woman's leg. It was grotesquely mangled, though the bone was not protruding from the skin. Chad knew that getting her down ten flights of stairs was going to be painful. He touched her head and looked her in the eyes, glad to see her responding when he spoke.

"I'm going to pick you up."

He could see the hesitancy in her face, but she just gritted her teeth, crying out only once when he lifted her. When he had her in his arms, he headed for the hall. Payson and Sam followed closely.

"We didn't find anyone else," Payson said.

"Good. Check the other rooms down the hall," Chad said as he headed back toward Anna, Gwen, and Manuel.

Gwen and Manuel quickly stood as soon as they saw Chad.

"Her leg's broken," Chad began, "but what really concerns me is the hematoma on the side of her face."

Smiling tenderly, Gwen reached out and touched the woman. "You're going to be okay."

The woman cried out again as Chad carefully lowered her to the floor so that he could continue checking the other rooms.

"Keep talking to her," Chad told Gwen and Manuel before turning his eyes to Anna, who was cradling her baby in her arms.

"How are you doing?"

"Don't worry about me. I'm fine," she said, though her expression was less convincing.

"Give me five more minutes, and we'll get you all out of here. I just don't want to leave anyone behind," Chad said as he turned to leave.

As he started down the hall, the floor beneath him began to tremble again, building quickly in intensity until he was unable to stand. The sound was deafening and terrifying. Chad threw his hands over his head to protect himself as best he could, sure that at any second the building would begin to crumble. He could hear debris crashing all around him, some of it falling on top of him as the quake persisted, its strength intensifying. Then, when Chad was sure the end had come, the tremor stopped. Pain radiated throughout his entire rib cage, but it was Anna's scream that stole his breath. He hurriedly began to dig his way out from under the wall that had collapsed on top of him, grasping his side with his hand until the pain abated somewhat and he was able to stand. Choking back the thick dust in the air, he started back toward the elevator, stopping in his tracks when he saw the reason for Anna's screams. The ceiling just to the right of where Anna and her new baby were sitting had completely collapsed, depositing a huge mound of rubble, including what looked like two vending machines from the floor above, in a heap just a few feet from her.

"Are you hurt?" Chad asked, his eyes rushing over her and the baby.

She shook her head frantically as she looked at the pile before her. "He's under there."

"Who?" Chad asked anxiously.

"Manuel," Anna said, a sob shaking her shoulders.

Chad glanced over at Gwen, who was also staring in horror at the mound of rubble. Then he turned toward the pile himself as a sinking feeling settled in the pit of his stomach. He hurried over to the debris just as Payson and Sam, who had been down the hall when the aftershock hit, came up beside him. Payson reached out and grabbed Chad's arm, then pointed above them where a third vending machine teetered just inches from falling through the hole in the ceiling.

"Be careful," Payson warned.

Chad nodded, knowing he still had to try. Casting one more anxious glance above, he began to dig through the rubble. Payson and Sam were quick to do the same. A moment later, Payson stopped digging and quickly turned away, his face drained of color.

"He's dead?" Chad asked, seeing the expression on Payson's face.

Payson confirmed his suspicions with a quick nod, then slowly began taking off his jacket so he could place it over Manuel's face. Chad glanced over his shoulder as Gwen knelt down and wrapped her arms around Anna, trying to console her, though she continued to sob. Everyone else was silent, the loss and the deadly reality of the situation hitting them afresh. Though only Anna had had a chance to get to know him, he was one of them—and now he was dead. As Chad glanced around at the small group, he couldn't help but wonder who would be next.

"How are we going to get out of here?" Sam finally whispered, breaking the silence.

Chad turned back around, his eyes going for the first time to the door leading to the stairs, which was now completely blocked. He let his breath out slowly, his hand going absently to his ribs as he scanned the contents of the pile. Though the vending machines would be heavy, he had no doubt that the three of them could move them. But when his focus shifted to a heavy metal floor beam that was pressed directly up against the door, Chad exhaled and shook his head. Barring the use of a crane, that beam wasn't going anywhere.

"We'll just have to clear it out," Sam insisted, already beginning to dig, his expression frantic.

Chad looked back to the pile and then to Payson, who shook his head, clearly thinking the same thing as Chad. Going down the stairs, at least through this door, was no longer a possibility. They were going to have to find another way.

CHAPTER ELEVEN

4:00 P.M. / Los Angeles; Two stories below Lincoln Tower

The parking garage amplified the sound of the earthquake, and the effect was terrifying. Jax placed his hands over his head, sure that at any moment he would be buried beneath a mountain of concrete. He screamed—at least he could feel air escaping his lungs—though the sound was drowned out by the deafening roar rumbling all around him. Mike was somewhere next to him, but the dust was so thick that Jax knew that he wouldn't be able to see him even if he tried. Instead he prayed, not sure if he was speaking out loud or just pleading over and over in his mind until the trembling finally stopped. Once it did, Jax began to cough violently.

"Hunter!" Jax shouted, coughing as he did.

"Can you still see the SUV?" Mike asked, choking on the dust himself.

Jax strained to see the spot where the two of them had been digging for the past two hours, but it was impossible to see more than a foot away. There had been an aftershock right after they had extracted Lakesha from the car. A pile of rubble had poured down on Hunter, completely burying him and the car. Jax and Mike had dug frantically after the aftershock had ended, and they had just found the roof of the car when another aftershock had hit, erasing all their efforts.

"I need to check on Lakesha and make sure she's okay," Mike shouted as the rumbling continued all around them.

After the first aftershock, Jax and Mike had carried Lakesha to a minivan not far from them that had received very little damage, in hopes that she would be safer there.

"Don't go!" Jax shouted. "If we get separated, we'll all die."

Mike must have believed him, because he stayed, though he did call out to Lakesha to make sure she was all right. After hearing Lakesha's voice assuring him she was okay, Mike turned his attention back to Jax, his face grim.

"Jax, I know he's your friend, but we've got to find a way out of here. There's no way he could have made it through that one. He was barely hanging on when we uncovered the car last time."

"No!" Jax snapped. "He's alive. I won't go without him."

Mike hesitated for a moment before finally nodding. "Let's wait a few more minutes until the dust starts to settle. I can't see a thing."

Jax nodded his head; if they didn't dig in the right place they would never find Hunter. Jax's body was cut and bleeding from diving into the SUV on top of the shattered glass, and after hours of lifting huge slabs of concrete, his hands were raw and his muscles burned. Too much more of this and he wouldn't be able to lift his arms, let alone chunks of cement.

"Does your flashlight still work?" Jax asked.

Mike pulled his flashlight from his utility belt and clicked it on. The beam shone across the rubble, catching millions of dust particles in its beam.

"It works," he said, quickly turning it off so they could preserve the batteries. They both knew the backup generator wouldn't last long; without the flashlight, they would be left in total darkness.

Jax had had a flashlight, but he had dropped it during the last quake and couldn't find it. Now they only had one source of light, and when that was gone, so was any hope of them finding a way out of there. The two of them waited a few more minutes before picking their way toward the large pile of rubble.

"Hunter! Can you hear me?" Jax shouted.

There was no answer. Jax thought he remembered where the car had been, but when he began digging, something inside of him told him to move a little over to the left. At first Jax ignored the thought, but then it came again, even stronger. This time, recognizing that maybe it wasn't just his own notion but a prompting—something he wasn't too used to getting—he immediately scooted over. Mike moved in alongside him. For the first twenty minutes, neither of them spoke. As the building continued to creak, Mike stopped and glanced up at the ceiling before picking up a chunk of cement and dropping it off to the side.

"So how do you two know each other?" Mike asked, clearly hoping to occupy his mind to keep the paralyzing fear at bay.

"We're roommates at BYU," Jax said, never taking his eyes from the debris as he continued to dig.

"Are you Mormon?"

Jax nodded as he dropped a heavy piece of cement behind him. "Yeah, only Hunter is a little more Mormon than me."

"What do you mean?" Mike asked, stopping as he began to cough.

Jax waited until Mike had caught his breath. "Hunter is about to leave on a mission for our church. He's been dreaming about it since he was twelve."

Mike lifted a brow, obviously surprised by this statement, though he didn't say anything. Instead the two continued to dig in silence for the next ten minutes, each helping the other with slabs of concrete that were too big to lift by themselves. Jax could feel his shoulders throbbing, but he didn't stop. He kept picturing Hunter all cramped up in the back of his Mazda when they had been on their way to L.A. Hunter had wanted to take a turn driving across the desert, but Jax had shot him down, not wanting to squeeze his own long legs into a tight space for that long. Hunter had shrugged it off with one of his easy smiles. Now the thought of him buried under all this rubble made Jax sick, the image forcing his muscles to endure far beyond what he had ever thought possible. Jax lifted another piece of cement out of the way and then another, trying to ignore the nagging voice inside his head telling him the chance of Hunter surviving was becoming increasingly slim. He shook his head, refusing to admit to himself that Hunter might never make it out of there alive.

* * *

Hunter scooped up another handful of mud and patted it onto the walls of his dam. Then he sat on his knees to admire his work. A lake, maybe two feet deep, had begun to form behind the muddy wall. Knowing that the dam wouldn't last for long, Hunter quickly began to take off his shoes and socks. Then he stepped into the middle of his own personal man-made lake. Feeling the mud squish between his toes, he smiled and then pulled a little green army man from his pocket, placing him on the top of the dam. Though he didn't have any other plastic men with him, Hunter could imagine a whole platoon surrounding the dam, looking attentively toward him.

"Alright, men," Hunter said with all the authority an eight-year-old could muster. "This is it: our final battle."

In his mind he could hear his troops cheer. He quickly reached behind him and grabbed a handful of rocks.

"Load the cannons," he demanded.

He imagined that the little men saluted their commander and then prepared for battle, taking up their positions. Hunter waited a moment before giving the signal. Making gunfire and explosion sounds with his mouth, Hunter began obliterating the dam with the rocks, sending mud flying everywhere. A moment later he sat in the middle of the mud, the battle over, his dam in ruins. He smiled.

"Another victory!" he shouted.

"It looks that way," a gruff voice behind him spoke.

Hunter whirled around. "Grandpa!" he shouted.

Grandpa Smith smiled, though the smile didn't last for long; nor did Hunter's focus, which quickly moved to the house several yards away, where a screen door had just slammed shut. Hunter's mom shouted at the departing form while Hunter's dad walked briskly to his pickup, climbed in, revved the engine, and then pulled out of the gravel driveway, shooting up dust.

Grandpa Smith let his breath out, then looked back at Hunter, his eyes sad. Hunter just shrugged; the scene was becoming all too common. Grandpa Smith placed his hand on Hunter's shoulder.

"Why don't you get cleaned up, and I'll make us some supper. Your mom asked me to watch you tonight while she works a second shift."

"Again?" Hunter groaned. "But she's always working."

Again the sadness returned to Grandpa Smith's eyes, though he quickly brightened. "We could make my famous flapjacks together if you'd like. Then when your dad gets home we could eat them out on the patio."

Hunter stuck his hand into the muddy water, fishing around for his soldier. "He won't be home 'til late either."

Grandpa Smith placed his hand tenderly on Hunter's muddy shoulder and then stood. "You can play for a few more minutes. Then come in and get cleaned up."

Hunter sat in the muddy water as he watched his grandpa walk away. Though the sun was still beating down, he suddenly felt chilled. He shivered, wondering why his body was so cold.

"Grandpa, wait!" Hunter shouted. "I'm coming with you."

Hunter tried to stand, but his body wouldn't move. "Grandpa, don't go!" Hunter shouted as he watched his grandpa slowly begin to fade from sight.

It was then that Hunter woke up, his heart beating wildly. For a second he simply lay there, hearing nothing but his own rapid breathing in the darkness. He tried to move, but his body wouldn't budge. Then, in a rush that nearly took his breath away, he felt the pain. It was all around him, the intensity almost overpowering. He tried to scream, but his lungs wouldn't allow it. Something was pushing down on him, making it hard to breathe. It was then, with a surge of terror, that he remembered what had happened. For a moment he wondered if he was dead, but the pain that ravaged through him assured him he wasn't. Where was Jax? And Payson? Had Payson been with them when the earthquake hit? Hunter couldn't remember. The images in his mind were so jumbled. He could feel the panic rising in his chest. He had to get out of there, but he couldn't move.

"Help!" Hunter gasped in desperation, the pain so intense he was having a hard time thinking straight. "Please!" he begged.

The words had no sooner crossed his lips, when he felt the pain beginning to ease and his coherency slipping, pulling him back into his mind. At first, snatches of memory played before his eyes, small glimpses of the moments that made up the whole of his life. Then, finally, he found his mind slowing, as if his subconscious had selected a particular moment and was pulling him into it. He knew the memory well, had replayed it many times before, though he had tried not to. Now he found himself experiencing it as if it were happening all over again.

Hunter lay in his bed with the covers kicked off on the floor and his window open wide. Though a slight breeze ruffled the curtains, the room was stifling. He climbed from his bed and headed down the hall toward the kitchen to get a glass of water. As he passed his parents' room he heard voices.

"Look, we both know this isn't going to work. I think it's time I moved out."

Hunter could feel his chest constrict as he pushed his ear up against the door.

"When should we tell Hunter?"

Hunter's father was silent for a moment. "We'll tell him tomorrow night when I get off work."

"He's only twelve . . . still just a boy," Hunter's mother began, her voice cracking. "He's going to be devastated."

"I don't see another any other option."

"You could quit drinking," Hunter's mom offered, her tone suddenly sharp.

"Oh, so this is all my fault?" his father snapped. "Maybe if you would come home once in a while, I would."

"Someone's got to pay the bills!"

"Don't give me that. We did fine when we were first married. It was you who wanted a bigger house and a new car. We were happy when it was simple."

"Well, it's not simple anymore, is it?" she said, her tone suddenly tempered.

Hunter's dad was silent for a moment. Then he started toward the door. "We'll tell him tomorrow."

Hunter hurried down the hall to his room, then quickly closed his door and threw himself on his bed, tears already stinging his eyes. How could they do this to me? *He felt the anger, the loss, the fear. They were no longer going to be a family. Just like that, it was over, and there was nothing he could do. He rolled over on his bed and looked out the window at the stars. He felt helpless and alone. Suddenly his thoughts turned to his grandpa. Once, when he and Grandpa had been fishing, his grandpa had told him about getting lost in the jungles of Vietnam. His platoon had scattered when the fighting had started, and he had gotten separated from them. He had lain low in the thick vegetation, fearing that he might be spotted by the enemy. Seconds had turned into minutes, then minutes into hours. Finally, when the heat had become too intense and his thirst overpowering, he'd begun to look for help. After searching the area for several minutes, he had finally come to the realization that he was all alone. Fearing that the enemy might still be lurking somewhere, he had cautiously begun walking in the direction he thought his platoon would go. After several hours, exhausted, he had slumped down to catch his breath. Nightfall was coming on quickly, and the jungle was coming alive. Somewhere off to his right he heard a snake slither across the grass, and farther into the trees he heard a large animal prowling, probably in search of food. Fear prickled up his back. He needed to find his platoon; it was his only chance. Knowing that he was lost and that he couldn't do it on his own, he had done the only thing he could. He had prayed. Getting carefully to his knees, not wanting to make any sound, he had begun to pray. No sooner had he ended the prayer when he heard a small branch snap. He quickly lifted his head and saw a man staring down at him.*

"Smith, you lost?" the man teased.

Twenty minutes later, Grandpa Smith was on a chopper headed back to camp.

With his grandpa's story still fresh in his head, Hunter slowly crawled out of bed and dropped to his knees. His family needed help, but there was nothing he could do—nothing but pray. Hunter was praying out loud when he was suddenly thrust back into the present, pain instantly monopolizing his every thought.

"It hurts," he cried out, a part of him wishing that he could just die so he wouldn't have to endure it any longer. "Help me," he breathed, though he figured it was useless. He could barely hear his own words. How could anyone else hear him? He closed his eyes and tried to force his mind from the agony and fear. After several seconds he again felt the fog begin to consume him, the intense pain too much for him to bear. Within seconds he was once again pulled back into the recesses of his mind.

"Hunter! Hunter Campbell! Are you paying attention?"

Hunter pulled his eyes from the scene outside the window to face his teacher, her brow creased.

"I'm sorry," he stammered, already feeling his face blush as all the other children in the class stared at him.

The teacher shook her head before turning back to the blackboard. Hunter watched her work the math problem for a moment before glancing back out the window, his thoughts already drifting. Two nights ago his mom and dad had sat him down after dinner and told him they were getting a divorce. He had already known it was coming, but the words were still a blow. Somehow, he had hoped that his prayer would make a difference, but it hadn't. Tonight his dad was coming over after dinner to get the last of his things, and then Hunter would only see him every other weekend. Hunter didn't understand. How could this happen? *He had tried to be a good boy, but none of that had mattered. Suddenly Hunter was angry. Without even realizing that he had decided to do so, Hunter picked up his math book and threw it toward the window, shattering it. His teacher, as well as the rest of the class, jerked around and stared wide-eyed at Hunter. At first his teacher looked angry, but then almost instantly her face softened.*

"Hunter, come with me," she said as she started toward the hall.

With every eye in the classroom on him, Hunter got up and followed. Some of the boys in the back snickered, but most everyone else was shocked into silence.

"Hunter," his teacher began as soon as the door had been closed behind them, "your mom called me yesterday and told me about her and your father."

The anger that had slowly begun to dissipate instantly ignited. "So?" he snapped. "I don't care if they get a divorce; I hate them both!" he shouted.

His teacher placed her hand on his shoulder, but her sympathy was too much for him. He ran down the hall and out the front doors of the school as she called him back. Ten minutes later, he found himself pounding on his grandpa's door. Grandpa Smith opened the door with a start, surprised to see him standing there. Hunter began to cry, though he fought to stop the tears. Grandpa Smith immediately wrapped his arms around him.

"It's okay. You can cry," he soothed.

"I'm not crying," Hunter said stubbornly.

His grandpa nodded. "I know, boy. I know."

* * *

Jax and Mike continued to dig, though their bodies were nearing the breaking point. At first they had communicated very little, saving their energy for the digging, but as the time wore on, the eerie silence became more than either one of them could take.

"What about you?" Jax asked, hoping for distraction. "How long have you worked here as a security guard?"

Mike huffed as he strained to lift another large chunk of cement. Jax quickly reached over and helped him.

"Only about six months, but I put in almost forty hours a week. Plus I'm taking classes at UCLA."

"Not much room for a social life," Jax offered.

"If I make it through school, I'll be the first in my family to get a college education."

Jax didn't comment; he had never had to work a day in his life. Sure, he worked out to keep in shape for football, but even that came naturally to him.

Just when Jax was beginning to doubt the feeling that he'd had to dig in that spot, he found the broken piece of rebar they had been using to pry up the bigger pieces of cement before the second aftershock.

"We're getting close," Jax said, sweat making clean rivers down the sides of his dirty face.

Mike didn't comment, only nodded as he grimaced and stiffly reached for another block, apparently experiencing the same numbing sensation Jax's own muscles were beginning to feel. Mike then glanced ominously up at the ceiling, as if wondering how much longer the beams overhead would hold out.

"I hope you're right," he finally said.

"Just keep digging!" Jax urged.

Within a couple minutes, Jax spotted a small portion of the car's roof. He felt a fresh wave of adrenaline.

"Hunter! Can you hear me?" he shouted, reaching his hand out and pounding on the exposed metal.

For a moment there was no sound, but then Jax heard a moan. He felt his heart leap. "Hunter! It's Jax. Hold on, buddy. I'm gonna get you out!"

Jax had not cried for as long as he could remember, but now he could feel tears mixing with his sweat. He glanced over at Mike, whose face was also filled with emotion.

"We've got to get him out."

Mike nodded, then the two began to dig again, their strength temporarily renewed. It took several minutes to clear off enough rock for Jax to finally catch a glimpse of Hunter. When he did, he felt his stomach tighten in a wave of nausea. A large slab of rock, several times bigger than the ones they had been removing, had fallen through the windshield of the car during the last quake and was pressing down on Hunter, blocking his way out. Jax glanced at Mike but didn't like the look on his face, so he quickly looked back at Hunter.

"You okay, man?" Jax asked, reaching his hand out and touching the top of Hunter's head. It was the only part of him left exposed.

Hunter opened his eyes. For a minute, he looked as though he couldn't quite place Jax, but slowly recognition lit his expression. "Jax," he mumbled, the word barely more than a whisper.

"Yeah, Hunter, it's me. I'm going to help you. I'm going to get you out of there."

Mike reached out and grabbed Jax's arm firmly, but Jax refused to look at him, unwilling to give Mike the chance to tell him it was hopeless. Instead, he jerked his arm away as more tears mixed with his sweat. The building above them rumbled again, showering down small rock-sized debris, which pelted their skin. Jax lifted his hand to shield his head, but as soon as the building had settled, he turned his attention back to Hunter, who appeared more coherent.

"Go," Hunter whispered, choking with the effort. "Leave me."

"No," Jax said firmly, sticking his hands down through the windshield to get a good grip on the cement. "I'm not going anywhere."

Hunter's face contorted as a wave of pain surged through his body.

"You've got to hold on, Hunter," Jax demanded, though his own voice was cracking. "You've got to fight!"

Hunter shook his head. "I can't," he whispered. "It hurts too bad."

Jax was desperate. He had to do something to keep Hunter's mind off the pain. His eyes widened as a thought struck him. "Okay, I've got a joke. So there are these two Mormons and a goose, and they're in this basement full of stolen food . . ." Jax stopped, suddenly realizing that he didn't know the punch line. He could feel the tears sliding freely down his cheeks as he watched Hunter's eyes roll back into his head. "No!" Jax shouted, his heart slamming hard against the walls of his chest. "Hunter! You can't die!" Jax was sobbing now, his shoulders convulsing in giant shudders. "You've got to live."

After several seconds, Hunter slowly opened his eyes and took another breath. Jax let his own breath go, a surge of hope rushing through him. "I'll get you out," he whispered fervently as he wiped at his wet face. "I promise."

"Jax," Mike began, taking him again by the arm. "We can't get him out. There's no way we can—"

"Yes we can!" Jax shouted, anger replacing the fear. Then, almost as quickly as the fury had appeared, it was gone. "Hunter loves God. God will help him. God can do this!"

Mike opened his mouth to say something but then closed it and reluctantly reached his own arm through the opening and grabbed hold of the rock. They both took a deep breath and then, using every muscle in their bodies, attempted to lift. Jax could feel sweat pouring down the middle of his back and off his forehead, stinging his eyes. He closed his eyes tight, focusing all his energy into lifting, silently begging God over and over to save Hunter. He was just a kid, a wide-eyed optimist that saw in others more than they would ever see in themselves. At one point as Jax felt his muscles begin to give out, he even pleaded that God would take him instead. But after thirty minutes of attempting to lift the slab from every angle possible, exerting all the energy they had, Jax pulled back from the car and dropped to his knees. God was not going to make the bargain. Jax was alive, and Hunter was struggling just to breathe. Jax wanted to scream, to dare the building to just fall on them now. But all he could do was cry.

* * *

James and Lawrence spent most of the six-hour flight in silence, each trapped in his own tortured thoughts. James was relieved when he felt the jet finally begin its descent. At least now he could do something besides just sit and think. He glanced out at the landscape below, praying that it wasn't as rippled as the land in and around Los Angeles. About an hour ago, CNN footage from another helicopter had shown the San Andreas Fault. During the quake, it had split wide open. James had gaped at the sight, feeling suddenly very insignificant and small.

"I can't get a chopper to fly us in. The government has stepped in and is commandeering everything," Lawrence snapped, clicking off his satellite phone and then tossing it on the seat next to him. "I guess four-wheelers are the best we're going to be able to do."

James didn't comment; there was nothing to say. Instead, he looked back out the window. Orange fields verging on ripeness stretched for miles.

"We might be in for a bumpy landing," the pilot's voice sounded over the intercom.

James tightened his seat belt as he looked out anxiously at the field they were quickly approaching. The pilot's initial assessment back in New York hit the mark. The landing strip was a tiny strip of dirt in the center of an orange crop, probably used by local crop dusters. Though the strip of land was narrow and promised a rough landing, there was cause for greater concern. James sat up with a start, his heart shifting into overdrive: A row of power lines ran the length of the field at the end of the runway.

"We're never going to make it," James breathed.

"We'll make it," Lawrence said, though he quickly tightened his own seat belt.

Seconds later, the wheels touched down, the force pushing James forward in his seat. He clutched his armrest as the jet bounded across the dirt, its hydraulic system screeching as the pilot fought to bring the small jet to a stop. James's eyes opened wide as the power lines raced toward them at a speed that didn't seem to be decreasing.

"We're going to crash!" James shouted.

He braced himself for impact. At the last possible second, the jet finally began to slow. But it wasn't going to be enough. They were still rapidly approaching the power lines. Tilting the plane so sharply that James feared it was going to roll, the pilot veered off into an open section of the field, finally bringing the jet to a bumpy and abrupt stop a hundred feet from the power lines, which now ran parallel to them. When he had pried his white knuckles from the armrest, James stood and faced Lawrence.

"I hope that pilot of yours just earned a nice bonus."

"More than you'll make in a year," Lawrence said, heading to the back of the craft to retrieve his supplies.

James shook his head, grabbed his duffel bag, and walked to the exit, relieved to still be in one piece.

"Man, I thought you were all goners."

James looked across the field at his childhood friend Kevin, who was dressed in fatigues and perched, wide-eyed, on a four-wheeler. There was another four-wheeler next to him, as well as a truck and trailer.

"You're not the only one," James said with a shake of his head as he descended the stairs before making his way over to Kevin. Once he reached him, they embraced, James slapping the man several times on the back.

"Thanks for coming, man," James said as he pulled back.

"Anything for McKenna," Kevin said, placing a hand firmly on James's shoulder.

"You know my daughter?" came a voice from behind them.

Both men turned to face Lawrence Bradford as he made his way over to them.

"Know her? I pledged my undying love to her. Of course, that was in the third grade," Kevin admitted with a smile aimed at James.

"I knew sending her to public school was a mistake," Lawrence said, dropping his bag on the ground with a thud.

Kevin eyed the man before him but instead of commenting, he turned to James. "I wish I could go with you, but they've called my guard unit up. If I don't show—"

James held up his hand. "You don't have to explain. The whole West Coast is a mess."

"I think I've got everything you're going to need," Kevin began, turning to a trailer hitched behind one of the four-wheelers. "There are several gallons of gas, food and water, and a few other odds and ends that might come in handy."

"I don't know what to say," James admitted, both relieved and overwhelmed with gratitude.

"Just do what you can to bring her home," Kevin said, his expression instantly serious. Then he turned to Lawrence and threw him a set of keys. "You're probably going to get that expensive designer suit dirty." With that, he wished James good luck, told him to give McKenna a big hug for him, then got in his truck and took off down the road, shooting clumps of dirt up behind him.

Lawrence glanced at his pilot, who had since joined them on the ground. "Find the nearest hangar to fuel up, then fly back and wait for us here."

"Yes, sir. And good luck," the pilot said with a nod as he turned and headed back to the jet.

Lawrence then looked James directly in the eyes, getting right to the point. "If you help me get McKenna out of L.A. alive, I'll cut you a check for a hundred thousand dollars."

"*What!*" James exploded, completely taken aback. "You think I'm doing this for money? McKenna doesn't have a price tag—not to me anyway. I'm going after your daughter because I care about her."

Lawrence lifted a skeptical brow. "I know you're flat broke. And don't tell me that money has never been an underlying motive in this fixation you have with my daughter."

"You don't know the first thing about me, Mr. Bradford," James said tightly, the muscles along his jaw rippling, "*or* your daughter."

With that said, James secured his helmet and turned his four-wheeler toward the setting sun, intent on one thing and one thing only: finding McKenna.

CHAPTER TWELVE

7:00 P.M. / Los Angeles; Thirty-sixth floor, Lincoln Tower

McKenna attempted to get to her feet, fighting the urge to cry out from the pain shooting through her knee. Though she and Nathan had stayed in the law office for several hours to hide from Sutherland and wait for help, they both knew it was time to get out.

"Give me your hand," Nathan said, offering his.

McKenna hesitated for just a second, trying to read the motive in his eyes, but as the pain in her knee intensified she slowly reached her hand out and allowed him to pull her up. Then she glanced around the room. The last quake had caused some of the ceiling to cave in.

"We need to get out of here," Nathan said, his own eyes scanning the destruction.

McKenna nodded, knowing that if they didn't get out soon, they might be trapped inside the building permanently. At the same time, she was terrified. "Do you think he's gone?" she asked anxiously.

Nathan was silent for a moment. "I don't know," he finally admitted. "But we're going to have to try anyway."

McKenna nodded, knowing that Nathan was right. The building was more unstable than ever, especially after the intensity of the last aftershock. She quickly placed the paddle under her arm for support before starting toward the door. Nathan took a quick peek into the hall before signaling McKenna to follow. Less than a minute later, the two were standing at the door to the stairs.

"I'll check if I can see anything," Nathan said as he took hold of the door handle.

McKenna felt light-headed; she wasn't sure which she was more afraid of: the threat of another aftershock or Alan Sutherland. Either way, there was a big chance she would never make it out of the building alive. McKenna leaned against the wall, her thoughts suddenly on James, regretting how she had handled things. Over the last few hours, different moments in her life had played over in her mind, little fragments, some so simple she couldn't believe she remembered them. But the one thing that stood out to her was that James was a part of everything. In middle school, she hadn't confided in a best girlfriend. It was James she had gone to, telling him her dreams, ambitions, and hopes. The day she had graduated from law school, it was his face she had sought out in the crowd, hoping to see his smile, reveling in the approval and acceptance he gave so freely. Then later, it was his shoulder she had cried on when she was frustrated about work, or her father, or life in general. He was always there, telling her that she was brilliant, encouraging her to go after her dreams and yet, at the same time, allowing her to be who she was. Then another image flashed through her mind: standing in her living room as James kissed her. She could almost feel his arms around her, the intensity of his emotion as he kissed her, and the feelings that had flooded through her when she had accepted and even welcomed the kiss. Then she had stood there and denied it all, insisting that all she felt for him was friendship. She shook her head, finally knowing the truth.

McKenna was pulled from her thoughts as Nathan swung open the door. "There's no sign of him."

McKenna felt a small surge of hope.

"Come on," Nathan began, holding the door open for her. "Let's get out of here before there's another aftershock."

McKenna hobbled past him, anxious to be on their way. Once she was in the stairwell, she was relieved to see that there were still a few people streaming down from the upper floors, trying to exit the building. If Sutherland was still inside, he would be less apt to make a scene with witnesses around. McKenna glanced at Nathan, who stayed beside her as they made their way down the stairs. Once again doubt welled up within her. Nathan could have made up the whole thing about Sutherland to cover himself. The fact that Sutherland had a gun didn't make him a killer. True, he had fired at Nathan, but only because Nathan—who had confessed to killing Mrs. Dillon—had pursued them, even throwing a heavy brass paperweight at him. Maybe Sutherland didn't want to kill them both to hide his own crimes; maybe Nathan had already killed Sutherland, back when McKenna had been hiding in the restroom. Had he invented this story to clear his own name? The plausibility of that scenario sent a chill up McKenna's spine. Nathan's father was a judge with influential connections. All he'd have to do was hire a lawyer to twist and manipulate the truth, and Nathan would get off scot-free. McKenna felt a flash of indignation rush through her, knowing that her father had sent her to do just that.

"Why don't you go on ahead a little, just to make sure he isn't waiting for us at the bottom," McKenna suggested, forcing her voice to sound steady and sure, though she felt anything but.

Nathan hesitated, but McKenna persisted. "I'll be right behind you."

Nathan slowed his step before relenting with a nod. "Are you sure you can make it down by yourself?"

"If she needs some help, I can help her."

McKenna turned and smiled gratefully at a woman close to her own age who was only a few steps behind them. "See," McKenna began, her eyes back on Nathan. "You go. I'll be fine."

Nathan finally surrendered and started down the stairs, making much quicker time by himself than they had made together. McKenna turned back to the woman who had quickened her step to make it to McKenna's side. "Thank you."

"No problem. Did you both get separated from someone?" the woman asked.

"Yes," McKenna said, offering nothing else as she watched Nathan slip around the corner of the stairwell.

"I can't believe all this," the woman said.

McKenna didn't comment, trying instead to think out her next move.

"What floor were you on when the first earthquake hit?" the woman asked as the two of them continued down the stairs.

When McKenna didn't answer, the woman reached over and touched her arm. "Honey, are you okay?"

"Huh?" McKenna turned her eyes to the woman. "I'm just a little shaken up," she said, seeing the concern in the woman's expression.

"I know what you mean. I was up at the top when it happened. The stairs had collapsed on the thirty-seventh and thirty-eighth floors, so we had to tie tablecloths from the restaurant together to climb down."

"Is everyone down now?" McKenna asked, relieved that the people at the top of the building had found a way out.

"No, not yet. It's going to take a long time. I was the last woman out, but all the men still have to make it down. Well, except for the ones who didn't want to wait and ended up climbing down the stairs—they went through the elevator shaft until they made it past the damage."

McKenna glanced over her shoulder as two men quickly approached. McKenna recognized them both. One of them was the man that had fallen out the window and who'd been dragged back in by the big man who had then been pinned under the pillar. The other man had also been helping with the rescue. McKenna crinkled her forehead, wondering why they didn't have the big man with them. Surely they wouldn't have left him after all they had done to save him.

"What happened to the man you pulled from under the pillar? Is he all right?" McKenna asked, causing both men to slow their pace.

The man who had fallen through the window shook his head. "What do you mean? We weren't able to lift the pillar," he began, the remorse still fresh on his face. "He bled to death."

His words hit McKenna like a sharp slap. She shook her head, her mind snapping back to the moment in the restaurant when Sutherland had told her that he and the other men had pulled the bigger man from beneath the pillar. Sutherland had lied. McKenna felt sick as this new information sunk in. She now felt more sure than ever that he had also lied about Mrs. Dillon's murder. Nathan had tried to warn her, but she had refused to listen. McKenna felt her heart begin to pound against the walls of her chest, the vibration seeming to turn her legs to liquid.

"It was so horrible," the woman next to McKenna said, though McKenna didn't even acknowledge her. Instead, she slowly turned to look over her shoulder, an icy chill spreading through her, forewarning her of what she would see. There, just a few steps away, his eyes trained on her, was Sutherland.

McKenna's first instinct was to burst through the door to the next floor and hide, but Sutherland was already pushing past the men, his eyes flashing a warning.

"McKenna!" he called out, causing everyone in the stairwell to glance back at him. By now he was right behind her. "I was so worried that you hadn't made it out."

"Well, I guess you're in good hands now," the woman said, stepping out of the way so Sutherland could take McKenna's arm. McKenna wanted to call her back, but Sutherland was already patting the gun bulging slightly beneath his suit before taking her firmly by the arm. "You better slow down with that knee or you'll never make it out of here," Sutherland said, emphasizing the last few words.

McKenna watched helplessly as the woman and the two men rounded the stairwell, heading down to the next level.

"In here!" Sutherland demanded, opening the door to the thirty-fourth floor.

McKenna hobbled through the door, her eyes quickly looking around for an escape, but there didn't seem to be one.

"Surprised?" Sutherland asked, a cocky grin spreading across his face as he shut the door behind him. "I think I was pretty convincing, don't you?"

McKenna felt the same loathing she had felt that day in court when Manning had toyed with her, letting her know that he had killed Mrs. Dillon and showing absolutely no remorse.

"My father knows I'm here," McKenna said, her eyes defiant.

Sutherland's face lit into a wicked grin. "Yes, and he's as expendable as Mrs. Dillon."

The earthquake and almost every moment since had been terrifying, but this declaration took McKenna to a new level of fear.

"Leave my father alone," she said, the terror that was coursing through her causing her voice to quiver.

"Maybe . . . if I get what I want."

McKenna could see in his eyes that her fear was fueling his power, so she held his gaze, though the very sight of him made her skin crawl. "And what is it you want?" she asked tightly.

Sutherland glanced at the closed door before turning back to McKenna. "In a few minutes, Nathan is going to run into that woman in the stairwell who was supposed to be helping you. He's going to ask what happened. Then, because the man will never be able to live with himself if he doesn't, he'll come back for you."

McKenna stared at Sutherland, not sure if she believed that Nathan would do that for her.

Sutherland, reading her expression, laughed derisively. "Oh, he'll be back. That's what's wrong with him—the man has a conscience."

"You obviously don't!" McKenna snapped, thinking about Mrs. Dillon.

"I'd say we're two peas in a pod. I hired a killer to do my dirty work, and you defended the same man, wiping the blood off his hands with a bunch of legal jargon and heated rhetoric painted all red, white, and blue. Not bad for a day's work."

"You're disgusting!" McKenna muttered, feeling the heat in her cheeks intensify.

Sutherland's jaw tightened, but he only jeered at her, revealing teeth that were too straight and white. "Be careful, counselor; we're not in a courtroom. I'm the judge and jury, and if you don't play this right, you're looking at a death sentence."

McKenna tried not to show her fear, but Sutherland must have seen it. His smile widened. "Good. Now, how about we go have a little chat with Mr. Rinehart?"

Sutherland grabbed McKenna hard by the arm as he escorted her out into the hall. Three men were heading down the stairs, but they paid little attention to the two of them, probably figuring that Sutherland was helping McKenna down to the ground floor. The two of them stood there silently as they waited for Nathan to make his way back. McKenna was still doubting that Nathan would return when she saw him come around the corner, his face draining of color.

"Nathan. I'm glad you made it back," Sutherland cooed, reaching his hand into his suit coat pocket and resting it on his gun, then gesturing with his head for Nathan to lead the way through the door next to them.

Nathan nodded, shooting an apologetic glance at McKenna before opening the door. Once the door was closed behind them, Sutherland withdrew the gun, his face deadly serious.

"Where is it?"

"What are you talking about?" Nathan asked, swallowing hard.

"Don't give me that. My office computer shows that company files were copied two days before I had Mrs. Dillon killed."

"I don't know what you're talking about," Nathan said, shaking his head.

"Oh, but I think you do," Sutherland said, maintaining his composure, though his eyes revealed that his patience was running dangerously thin.

Nathan glanced quickly at McKenna as he considered his options, then turned back to Sutherland, apparently seeing no other alternative. "It's safely tucked away."

Sutherland smirked, though his face was quickly turning a deep scarlet. "You went and got yourself a little insurance, did you? Smart." As he turned to McKenna, the smirk vanished. "Too bad the lady doesn't have any." Then he raised his gun, pointing it directly at her.

McKenna could feel the blood rushing from her head.

"Don't shoot!" Nathan shouted.

Sutherland aimed the gun at the ceiling, then tilted his head expectantly.

"It's in my office safe," Nathan offered begrudgingly.

"Well, then, let's go," Sutherland said, motioning them both toward the door with his gun.

"Sutherland, this building's coming down. That disk and everything on it is going to be destroyed," Nathan said, his expression suddenly desperate.

"It's a nice thought," Sutherland began, still motioning them toward the door. "But I can't take that chance."

McKenna glared at the man. A "nice" thought that the building would come down, killing all the innocent people still trapped inside? The very notion was infuriating. The man cared for nothing but himself. That realization only gave more credence to McKenna's next thought—there was no way Sutherland was going to let either one of them live once he had that disk. Their lives were debris on a path he had every intention of bulldozing.

"You know what I hate most about my job?" McKenna asked, glaring at Sutherland.

"What's that?" Sutherland asked, almost amused.

"Looking into the faces of people who will do anything for money."

Sutherland laughed, though the effort sounded more like a snarl. "No, counselor," he began, his tone condescending. "This isn't just about money. It's about power. Power is a tonic infinitely more intoxicating than wealth. With money I could buy respect; with power, I'll command it!"

"Where you're going, you'll have neither respect nor power, just an endless, nightmarish infinity."

"How poetic," Sutherland sneered, grabbing her hard and pushing her toward the door.

McKenna's leg was on fire by the time they reached Nathan's office on the thirty-sixth floor, but the condition of every office in West Link—especially Nathan's—temporarily monopolized her attention. Desk drawers and file cabinets had been yanked open, the contents scattered all over the floor, while paintings had been ripped from the walls and furniture sliced open, exposing the stuffing. McKenna quickly glanced up from Sutherland's handiwork as he began to speak.

"Enter the combination," he barked, "but don't open the safe. Just step back when you're done."

Nathan nodded as he began to slowly press the numbers on the pad next to the safe. McKenna watched Sutherland. At first he kept swinging his attention from Nathan to her, making sure that neither tried anything, but as Nathan neared the last numbers, Sutherland began to focus, his need to secure the disk clearly dominating his other concerns. And that was exactly what McKenna had been counting on.

Though Sutherland had taken her crutch from her, tossing it across the floor so she couldn't use it as a weapon, she slowly eased her hand toward a small marble replica of the *Venus de Milo* on Nathan's desk while still watching him from the corner of her eye. Sutherland was licking his lips nervously, his eyes trained on the safe. McKenna lifted the sculpture once she reached it, and then, praying that Sutherland wouldn't pull the trigger and kill Nathan when the statue hit him, she threw it. Sutherland glanced toward her at almost that exact moment, his eyes widening in alarm. But he didn't have time to react. The statue hit him in the side. McKenna heard the gun fire, the sound making every muscle in her body tighten, but instead of the bullet hitting Nathan, it lodged in the safe next to him. Nathan whirled around before slamming his body hard into Sutherland, who stumbled backward, then fell to the floor, his gun skidding across the tile. As the men struggled, McKenna's eyes followed the gun as it hit a bookshelf across the room. She hobbled over to it, ignoring the jarring pain in her knee, then bent and picked it up.

"Get up!" she demanded, her tone authoritative, though she was shaking uncontrollably. She reached her other hand up to help steady the gun, but it still continued to shake.

Nathan grabbed Sutherland, who was bleeding from his nose after a few well-placed punches Nathan had managed to throw while McKenna was retrieving the gun, then dragged him to his feet. Nathan tossed the man toward a chair and then started toward McKenna, reaching his hand out to take the gun.

"Good job," he said, taking her by the arm so that she wouldn't fall.

"I thought we were both dead," she said, the adrenaline that had been coursing through her body now turning her limbs to jelly.

Nathan nodded his head as he turned his eyes back to Sutherland. "We almost were." Then he started toward the safe, keeping the barrel of the gun trained on Sutherland. A few seconds later, he returned to McKenna's side with the disk in his hand. He held it up for Sutherland to see. "This is going to put you away for life."

Nathan reached over and picked up McKenna's crutch, handed it to her, then told Sutherland to get up. Sutherland glared at Nathan, but, after wiping at the blood on his face with his sleeve, he stood. McKenna felt an uneasy shiver crawl up her spine as something in Sutherland's calculating gaze assured her that this was far from over.

CHAPTER THIRTEEN

8:05 P.M. / Downtown Los Angeles

James was overwhelmed by the immensity of the destruction all around him. People were walking aimlessly down the center of the street he and Lawrence Bradford were now traveling, trying to stay clear of the debris that periodically fell from the buildings on either side of the road. The destruction had spanned almost the entire distance from where the Bradford jet had touched down to where they were now, in downtown Los Angeles. Huge cracks in the ground zigzagged across the land, tearing up roadways and making travel, even on four-wheelers, extremely difficult.

The fires James and Lawrence had seen on TV had also spread, saturating the air with smoke and ash. James could feel a tightness in his chest, not only from the smoke, but from the increasing anxiety that seemed to heighten the closer they got to Lincoln Tower. James had not once allowed himself to believe that McKenna was dead, but now, seeing the destruction before him and being in the center of it all, his hope began to waver. The despair he felt was almost unbearable. How could he go on without McKenna?

James was pulled from his thoughts as they neared an intersection. A soldier ran toward the stream of light provided by the four-wheeler's headlights and began waving for the vehicles to stop. James saw the problem right away. A woman was pinned under a streetlight that had been struck by a car. James immediately pulled his four-wheeler up next to the guardsman.

"Do you have any rope?" the soldier asked, his uniform already stained and ripped in several places.

James hopped off the four-wheeler and ran around to the small trailer in back, withdrew the rope, and began tying it to the back of his four-wheeler. When he was done, he handed it to the soldier, who immediately tied it around the pole. James looked down at the woman trapped beneath. Though she was conscious and looked terrified, she didn't appear to be in any pain. James bent down next to her.

"We're going to move the pole," he said, trying to sound confident.

"I can't feel my legs," she cried, reaching her hand out and clinging desperately to his sleeve.

James felt a hard lump forming in his throat as he looked at the pole across her abdomen, knowing that she likely had a spinal cord injury. "Just hold on. We'll get you to a hospital."

She nodded, and James was relieved that at least she was able to move her upper body, even if she couldn't feel her lower.

Within a few minutes, James, the soldier, and even Lawrence—who had been reluctant to get off of his own four-wheeler for fear that someone would steal it—had helped move the pole off the woman. Seeing the extent of her injuries and knowing she would probably die if she didn't get medical help soon, James grabbed his backpack from the trailer, draped it over his shoulders, and emptied the other supplies onto the ground. He then quickly helped the soldier lift her into the almost empty trailer. After squeezing the woman's hand and assuring her that she would be all right, James extended the key for the four-wheeler to the soldier.

The soldier shook his head. "You'll have to take her," he said firmly. "I've got to stay here and help as many people as I can."

"I can't!" James exclaimed, feeling a wave of panic as he continued to hold the key out to the man.

"If you don't take her, she'll die," the soldier said bluntly.

"We can't," Lawrence interrupted, his words forceful. "We came here to find my daughter, not to help a total stranger."

Someone from across the street was already screaming for help.

"Do what you have to," the soldier said, his eyes on James.

James was silent for a moment before he slowly nodded his head. "I'll take her."

"*What?*" Lawrence bellowed.

Ignoring Lawrence, the soldier quickly gave James directions to the nearest hospital, then hurried across the street.

"What do you think you're doing?" Lawrence exclaimed once the soldier was gone.

James took a long steady breath. "If McKenna were here, she would do it. She wouldn't just leave this woman to die," James said, his gaze steady.

Lawrence looked like he was ready to explode, but he didn't say a word. How could he? James was right, and they both knew it. Instead, Lawrence climbed back on his four-wheeler and turned the key. "You do what you want, but I'm going after my daughter."

James climbed onto his own four-wheeler and started the engine. "Take care of yourself, Mr. Bradford."

Lawrence shook his head in disgust and drove away. Although deep down James knew that he was doing the right thing, he couldn't help feeling that he had just betrayed his best friend, leaving her to fend for herself.

"Hold on, McKenna," he breathed, taking one last look at the road that led to Lincoln Tower.

"It hurts," the woman in the back of the trailer called out, pulling James from his thoughts.

James quickly turned around in his seat to face her. "What hurts?"

"Everything," she cried.

James exhaled slowly, knowing that if she was in pain, she wasn't paralyzed. "Hold on. I'll get you to a hospital."

She bobbed her head feebly, her body trembling. "Please, hurry."

James felt heartless passing by so many stranded and injured people, but at the same time, he knew that he needed to get this woman to the hospital so he could find McKenna. Tatum's declaration that McKenna might be trapped in Lincoln Tower with a killer had played over and over in his mind the past few hours. It was bad enough that McKenna's life was in danger from a natural disaster, but it was trumped by the fact that she was going through it all with a man who might profit from her conveniently coming up missing—or better yet, dead.

After getting lost several times and having to take multiple detours because of all the destruction, James finally made it to the hospital. A triage with temporary lighting provided by a generator had been placed in the parking lot because the hospital was already packed to capacity. Helicopters were flying some patients to other cities, but even so, the parking lot and lawn surrounding the hospital were filled. James shook his head in awe and then turned around on the four-wheeler to face the woman, whose name he had learned was Stacy.

"I'll be right back," James said as he pulled a flashlight from his duffel bag. "I'm going to see if I can get someone to help us."

The woman barely acknowledged James, clearly consumed by the pain she was experiencing. James made his way through the throng of people, watching faces as he passed, just in case McKenna had been able to get out of Lincoln Tower and had somehow made her way here.

"Excuse me," James said as he passed a nurse who was bending down next to a man writhing in pain. "I have a woman who needs help."

The nurse didn't even look up; she just pointed toward a tent that had been set up across the parking lot. "Take her there. A nurse will assess her situation and place her according to the severity of her condition."

"Thank you," James said as he hurried back toward his four-wheeler.

Stacy only moaned as James took her into his arms. "They're going to help you," he assured her.

James scanned the immense crowd as he passed, knowing that many of these people would die before they were ever seen. Still, he carried Stacy to the evaluation area. He placed her gently down on a cot that had just been vacated and walked quickly to a nurse who was bandaging a little boy's shoulder, the bandage already turning crimson.

"Please, she needs help," James said, pointing over to Stacy.

"Just a minute," the nurse said. She finished wrapping the boy's shoulder before finally turning to James, eyeing him for the first time. "Where's your injury?" she asked, her eyes already going to the other wounded around them.

"No. Not me," James corrected as he gestured toward Stacy. "I found her trapped under a streetlight downtown."

The nurse glanced toward Stacy but quickly turned back as another man stumbled toward them, his head bleeding profusely. The man opened his mouth to speak, but then his eyes rolled back into his head as he slumped to the ground. The nurse quickly felt for a pulse, then reached for her bag, retrieved a compress, and applied it to his head. James stood back and watched, the massive amount of blood making his stomach churn. Then the nurse turned to an orderly who was just a few feet from them, carrying an armful of supplies.

"Hold this compress to his head while I get a physician," she demanded. The orderly obeyed, and the nurse stood to leave, but before she did, she glanced briefly at James, her face strained with fatigue. "I'll be over to help your friend as soon as I can."

James nodded and then slowly glanced around at the mass of people clustered in and around the temporary triage, while others streamed into the hospital, all of them frightened, most of them injured, and each of them vying for attention from the few doctors on the scene. James felt numb. He had no idea how long it would be before someone could evaluate Stacy. But even as he glanced in the direction of Lincoln Tower, he knew he wouldn't leave. He couldn't, not until he knew Stacy was in good hands. And with so few emergency personnel, that wasn't likely to be soon.

* * *

Justice could feel the heat through his uniform and knew he was too close, but he still couldn't stand down. He and his men were the only thing standing between this fire and the rest of downtown L.A.

"It's too far gone!" Thomas Porterman shouted over the roar of the blaze.

Justice stood his ground and continued to train his hose on the flames, but they only seemed to climb higher.

"Captain!" Thomas yelled again, starting toward Justice. "We've lost it here. We've got to pull back or we're going to start losing men."

Justice turned for the first time, his eyes on the man next to him. Thomas was covered in ash, his face black and streaked with sweat. Justice knew that he was right, but he also knew what this would mean. To save his own men, he would have to sacrifice another section of the city, lessening the distance between the fire and Lincoln Tower. People, *innocent people*—maybe even his wife—would die. But if he didn't do it, and do it quickly, he would lose his men, and then there would be no chance of stopping the blaze.

"Okay!" Justice finally shouted, glancing around at all the eyes now trained on him. "Pull back. We'll regroup and go at it from another angle." Then he turned to Thomas. "Go find out how much longer until we get some outside help. Without reinforcements or air drops, we don't have a chance."

"You got it," Thomas said as he turned and headed over to the battalion chief, who was talking to one of the other captains on the scene.

Ten minutes later, Justice and his men had repositioned themselves, though Justice saw little improvement from the last stance. His men were tired, filthy, and beginning to lose hope. He could see it in their faces.

"Arizona and Nevada are sending in fresh guys. They should be here within the hour," Justice offered, looking at the circle of men around him.

"An hour!" Brian Lindstrom exclaimed, his face black with soot. "We need help *now*."

Justice knew it was true, but that didn't change the facts. "We should be getting some more guys from in and around California any minute. And we should start seeing a few air drops too. But until then, we've got to fight this fire like our lives depend on it, because they do."

Brian shook his head in frustration, but the other men nodded. They had a job to do, and every second they wasted meant lives. Justice began issuing assignments, sending the men in small groups in different directions. He decided to keep Brian Lindstrom and Thomas Porterman with him, as well as Archer Whitle, a young kid that Justice couldn't help but like. Archer was only twenty-two, but he had married and divorced young and had two little boys. What impressed Justice was that despite a few mistakes in his past, the kid was trying to get his head on straight, working as a firefighter to take care of his boys. Justice also knew that Archer had plans to take a few college classes in the fall.

"Alright," Justice began, eyeing the three men before him as he gestured to the building behind them. "Let's start on that apartment complex."

Thomas and Archer nodded as they started dragging their hoses in that direction, but Brian just shook his head, his eyes wide as he stared at the apartment complex that was quickly being consumed by the blaze.

"There's no way we'll be able to put this out ourselves," he shouted, gesturing at the apartment complex and the raging fires beyond.

Justice didn't like the look in Brian's eyes. The kid was clearly petrified, and Justice had seen him back away from a fire on more than one occasion. Although that was expected to a certain degree with rookies, for the past few months Justice hadn't seen any improvement. In fact, if anything, Brian's hesitancy and anxiety seemed to be increasing, and that bothered Justice. Indecision in fire fighting was as dangerous as tossing gasoline on the flames—and just as deadly.

"Help's on the way. But it takes time, and that's something we don't have a lot of," Justice said, keeping his eyes on Brian.

Brian finally nodded, but Justice could still see the trepidation on his face. In any other situation, Justice would have pulled him from the job, but today he didn't have an option. Putting out this fire was going to take every man they had, and a good-sized miracle besides.

"Stay close to me," Justice called over his shoulder to Brian as he moved ahead, rationalizing that at least if they were together, Justice could keep an eye on him.

Brian didn't reply, but for the next ten minutes he obeyed the order. In fact, Justice was beginning to think that they might be gaining some ground when Archer pointed toward the top of the complex.

"There's someone on the ledge," Archer shouted, pointing frantically up toward one of the apartments.

It took a few minutes for Justice to see the figure through the thick, dark, smoke that was now billowing out of the building, but at last he spotted someone. A man was on one of the small balconies that jutted out from the building and was waving his hands frantically.

"We've got to get him," Archer shouted, his eyes on Justice.

Justice knew that they didn't have time to position the fire truck that was two buildings away and raise the ladder. By the time they did all that, it would be too late. But another idea struck Justice, propelling him over to the truck, where he pulled a large tarp from one of the compartments. The tarp was older than Justice would have liked; it hadn't been replaced with a new one since tarps were rarely used in evacuations anymore. Usually, the risk of the victim striking and killing one of the firefighters was too great, but Justice didn't have any other alternatives. If he didn't chance using the tarp, the man would die—Justice was certain of that. With that thought clinching the decision,

Justice ran back toward the apartment complex, the tarp slung over his shoulder.

"Hold it tight," Justice shouted to his men, taking a firm hold on the material himself before lifting his eyes to the man directly above them. The man had climbed over the railing so he could get farther away from the flames and was screaming for help.

"Jump!" Justice shouted, hoping that the man who was three floors above them could hear him over the increasing volume of the blaze.

Every muscle in Justice's body tightened as he watched the man let go of the banister, his arms flailing around in circles as his body picked up speed, heading straight for them. For a second, Justice thought he was going to miss the tarp and hit one of the men. Although it was close, the man hit the edge of the tarp, the force ripping the material and causing him to hit the ground with a thud. Justice dropped to his knees, searching the man's body for any sign of life. For a second, the man didn't move, but then he began to cough, and his eyes slowly opened. Justice exhaled in a burst of relief as he glanced around at the other firefighters who were doing the same.

"Are you okay?" Justice bent and asked the man.

"There's a woman . . . and a baby," the man gasped, grabbing hold of Justice's arm as an EMT bent down next to him.

"Where?" Justice asked, snapping his head back to stare at the balcony above him, though all he could see was smoke.

"Right there!" Archer shouted, pointing to a balcony on the same floor the man had just come from, but a couple of apartments over to the left.

Justice felt his stomach churn. In the light of the fire, Justice could see a woman standing on her balcony with a tiny bundle in her arms. Justice looked down at the tarp that was now ripped almost in half. Then he glanced at his men, their expressions as horrified as his own.

"I can't just sit here and watch them burn," Archer said, his voice almost frantic.

Justice glanced back over at the fire truck, still two buildings away where another group of firemen had the ladder raised and were attempting to rescue someone stranded on the roof. Justice turned back to Archer, but before he could say anything, the young fire-fighter began throwing off his gear.

"What are you doing?" Justice shouted.

Archer pointed to a tree just to the left of them. "Give me the tarp," he demanded.

"What are you going to do?" Brian asked, voicing the question on everyone's mind.

"Just give me the tarp," Archer said, dropping his air tank to the ground with a clank.

Justice wasn't exactly sure what the man had in mind, but at this point none of them was willing to just sit there and watch a mother and her child die. Justice reached down, grabbed the tarp, and handed it to Archer, who immediately ripped the torn tarp in two, tossing one half on the ground and the other over his shoulder.

"Be careful," Justice said, standing back and watching as Archer jumped up and grabbed one of the lower branches, wrapping one leg around it to pull himself up.

Justice turned to Brian and Thomas. "Get your hoses. Let's give him some cover."

The three of them began spraying their hoses at the flames shooting out from the apartment just below where the woman stood. Justice's pulse quickened as the woman began to climb over the railing and onto the balcony, still clinging awkwardly to the baby. Justice knew why she was doing it. He could feel the heat from the fire through his heat-resistant suit, and he knew that it was probably almost unbearable for the woman. Justice glanced up at Archer, who was climbing higher in the tree, edging toward the woman who was calling out to him in a state of near hysteria.

"He's not going to make it in time," Brian said, glancing at Justice as if to gauge his reaction.

Justice didn't say anything; they were all very much aware that the woman and her child had only seconds to live.

"He'll make it," Justice said, though his words, even to him, seemed to lack conviction.

Justice glanced up as Archer shimmied out onto a branch directly in front of the woman. But even after climbing out as far as he could, the woman was still just out of reach. He quickly wrapped his legs securely around the limb and then began pulling the tarp from off his shoulder. Working frantically, he tied one end of the tarp around his own waist, then the other around the limb.

"What's he going to do?" Brian asked, craning his neck back as far as he could.

Justice kept his eyes glued to the scene. "He's going to swing out and grab her before she falls."

"But once he has her, he won't be able to pull himself back into the tree," Thomas said.

"*Hurry!*" Justice shouted to Thomas, who had already dropped his hose and was on his way over to the tree. "Help him!"

Justice jerked back as an explosion rocked the building. The flames shooting out from the apartment just below the woman climbed higher, almost reaching her feet.

The woman shrieked, and, for a second, Justice thought she was going to fall, but she continued to cling to the railing. After a minute of Justice aiming his hose at the flames, they began to abate, disappearing back into the room.

"I'm almost there," Thomas shouted to Archer.

"I can't wait!" Archer shouted back, teetering as he stood up, balancing himself on the branch as he prepared to jump toward the woman.

Fearing that he was about to watch Archer plummet to his death, Justice's gaze remained riveted as Archer leaped out toward the woman, catching her around the waist. The woman screamed but held tight to the infant in her arms as they swung back toward the tree and then, with less momentum, back toward the building. Justice continued to point his hose at the apartment below, knowing that if the flames again reached the level they had after the explosion, they would completely envelop the three people now dangling three stories above the ground. Thomas finally reached them and began pulling them up, though it was taking much longer than Justice would have liked. But after several minutes of straining his body to the limit, Thomas finally pulled the three to safety.

"Do you need help?" Justice called up.

"What we need," Thomas called down, "is Chad. These kinds of stunts are his specialty—*not mine!*"

Justice felt a lump forming in his throat as he thought of his friend. Where was Chad? Had he found Anna yet? Justice watched as Thomas began to carefully make his way down the tree with the small bundle gripped tightly in the crook of his arm. Though Justice tried not to think about it, the sight made him wonder if he would ever get to see his own child.

CHAPTER FOURTEEN

8:05 P.M. / Los Angeles; Lincoln Tower

"Manuel can't be gone," Anna cried, her eyes red and moist from crying on and off over the past four hours since Manuel had been killed. "He talked with me in the elevator, promised me we would make it out." Tears were streaming freely down her checks and falling on the baby who was in her arms. "And now he's dead, and we're trapped in here just waiting until it's our turn."

Chad walked to her side to comfort her, but as he began to bend down next to her, he let out a grunt, his hand shooting to his ribs.

"Are you all right?" Payson asked, taking him by the shoulder.

"I'm okay," Chad said too quickly.

Payson knew that Chad was in a lot more pain than he was letting on, but before he could press the issue, the lights provided by the backup generator began to flicker. Everyone looked up apprehensively, but after only a moment, the flickering stopped and, though the lights had dimmed considerably, they remained on. Sam broke the silence that had fallen over them as he quickly stepped toward the metal beam pressed up against the door to the stairs, placing his shoulder firmly against it, his face filled with panic. "We've got to move this," he said, grunting as he pushed. "We've got to get out of here!"

Chad shook his head, his eyes on the beam. "We've tried for hours now. That thing isn't moving."

Payson knew he was right, and deep down, Payson figured that Sam knew it too, but he watched as Sam continued to push until his face was red and his limbs were trembling. After several minutes, unable to move the beam even a fraction of an inch, he reluctantly stepped back, panting.

"Well, what then?" he exclaimed in frustration. "We're running out of time. Once the generator goes out, we're going to be stumbling around here in the dark."

Payson watched as Gwen stepped over to Sam and took hold of his arm, the gesture seeming to calm him considerably. Payson looked away, not wanting anyone to see the ache he was feeling. His anger over seeing Gwen and Sam together earlier had dissipated, but the longing remained. Though Payson had been telling himself repeatedly that it was over, that he had to move on with his life, the truth was that he couldn't imagine life without her. Payson forced himself to take a steady breath as he glanced at Chad, who seemed calm despite the situation.

"There is one other way," Chad said as he glanced toward the elevator shaft, his hand still protectively resting over his side.

"There's no way we'd be able to get her down that shaft!" Sam blurted out, seeming to read Chad's mind as he glanced first at the shaft, then at Kimberly, the woman they had found trapped under a wall divider. "And what about Anna and the baby?"

"Do you have a better idea?" Chad snapped in frustration. Then his face softened. "Look, I'm aware of all the obstacles before us. Trust me. But I think if we work together, we can make it down. We certainly can't wait around any longer."

Sam threw his hands up in exasperation, but then reluctantly shook his head. "It looks like we don't have a choice," he said in a low voice.

Chad nodded and then placed his hand firmly on Sam's shoulder. "We need something to carry the baby in. That paper sack is too risky. One tear and . . ." Chad didn't finish; instead he glanced over at Anna, whose eyes were still leaking tears. "I've got something," he said, reaching for the backpack he had placed on the floor, then removing the rappelling equipment that was inside. "This should work fine."

"What about Kimberly?" Sam asked in a hushed tone as he glanced over at her. She was lying on the ground with Sam's jacket still draped over her. Though the coloring in her face had returned, the large purple bruise across her forehead had continued to swell. "How are we going to get her down?"

Chad held up the rappelling equipment. "We'll lower her down. But first we'll need to brace her leg. Why don't you and Payson go scavenging through a few of the rooms to see if you can find something we can use to make a brace?"

"I'll go with you," Gwen said, stepping next to Sam and Payson.

Chad nodded, then walked over to Kimberly while Payson, Gwen, and Sam started down the hall. At first no one spoke. Though getting out of the building was paramount in everyone's mind, Payson could still sense an awkward undercurrent among the three of them.

"I think I remember seeing a couple of wooden chairs in the room we found Kimberly in. The legs would make a good brace," Payson said, anxious to distance himself from the tension in the air. "I'll head back that way."

"I'll go with you," Gwen said, causing both men to stare at her.

For a minute, Payson thought that Sam was going to object, but after flashing Gwen a questioning glance, he only nodded his head.

"I'll see if I can find some food," Sam said as he continued down the hall, heading for the first room.

As he stood in the hall next to Gwen, Payson suddenly felt as if he couldn't breathe.

"Which room was it?" Gwen asked.

Payson, temporarily at a loss for words, just turned and began leading her in the opposite direction from which they had been walking. Once they reached the room, Payson walked right to a chair that had been knocked over. He reached down and began to unscrew one of the wooden legs while Gwen took a seat in another chair. For a moment, neither of them spoke. Payson glanced up at her once when he was sure she wasn't looking and was suddenly struck by how pale she looked.

"Are you okay?" Payson asked.

Gwen, who apparently had been lost in thought, quickly raised her eyes. "What?" she asked, her pale cheeks blushing slightly.

"You look a little pale," Payson said as he removed the first leg, placing it on the floor next to him. "Are you hungry?"

Gwen started to shake her head, but then she jumped to her feet and ran to the other side of the room. Payson started after her, but she yelled over her shoulder for him to stay where he was. The sounds he heard immediately told him why she had made the request. He turned around, not wanting to embarrass her as she vomited in the corner. When she was done, Payson walked to the water cooler and got her a cup of water.

"Here," he said, placing the paper cup on a desk next to her.

Gwen didn't turn around, but Payson could hear her crying.

"Are you all right?" he asked, concerned. "Are you hurt somewhere?"

Gwen shook her head but didn't turn to face him.

Relieved by her answer, he placed his hand on her shoulder. "Gwen, we're going to get out of here."

"I just don't know," Gwen said, her whole body trembling.

"What do you mean, you don't know?"

Gwen reached for the water, rinsed her mouth out, then wiped her tears. "Nothing. I'm just scared, that's all."

Payson nodded, understanding completely. "I know. We're all scared."

Gwen turned to face him. "Thank you," she said, her eyes wet.

"For what?"

"Coming back for me and Tristin," she said, the sincerity in her gaze stealing Payson's breath.

Payson instantly wished she hadn't come with him, that she had stayed with Sam. Having her this close to him, looking into those liquid blue eyes, and feeling that same ache he had felt every day for the past few weeks was almost more than he could take.

"Sam would have gotten you out," he finally said, starting back toward the chair so he could remove the second leg.

Gwen took a deep breath but didn't comment. Payson quickly removed the leg of the chair, desperate to get out of there.

"I want you to know, Payson, that I really do want you to be happy," Gwen began, her voice tender. "You're going to find another girl, and she's going to be—"

"Don't," Payson said, fighting to remain calm. "Please . . . just don't."

Gwen opened her mouth, looking like she wanted to say something else, but then dropped her head and nodded. "I'm sorry."

Payson stood with both chair legs in his arms but didn't look at her. He couldn't. Instead, he started for the door. "We better go find Sam."

Gwen stood, but as she did, she had to grip the chair she had been sitting in to keep from falling.

Payson immediately jerked around and grabbed her arm, sending the wooden chair legs flying.

"Are you okay?"

"I guess I'm just a little light-headed," she said, her face pale and her skin clammy.

"Are you sure you're not hurt anywhere?" Payson asked, his eyes racing over her, searching for any sign of trauma.

She shook her head. "I'm okay. I just haven't eaten anything today, and now with all of this . . ." She swallowed hard, and Payson could tell that she was fighting another wave of nausea.

"Do you want me to see if I can find you something to eat?"

Gwen raised an eyebrow sharply, her face now slightly green.

"Sorry," Payson said sheepishly. "Maybe you better just sit down for a minute."

Payson took her by the elbow as he led her to a chair. He took a seat on the edge of a desk not far from her, his eyes on the shattered windows across the room that looked out onto the fires lighting the city below.

"How are *you* feeling?" Gwen asked, her eyes going to the scarf around Payson's head.

Payson still felt the effects of the loss of blood, but at the moment he had completely forgotten about the cut on his head. "My mom always said I was headstrong. I guess it's a good thing."

Gwen smiled and then looked away. For a minute or two, neither of them spoke, but once the color started returning to Gwen's face, she did the one thing Payson least expected: She laughed, her dimples deepening for the first time all day.

"What's so funny?" Payson asked, his curiosity piqued.

"I was just thinking about the first time I met you," she said with a weak smile. "Do you remember?"

Payson nodded, then turned and looked back out the window.

"Tristin and I were at a dance on campus. Hunter came up and said that his friend—you—had lost his phone number and wanted to know if he could have mine."

Payson smiled in spite of the mixed emotions the memory invoked.

"That line was so completely tenth grade, but Hunter's smile was so genuine and infectious that I liked him instantly," Gwen admitted, her face almost wistful. "Then he pointed to you and began to name off all of your *supposed* good qualities."

Payson shook his head and lowered his eyes to the floor, his mind suddenly on Hunter and Jax.

"He said you were a returned missionary with a good GPA and that you had aspirations of becoming an architect. Then he threw in the fact that all the men in your family still had their own teeth and hair well into their sixties."

Payson finally lifted his eyes to Gwen.

"What's wrong?" Gwen asked, seeing his pained expression. Then her eyes widened in horror. "Hunter came with you to L.A., didn't he?"

Payson nodded. "He and Jax both. I left Jax in the lobby and Hunter in the parking garage."

Gwen lifted her hand over her mouth to stifle a cry as her eyes flooded with new tears. Payson could feel his own eyes beginning to mist as he reached out and took her free hand.

"I'm sorry," Gwen cried. "It's all my fault."

"It's not your fault," Payson began, pricked by his own guilt for having dragged Hunter and Jax to Lincoln Tower, though he didn't regret for a second coming himself. "You didn't even know I was going to be here."

"I didn't want to hurt you, and that's all I've done."

Payson briefly thought about reminding her that she *had* started dating another guy—while seriously dating him—but the impulse quickly died. What did it matter? It was over, and despite the pain he was feeling, he had no desire to hurt her.

"Do you think you're steady enough to walk?" Payson asked, getting to his feet.

She bobbed her head, though the color had not completely returned to her face. "You need to go after Hunter and Jax," she said, her eyes suddenly intense.

"They'll be okay," Payson said, though he didn't feel as certain of that fact as he tried to seem.

After a moment, he and Gwen walked to the elevators in silence. Chad was still bent down talking to Kimberly while Sam busily sorted through a gym bag he had found in one of the rooms. He'd stuffed it with snacks from a little kitchenette in one of the offices.

"I found some snacks, a clean towel, a stinky pair of sneakers, and a couple of toothbrushes still in their packages," Sam said with a smile as he dumped the contents of the gym bag out onto the floor and retrieved a bag of peanut M&Ms, which he promptly ripped open with his teeth.

Anna, who was nursing her baby with a receiving blanket over her shoulder, declined when Sam offered her a Snickers bar. Payson picked up the towel that Sam had found, taking it and the chair legs to Chad.

"Thanks," Chad said, placing the wood next to Kimberly's mangled leg before ripping the towel into strips.

Kimberly's eyes were dilated and filled with apprehension as she watched him lift her leg so he could strap the wood to it with the strips of towel. She cried out, then reached for and grabbed Payson's hand, her face twisted in pain.

"You're going to be okay," Payson reassured her. "You'll be out of here soon."

She nodded her head, her eyes still wide.

"I'm going to need someone to go down first and be ready to help her once we lower her down," Chad said, glancing up at Payson. "I'd send Sam, but I'm going to need him to help me lower her."

It was obvious to both men why Chad had picked Sam to help him lower Kimberly—Sam outweighed Payson by at least twenty pounds—but Payson was still hesitant. Though he was willing to help in any way he could, he didn't want to leave Gwen.

"Don't worry," Chad began, shooting a quick glance at Gwen. "I'll make sure she gets down all right."

Payson tilted his head curiously, wondering how Chad, whom he had just met, could sense how he felt about Gwen.

Chad just smiled. "It's written all over your face."

Payson let out a sigh and then glanced over his shoulder as Sam left Anna's side and walked over to sit down next to Gwen, who was sitting with her back up against the wall. She looked so small next to him, almost fragile. "That's the problem," Payson mumbled.

Chad seemed confused by Payson's comment, but he let it go. "Will you do it?"

Payson nodded.

Chad placed a hand on his shoulder and then went back to work securing the brace to Kimberly's leg. Payson glanced back over at Gwen. Her short, dark hair, as fashionably disobedient as ever, seemed to intensify the paleness of her face. Payson watched as Sam slid his arm around her shoulder, his brow furrowed in concern. He whispered something to her, and she nodded, her eyes again flooding with tears. Payson felt his throat catch. He needed to get out of there, and the sooner the better.

* * *

McKenna made her way down the stairs, careful to keep a safe distance from Alan Sutherland, even though she knew Nathan had a gun aimed at his back. She had no doubt that Sutherland would kill them both to maintain his freedom if given the opportunity. But what McKenna didn't suspect was how quickly the opportunity would present itself.

McKenna, Nathan, and Sutherland had only made it down two flights of stairs, going at a painfully slow pace because of McKenna's knee, when a man came running down the stairs at full speed. McKenna could hear him approaching long before she saw him, and though she attempted to get out of the way, her efforts were in vain. The man clipped her crutch with his foot, sending it flying and causing her to lose her balance and fall. She fell down several stairs, her body tumbling end over end, before finally sprawling face-first on the next stairwell. Though pain radiated sharply from her head and her already bruised and battered knee, her entire body seemed to go numb as she heard a shot ring out above her. McKenna twisted around on the floor just in time to see Nathan and Sutherland struggling for the gun, which was now raised over both their heads, although still in Nathan's hand. McKenna reached for the handrail on the wall and then slowly lifted herself to her feet, though the pain was excruciating. Then she watched helplessly as the two men struggled for the gun. Just when it seemed that Nathan was about to break from Sutherland's grasp, Sutherland reached into his pocket with his free hand and thrust something toward Nathan's chest. Nathan grunted, his eyes suddenly wide and unblinking, and then he dropped his arms, the gun no longer in his hand. As McKenna watched in horror, Nathan lost his balance and tumbled down the stairs, sprawling out in front of her with a baseball-sized splotch of blood on the front of his crisp, white shirt. McKenna slowly lifted her eyes to Sutherland as he wiped a bloody letter opener—the one he had been using to screw open the vents earlier—onto his expensive slacks before tucking it back into his pocket.

"Hey, what happened? Was that gunfire?"

McKenna's eyes lifted to two men who had just rounded the stairwell several feet above her, where Sutherland now stood. Caught off guard, Sutherland quickly turned around to face the men while holding the gun at his side so they couldn't see it.

"No. I think it was some kind of explosion," Sutherland offered, his voice tight but his tone still convincing.

"Go back upstairs," Nathan breathed, reaching out and grabbing McKenna's ankle.

Startled, McKenna swallowed back the urge to scream. Her focus shot to Nathan, who was on the ground next to her feet, his face pale and his voice raspy. "There's a CPA office across the hall from West Link. The guy in the first cubicle has a satellite phone. And take this," Nathan said quickly, pulling the disk from his pocket and extending it to her. McKenna hesitated for only a moment before quickly taking the disk and sliding it into the pocket of her slacks.

"Go!" Nathan urged, his face a sickly shade of gray.

Troubled by the thought of leaving him but knowing that if she wanted to live she needed to hide, McKenna glanced back up at Sutherland. He still had his back turned to her, his focus on the men on the stairs who were quickly making their way toward him. McKenna looked back at Nathan, wishing there was something she could do for him. Then her eyes came to rest on the door next to her. Thinking quickly, she slipped unnoticed through the door, the pain in her body temporarily dulled by the surge of adrenaline pumping through her. She knew she had only seconds before Sutherland would notice that she was gone, but she also suspected he would at least make a show of helping Nathan—for a time, at least—to keep up pretenses. This would buy her some time, but it wouldn't be much, especially considering how frustratingly slow she was able to move.

With her heartbeat thrumming all the way up the nape of her neck, she hobbled down the hall, her eyes racing wildly for a place to hide. She passed by the first room before taking refuge in the second. At first glance, McKenna guessed that the expansive office was a travel agency. There were posters of striking beaches and exotic foreign cities plastered all over the walls. McKenna zeroed in on a large oak desk positioned by the window. But just as she was about to start toward the desk, she heard something in the hall. The noise was faint, and for a minute McKenna doubted that she had heard anything at all. Then, standing perfectly still, with only her rapid breathing punctuating the silence, she heard it: the undeniable sound of a door swooshing closed. Sutherland was coming after her.

McKenna started toward the desk, fighting the urge to rush so that the steady thud of her makeshift crutch wouldn't echo too loudly on the tile floor. Once she reached the desk, she glanced around in desperation for a place to hide the crutch, since there was no way it would fit under the desk. Her eyes finally fell on the full-length curtains pushed back at the sides of the window before her. She quickly placed the crutch behind the curtain, grateful the sun had gone down so there wouldn't be any light coming in to cause a silhouette. Then, having no time to do anything else, McKenna climbed awkwardly under the desk, biting her lip to keep from crying out from the dizzying pain shooting up her leg as she bent it. She had only been under the desk seconds when she heard the soft clip of a hard-soled shoe touch down on the tile in the room. McKenna held her breath, though folding her battered body into such a confining position made her head swim with agony. She closed her eyes, willing him to leave, but she heard nothing and felt only the chill of his eyes racing over the room. Then, when she was sure that she couldn't take another moment of the pain and the terror, she heard the soft scrape of footsteps as he turned, and the gentle swoosh of the door closing behind him.

McKenna let her breath out in a rush. Then she waited, her ears tuned in to the slightest sound, knowing Sutherland was still nearby, checking the rest of the rooms on the floor. After what felt like a lifetime, she heard the larger swoosh of the heavy door leading to the stairs. The relief that shot through McKenna left her body weak and tingling, though she knew that might have also been due to the fact that her legs had gone to sleep.

Waiting another minute or two, just to be certain that Sutherland was gone, McKenna slowly climbed out from under the desk. A cold shudder raced through her as she reached for the paddle, still hidden behind the curtains, and her mind raced to her next move while she waited for the blood to return to her legs. She was fairly certain she was on the thirty-fourth floor, two floors below Nathan's office. She would only have to make it up two flights of stairs, though with her knee almost double in size, that would be a feat in and of itself. She was counting on the guess that Sutherland would never expect her to go up, given the condition of the building, especially with the lights provided by the backup generators flickering almost constantly. Once she reached the office, she could take the satellite phone, if it was still there, and call for help. Her only other option was to climb down thirty-four flights of stairs with Sutherland possibly lurking around every corner. With that last thought outweighing all other factors, McKenna started toward the stairs.

It took longer than McKenna would have liked to make it down the hall, but eventually she made it to the door leading to the stairs. After taking a moment to catch her breath, she slowly opened the door and peeked out into the hall. The first thing she noticed was that Nathan was no longer there; the only evidence that he had been there was a smear of blood on the floor. She let herself feel a glimmer of hope, knowing that the two men in the hall probably wouldn't have wasted the effort on a dead man, especially when there were injured people to help. That meant Nathan was alive, at least for now. With that thought buoying her up, McKenna stepped out in to the empty stairwell and began the painful climb. Every few steps she would glance over her shoulder just to make sure Sutherland wasn't behind her, though she was sure she was being paranoid. Sutherland, though greedy and methodical, would rely on logic. He would know that no one in their rational mind would trek back into a building that was surely coming down, and so he would head down, at least initially, to search for her. But McKenna knew that eventually he would realize what she had done, and then he would be back. McKenna shuddered and attempted to push the thought to the back of her mind. Right now she needed to find that satellite phone. If she was going to make it out alive, she was going to need help.

CHAPTER FIFTEEN

8:05 P.M. / Los Angeles; Lincoln Tower parking garage

Hunter could feel himself fading in and out of consciousness, the pain so intense that he could hardly stand it. From time to time he heard sounds, maybe voices, but he wasn't sure. His head was foggy, and it took too much energy to concentrate. Instead, he found himself slipping back into his memory for relief.

It was the same day Hunter had left school and gone to his grandpa's after breaking the window in his classroom. Though he was embarrassed, he had cried until he couldn't cry anymore. His grandpa had just held him and let him get it all out. Then the two had gone into the kitchen. After placing a quick call to Hunter's parents to let them know where he was, Grandpa had cooked him up a couple of sloppy joes. Grandma Smith had died when Hunter's mom was just little, leaving Grandpa to feed, clothe, and take care of his little family. Fortunately, for his family's sake, Grandpa had turned out to be a great cook.

Hunter was three-fourths of the way through his second sloppy joe when his mom walked through the front door. She shot a quick look at her father, who immediately began to mumble something about mowing the grass before he slipped out the back door. Then she turned her eyes to Hunter. She walked to him, her eyes tender.

"I'm so sorry, Hunter."

He wanted to shout at her, to make her feel as bad as he did, but he couldn't. Instead, he again felt tears burning his eyes.

"We never wanted to hurt you," she continued as she took the seat next to him.

He looked down at his plate. Though he wouldn't lash out at her, he wasn't ready to let the anger go.

"What's happening with your dad and I doesn't change how I feel about you. I love you."

"Do you love him?" Hunter asked, looking her straight in the eyes.

She let out a long sigh, her eyes sad. "Hunter, it's complicated."

Hunter stood up abruptly. "I'm walking home."

His mom immediately stood as if to stop him, but then almost as quickly changed her mind and turned to the side to let him go. Hunter ran out the front door and down the road. He ran as fast as he could for three or four miles. Then, when he was too tired to run anymore, he cut through a park not far from his house and plopped down on a bench. Still struggling to catch his breath, he closed his eyes, wishing he could drown out the world.

"I give up," he snapped bitterly, feeling a rush of blood pounding through his veins.

"Anyone sitting here?"

Hunter opened his eyes with a start to see two young men in suits looking down at him. Embarrassed, he quickly stood up. "It's all yours," he said as he started to leave.

"You look like you just lost your best friend," one of the guys said. He had short brown hair and was wearing a suit that looked like it had probably been a tight fit twenty pounds ago.

"Why do you care?" Hunter snapped, surprising even himself with his rudeness.

The other young man laughed, his expression relaxed and friendly. "I guess he told you," he said to the guy next to him. Then he extended his hand to Hunter. "I'm Elder Gates, and this is my companion, Elder Steller."

"Elder?" Hunter asked, looking at him curiously. He was also wearing a suit like his friend, though it fit right and was in better condition, if not a little threadbare through the knees.

"We're missionaries for The Church of Jesus Christ of Latter-day Saints," Elder Gates offered.

Hunter acknowledged the man's words with a nod and then turned to leave, anxious to get away.

"You do believe in Jesus Christ, don't you?" Elder Steller, who had taken a seat on the bench, asked.

Hunter turned back around, at once irritated. "Yeah. But it hasn't done me any good so far."

Elder Gates nodded. "Sounds like you're going through a hard time right now."

"Look, I've got to get home," Hunter said, suddenly wanting to run again.

"I hope everything works out for you," Elder Gates said, something in his expression conveying that he really meant it. "We're going to be in the area for a while. Maybe we'll see you around."

"Maybe," Hunter said with a shrug as he started across the grass.

"Hey, kid!" Elder Gates called out.

Hunter stopped and glanced over his shoulder.

"Remember . . . the rainbow didn't come until after *the storm."*

Hunter wanted to blast the guy with a few choice thoughts of his own, ones that his mother certainly wouldn't have approved of, but Elder Gates looked sincere, like he genuinely wanted to help. Hunter finally shook his head, then turned and started away, the storm inside his own soul still raging.

The image faded, and Hunter began to moan, the recollections that had been flashing through his head now hazy as his mind teetered between reality and reminiscence. Flashes of the enormous mound of rubble burying him alive began to assault him, the image causing the pain in his body to intensify. He squeezed his eyes shut, forcing his thoughts deep into the security of his cognitive past where physical pain couldn't penetrate. But again the images returned, and he was suddenly in his childhood home, in his room with the door shut. He knew the memory well and quickly found himself pulled into it.

He was lying on his bed with one arm draped over his eyes. His father would be leaving in a few minutes, as soon as he had gathered the last of his things. The anger, sadness, and fear he had been feeling for days had subsided, leaving him feeling numb. It was then that he heard the knock at the front door. Hoping that it was his grandpa, Hunter quickly got up and hurried down the hall to the front room. But instead of seeing Grandpa Smith standing in the entryway, he saw the same two guys he had seen earlier in the park. Elder Gates, who was shaking his mother's hand and saying something about sharing a message with her about Jesus Christ, glanced toward him. A look of surprise flashed across the young man's face, though it was quickly replaced by a broad smile.

"Hi!" Elder Gates said, extending his hand to Hunter. "I said we'd see you around, but I didn't think it would be this quick."

"You know them?" Hunter's mom asked, looking at Hunter inquisitively.

"We met in the park today," Hunter said.

Hunter's mom nodded as she glanced back at the men. Hunter expected her to make up some excuse not to invite them in, especially considering the circumstances, but after another thoughtful glance at Hunter, she opened the door wide and welcomed them both into their home.

"Would you like something to drink, maybe a cold glass of iced tea?" she asked.

Elder Gates shook his head. *"No thank you, ma'am. We don't drink tea, but water would be great if it's no trouble."*

"Sure," she said as she gestured for them to take a seat on the couch.

She had only made it halfway across the room when Hunter's father emerged from the hall with two bulging suitcases and another bag slung over his shoulder. He immediately stopped, his eyes going to the young men on the couch.

Both elders stood. *"Hi,"* Elder Gates began, walking across the floor and extending his hand. *"I'm Elder Gates and this is my companion, Elder Steller. We're missionaries for The Church of Jesus Christ of Latter-day Saints."*

Hunter's dad gestured to the suitcases. *"Well, as you can see I'm on my way out."*

Elder Gates looked at the suitcases and then glanced at Hunter, who was fighting hard to hide the emotion that he knew must be written all over his face. Elder Gates nodded, seeming to put all the pieces together. He was silent for a moment before straightening and looking directly at Hunter's dad. *"What if I told you that the message I've been sent to give you could change your life forever? Would you listen then?"*

"I'd say you're probably in the wrong line of work. You should consider selling used cars with a line like that." Then he sighed and shot a quick glance at his soon-to-be ex-wife. *"Besides, at this point, I don't think there's anything you could say that would make a lick of difference in my life,"* he said, the discouragement thick in his voice.

Elder Gates smiled kindly and then glanced over at Hunter. *"Why don't we find out?"*

The image slowly faded as Hunter's subconscious pulled him into another memory.

It had been three weeks since the missionaries had shown up for the first time on their doorstep. In that time, Hunter couldn't believe the transformation that his family had gone through. Everything the missionaries had taught them had rung true for all of them. It was as if they were relearning things they already knew. Hunter glanced across the living room at his parents and then at Elder Gates and Elder Steller. Though it would take time for Hunter's parents to rebuild their relationship, they were smiling again, even laughing together. Hunter smiled himself, hardly believing that life could be this good. Then the phone rang.

Hunter began to moan, knowing the news that the call would bring, knowing how his life would change forever.

Hunter's mom took the call. After a quick greeting, her hand shot to her mouth, and she let out a cry, one that made Hunter feel sick. Hunter's dad was on his feet in an instant.

"What is it?" he said, taking his wife by the arm.

For a second, she just stared off as if he hadn't spoken, then she slowly turned to face him, tears streaking her cheeks.

"My dad . . . had a heart attack," she said haltingly.

"A heart attack!" Hunter's father repeated in disbelief. "What hospital's he in?"

Hunter's mom shook her head slowly back and forth, her expression dazed. "He's not. He's dead."

Hunter felt as if someone had just reached into his chest and withdrawn his beating heart. He stared at his parents, his vision already beginning to blur. This couldn't be happening. Grandpa Smith was his rock. When the rest of his life had been falling apart, his grandpa had always been there for him, steadfast, immovable. Now, in an instant, he was gone.

"No!" Hunter cried out, shaking his head. He fought to pull his mind back to the present, preferring the physical pain to the overwhelming despair and grief he was feeling now. But the image was quickly replaced by another—one that brought a measure of joy to equal the pain of the last.

Hunter was standing next to a baptismal font, his hair wet. His mom stood next to him dressed in white, her hair also damp. She was smiling, her entire face lit up. Hunter couldn't remember a time when he had seen her look this beautiful. She was almost glowing. Hunter wished that

Grandpa Smith were here to see her this happy, but even as the thought crossed his mind, something inside him told him that he was. Feeling warm all over, Hunter smiled at his mom as she squeezed his arm, her eyes moist. Then they both turned back toward the baptismal font. Elder Stellar was standing in the waist-high water next to Hunter's dad, the two of them both dressed in white. Elder Stellar pronounced the sacred words of the baptismal prayer, then dipped Hunter's dad all the way back into the water, covering him completely. When Hunter's father reemerged, water still streaming from his body, he turned and looked at his wife and son. He smiled, his eyes filled with a kind of wonder that Hunter was only beginning to understand. He smiled back, feeling the muscles in his throat constrict.

Elder Gates, who was standing next to Hunter, placed his hand on his shoulder. "You know, one day you'll be a missionary," he whispered, his eyes shining.

Hunter could feel the man's words burn throughout his entire body, igniting a fire that would never be extinguished. He smiled back, suddenly filled with a new purpose. He wanted to be able to help change lives in the same way that these two elders had his. He wanted to make a difference. He wanted to be a missionary!

* * *

Jax lay across the rubble, his entire body aching. His throat and lungs burned from inhaling the thick dust that seemed to fill every inch of the parking garage, and he could no longer lift his arms without a concerted effort. But all of that paled in comparison to the pain that gripped his chest every time he looked down at Hunter still trapped beneath an immovable slab of concrete. Over the last hour, Jax had watched the life slowly drain from Hunter's face. For most of that hour, Hunter had not even been coherent. Mike had finally walked in the direction of the minivan, where they had placed Lakesha, to look around for a way out. Jax had stayed next to Hunter, unable to leave him to die alone in the dimly lit, concrete room.

"Please, God," Jax begged, feeling a flicker of anger, tempered substantially by exhaustion. "*Help him.* Don't let him suffer like this."

Jax jerked around as someone placed a hand on his shoulder.

"Is he gone?" Mike asked hesitantly.

Jax took a steady breath before shaking his head. "He's still holding on. How's Lakesha?"

"She's in a lot of pain."

"Did you find a way out?" Jax asked, though he held out little hope.

Mike shook his head. "We'll just have to wait for someone to find us."

Jax looked up at the stressed beams overhead, knowing that the building would never last that long, though he didn't say so. Instead, he scooted over a little as Mike sat down and put his head in his hands.

"I guess I'm not going to be the first in my family to graduate from college after all," Mike said with a sad shrug, his tone revealing more remorse than self-pity.

Jax looked down at the rubble. "I never really cared about school. College was just a stopover while I waited to join the family business. I studied just enough to get by; I never got any real satisfaction from the actual learning," he admitted matter-of-factly, though the sting he felt from his candor was surprisingly keen.

Mike nodded but didn't comment. "So, do you have a girlfriend?"

Jax laughed. "One for every day of the week." Then his smile faded. "But I've never really loved anyone—except myself," he admitted frankly as he lowered his eyes and looked down at his battered hands, feeling the shame of his words.

"What are you talking about?" Mike exclaimed, shaking his head in disbelief. "You walked out of this death trap, and you came back in for a friend. If that isn't love, I don't know what is."

Jax glanced up at Mike, wanting to believe his words but still feeling the weight of his guilt. Then he looked back down at Hunter. Jax and Mike were silent for a moment, both feeling the loss of so many lives cut short.

"I hope it's over quick . . . for all of us," Mike finally said as he looked first at Hunter, then at Jax.

Jax nodded; the same thought had crossed his own mind several times in the last thirty minutes.

"Do you believe . . . you know . . . that there's something more?" Mike asked hesitantly.

"You mean like heaven?"

Mike nodded, appearing a little embarrassed by the question.

Again, the remorse returned. Jax thought of the countless times he had partaken of and passed the sacrament, and of the promises he had made at his baptism: to always remember the Savior and to be like Him. Jax felt the void more poignantly than ever before. Though for the last few years he had believed, he had not kept his promises. "I guess I've always just taken all that for granted," he admitted.

"It's different when it's staring you in the face," Mike said, his bloodshot eyes surveying the massive destruction all around them.

They both looked up as a shower of pebble-sized debris rained down just to the left of them. Jax's muscles tensed as he waited to see if there was going to be another aftershock, but after almost a full minute of silence, the tension that had built across his shoulders began to subside. He turned back to Mike, whose eyes now seemed glued to the red SUV across the parking garage.

"What is it?" Jax asked curiously.

Mike didn't answer immediately but continued to stare at the vehicle, his brow creased in thought. Jax was about to ask again when Mike suddenly stood, his expression determined.

"Maybe we could move the SUV."

Jax shook his head. "There's no way. The tires are wedged in the middle of all that debris, and some of the pieces are larger than the one on Hunter. If we can't move this one," Jax said, pointing at the slab, "then what makes you think we can dig the tires out of that mess?"

"We can't," Mike said simply. "But if we can start it, we might be able to drive it out."

"Then what? The elevator shaft is blocked. There's no way out."

"Maybe . . . maybe not. The third shaft has been closed for repair. If we could move the SUV, it's possible we could pry those doors open and get out through there."

Jax looked over at the elevators, knowing it was a long shot.

"Look, it's better than just sitting here waiting to die," Mike pressed, his eyes more alive than Jax had seen them in hours.

Jax began to shake his head and then glanced down at Hunter. "Even if we could find a way out, I couldn't leave him here alone to die."

"What about Lakesha? Do we just let her die?" Mike asked, his tone rising sharply. "Hunter's going to die—but she could live."

Jax continued to look down at Hunter for several seconds before slowly turning toward the minivan and the woman he knew was inside. Mike was right, but that didn't ease the pain that tore at his chest.

"Hunter gave his life to save Lakesha," Mike continued, keeping his tone calm. "Do you want his sacrifice to be for nothing? Is that what he would want?"

Jax knew the answer, but he was struggling to accept it. He wanted to cry, scream, anything but feel the emptiness that welled inside him as he sat watching Hunter slowly die. Jax finally shook his head, then lifted his eyes to Mike, swallowing past the hard lump in his throat. "No," he said simply. Then he reached down and touched the top of Hunter's head, though he knew his friend was unconscious. "I'll be back," he whispered, unable to hold back the flood of emotion that rose in his chest. After a minute, he stood and turned back to Mike, wiping at the damp streaks on his dirty face. "Let's go," he said, starting toward the SUV.

As they passed the minivan, just feet from the SUV, Mike and Jax stopped. Lakesha, who was stretched out across the middle seats of the vehicle, her legs badly broken, had begun to cry.

"It's okay," Mike soothed, trying to calm her down. "We're going to find a way out of here."

Jax was much less certain, but he didn't say so. Instead, he continued toward the SUV. He had just slid into the driver's seat when the lights in the parking garage clicked off with a low hum, plunging everything into total darkness. Lakesha let out a scream, which only intensified the rhythm of Jax's violently beating heart.

"Don't panic. Everything's all right," Mike called out to Lakesha.

Jax felt his stomach clench. They only had one flashlight, and once the batteries were dead, so were they. It would only be a matter of time. He held his breath, waiting for the lights to come back on, but after a few moments, it became painfully apparent that the backup power from the generators was exhausted. Mike flicked on his flashlight and then carefully made his way to Jax.

"We're running out of time," Mike said once he reached him.

Jax nodded before glancing toward the ignition, hoping to find a set of keys, though he knew the chances were slim. Once his suspicions were confirmed, he began to search the glove box, as well as under the mat and the overhead visor, for a set of keys. Having no luck, he turned back to Mike.

"Please tell me you have a juvenile record for car theft, because I don't have a clue as to how to start this thing."

"Try the console between the seats," Mike suggested.

Jax quickly opened the little compartment positioned between the leather seats while Mike, who was standing next to the driver's side window, shined the flashlight toward it. When he opened the console, Jax flashed a smile back toward Mike and then withdrew a small handbag.

"Check for keys," Mike urged.

Jax quickly shook the bag, and his smile grew broader when he heard what sounded like the clinking of metal. He reached in and withdrew a set of keys.

"Yes!" Mike exclaimed enthusiastically.

Jax fumbled with the keys, trying to determine which was the key to the ignition, while Mike stepped back from the vehicle.

After a moment, Jax held up the largest key on the ring and then glanced briefly at Mike. "I hope this works."

"It will," Mike said, taking another step back.

With trembling hands, Jax slid the key into the ignition. It was a perfect fit. *"Please!"* Jax whispered as he pumped the gas pedal, the beating of his heart coming in thunderous jolts. "Let it start." Then, with Mike watching in breathless silence, Jax turned the key. The vehicle immediately purred to life, shooting smoke out of the tailpipe.

"It works!" Jax shouted, a surge of euphoria and relief coursing through his body.

Not wasting another second, Jax hollered for Mike to get farther back, then shifted the SUV into drive and pressed down on the gas. The tires began to spin, spitting dust and debris out from beneath them, but the vehicle didn't move.

"Come on! Come on!" Jax shouted as he pushed the pedal all the way to the floor.

Finally, with the engine roaring, the vehicle lunged forward, jerking Jax sharply in his seat. He held tight to the steering wheel, his body tingling with adrenaline. Just a few more feet and he would be out of the debris, and the SUV would be clear of the elevator shafts.

But as thoughts of escape and rescue ran through his mind, Jax heard a grinding screech coming from the bottom of the vehicle, causing it to come to an abrupt halt, though the tires continued to spin.

"No!" Jax shouted, pressing the gas pedal all the way to the floor again, but the vehicle refused to budge. He slammed his palms down on the steering wheel and tried again, but the results were the same.

"It's high centered," Mike called out.

Jax took his foot off the pedal, then placed the SUV in park and quickly climbed out. It only took a glance to see that Mike was right. There was a huge mound of cement under the belly of the vehicle, lifting it a few inches above the ground so that the rear tires didn't even touch the pile of rubble.

"I can't believe this!" Jax shouted as he kicked one of the tires, then walked away from the SUV, fighting the urge to scream. Knowing that he was going to die was awful, but thinking for just a split second that he might live only to have the last shred of hope jerked out from under him was too much.

"Maybe we could move some of the smaller chunks of cement," Mike said as he pointed the flashlight beneath the SUV.

Jax didn't even turn around. "It's no use," he mumbled, finding a warped sense of solace in his self-pity. "Why try?" As soon as the words were out of his mouth, Jax felt the guilt. He glanced in the direction where Hunter was still trapped, though the room was a mass of blackness. Hunter was going to die, if he hadn't already, but Jax was alive. He still had a chance at life, and *he* was the one complaining. He slowly turned around, his decision made.

Jax walked back toward Mike, who was on his belly trying to drag some of the smaller pieces of rubble out from under the vehicle. Jax took a breath and moved to help Mike dig, but as he approached, his eyes fell on a length of wood protruding from a pile of debris just to the right of the vehicle. He stopped, suddenly struck with an idea.

"Hey, shine the light over here!" he called out to Mike as he veered toward the strip of wood.

"What are you doing?" Mike asked, getting to his feet and aiming the flashlight toward him.

"We've got to put something under the tires for traction," Jax said, grabbing hold of the wood and yanking it from the pile despite his raw hands.

Mike nodded in agreement. "Do you think it'll work?"

"It's got to," Jax said as he walked toward the back of the vehicle.

He had lowered himself on his stomach and was attempting to wedge the wood under one of the back tires when his attention was drawn to a puddle under the belly of the vehicle. Jax breathed in and felt his stomach contract sharply. There was no doubt as to the identity of the fluid.

"The fuel tank's been punctured," he said as he reached out and put his finger over a pea-sized hole in the tank, temporarily stopping the slow but steady drainage of gasoline.

"What do we do?" Mike asked, his face rapidly losing its color.

The purring engine, which Jax had purposely left on, seemed instantly louder with his head only inches from the gas tank. "There's not too much we can do except pray this thing doesn't backfire when we're moving it. One spark and we won't have to worry about aftershocks, because this place will be a fireball."

"That's comforting," Mike said, the flashlight in his hand still trained on the fuel tank as he temporarily closed his bloodshot eyes and rubbed them with his free hand. When he opened them, he looked at Jax and shook his head as if in surrender. But then a slow, tired smile began to spread across his lips. "Hey, if we sit here and do nothing, we're dead men," Mike said with a shrug. "I say we at least go down trying."

Jax hesitated for just a moment as his eyes flicked once more toward the punctured fuel tank. The gas fumes were getting steadily stronger. Then he nodded his head decisively. "Let's get this piece of junk off these rocks," he said, turning his eyes back to Mike.

Mike nodded his approval, then watched as Jax secured the length of wood under the first tire before crawling all the way under the SUV on his belly and placing several small chunks of cement under the other tire so that it was no longer off the ground. Then he crawled out from under the vehicle, dusting off his pants.

"Thanks for coming back into the building with me," Mike said as Jax stood.

Jax looked at the man before him. Though the two had only met a few hours ago, they had formed a bond that even Jax didn't fully understand. He suspected that no one, besides someone who had lived through something like this, *could* understand. "I'm not ready to die," Jax admitted honestly.

Mike nodded, Jax's declaration clearly a reflection of his own thoughts. "Good. Neither am I."

With that said, Jax climbed back into the SUV, closed the door, and took hold of the steering wheel, his palms suddenly sticky with sweat. The fumes from the gas were strong. Jax knew that it would only be a matter of time before all the gas had drained out of the tank and moving the vehicle was no longer an option, dooming them to die a slow death in this dark, underground crypt. But he was also aware that if driving off the rocks caused even one spark, they would all be dead in seconds. Neither was an option Jax wanted to consider, but with the fumes filling the interior of the vehicle, he knew he would have to take the risk.

"This is going to work," Jax said, the words sticking in his dry throat as he glanced over at Mike.

Mike took a deep breath and nodded his head, though his face was filled with the same dread Jax felt. As Jax placed his hand on the gear shift and lowered his foot over the gas pedal, he quickly closed his eyes. Like all the other times he had prayed since he had been trapped in the bottom of the high-rise, the prayer was silent and brief, evoking intense emotions. This time, however, much to Jax's surprise, the prayer was followed by a measure of peace that filled his entire body. The tingling sensation started at his head and spread until it completely enveloped him. It almost felt as though someone had wrapped their arms around him, encircling him, telling him that regardless of the outcome, everything was going to be okay.

With this sense of peace still wrapped around him, Jax pushed down on the gas pedal. At first, the wheels began to spin, though there was very little movement from the vehicle, but then in a lurch it began to move, the motion jerking Jax backward as he continued to hold tight to the steering wheel. After a few more seconds, with the engine protesting the abuse it was receiving, the SUV was out of the debris. Jax screeched the vehicle to a stop, then immediately pulled the key from the ignition.

Mike's shouts were echoing through the garage. "You did it!" he exclaimed. "I can't believe it."

Jax could hardly believe it himself. He exhaled sharply as relief coursed through him before climbing from the interior of the vehicle. "You're not the only one," he admitted as he started toward the shaft.

Gasoline was everywhere, and the vapors were strong, once again causing Jax to shake his head in wonder. It was nothing short of a miracle that driving over those sharp chunks of cement hadn't caused a spark, ending their lives in an instant. Jax's and Mike's wonderment was short–lived, however, as they got a good look at the elevator shaft. Jax had known that two of the shafts would be impassible because of the elevators that had plummeted to the ground, completely sealing those exits. However, as he looked at the third elevator, the one marked out of order, he realized that it didn't look much more promising. The elevator doors appeared to have buckled, causing a small gap in the center of the doors. Apparently the force from the adjacent elevator hitting the ground at high speed had caused the damage. Jax shook his head, hardly believing that this was happening.

"Do you think we'll be able to squeeze through there?" Mike asked skeptically, his eyes filled with the same doubt and fear that knotted in Jax's stomach.

"We're about to find out," Jax said as he slid one of his arms through the gap, followed by his head. "Okay, give me a push," he said before slowly exhaling in an attempt to contract his thick chest.

Mike placed his hands on Jax's shoulder and began to push, but after only a few seconds it became painfully obvious that the gap was simply too narrow.

"You try," Jax said as he stepped back.

Mike stepped up and began to slide his own body in between the breached doors. He was able to get farther in than Jax, but was still unable to squeeze through completely.

"We've got to pry it open a little more," Jax said as he began to look around. "We need a piece of rebar or something."

Mike shined his flashlight across the parking garage. The dust hung in the air like a low-lying cloud. Then he glanced back at the SUV, his whole face lighting up. "A jack!" he exclaimed. "The SUV's got to have a car jack."

Jax was already on his way over to the vehicle. He threw open the back doors of the truck, then reached for the spare tire that was encased in a side compartment. After pulling out the tire, he reached back in, feeling for a jack. A second later, he stepped back from the SUV with a jack in his hand and a look of triumph on his face.

A moment later they were standing in front of the elevator. They had propped the flashlight on a cinder block aimed at the doors and then placed the jack between the doors. Jax and Mike looked at one another. There was no need to say it: This was their last chance. If they weren't able to pry these doors open enough for them to squeeze through, it was all over.

Feeling a trickle of sweat make its way down the center of his back, Jax began to turn the handle on the jack. Within seconds it was wedged in tight. Jax glanced briefly at Mike, but his eyes were glued on the doors, as if he could somehow will them open. Taking another deep breath, Jax pushed on the handle with all he had. His arms and shoulders still ached from all the heavy lifting they had done trying to dig Hunter out from the rubble, and the skin on his hands had been rubbed raw, but none of that mattered right now. All he cared about was opening the gap in the doors just a few more inches. That was all that was separating them from freedom.

"Come on!" Jax pleaded, his arms and legs trembling and his head dizzy both from overexertion and the increasingly strong gasoline vapors.

After several minutes, exerting every ounce of strength that he could muster, he dropped his grip on the handle and stood back, shaking his head. It was no use. The gap between the doors had only widened maybe half an inch, if that.

"Let me try," Mike said, stepping up next to Jax.

"It's not going to work," Jax said as he stepped aside, still struggling to catch his breath.

Mike didn't reply, only grabbed hold of the handle and began to push.

He grunted as he dug his feet in and intensified his efforts, but after several minutes, he finally stood back, his arms falling limply to his sides.

"It won't budge," he gasped as he sat down next to the elevator doors, his head and shoulders slumped in defeat.

Jax bent next to him and took in several long breaths, though that only started him coughing. "We'll try again in a minute. Just catch your breath."

Mike looked down at his hands, where blood was now draining freely from the open sores. "I don't think we're going to get it open."

"We'll get it open," Jax said, still struggling to breathe.

Mike nodded, though a look of defeat clouded his eyes. He reached over and flicked off the flashlight, leaving them in total darkness. "We'd better conserve the battery."

As a little boy, Jax had accidentally gotten locked in a cellar in an old house down the road from his grandparents' farm in Idaho. He had spent three hours alone in the dark before the police had finally found him. Now all those memories came flooding back, causing him to shudder violently.

"You all right?" Mike asked, his voice breaking the eerie silence.

"I'm fine," Jax said quickly.

"Hey! Where are you?" Lakesha called out from the minivan, her tone high and panicked. "What happened to the flashlight?"

"Everything's okay," Mike called back, temporarily flicking the flashlight on so she could see where they were. "We're just conserving the battery."

Jax sat down next to Mike and stretched out across the rubble, too tired to care about the rough-edged pieces of cement that jabbed at his back. All he could feel were his throbbing muscles. After a few minutes of hearing only the creaking and moaning of the building above them, Jax knew he wouldn't be able to take much more of sitting silently in the dark, wondering if they would ever get out of there.

"So tell me about the girls in California," Jax said, desperate to concentrate on something other than the unnatural noises resounding all around them.

Mike's voice was heavy with fatigue. "I spend so much time working and going to school that I don't have much time to date. There is this one girl, but I'm not sure she even knows my name."

"What's hers?"

"Afton Tims. I see her in the library up on campus, and we even have a class together, but every time I try to talk to her, I come off sounding like some rambling kid who grew up on the wrong side of the tracks. Which is about right."

"So she's smart and beautiful and way out of your league," Jax offered, summing it up neatly.

"That's about it," Mike said with a tired sigh.

"Wrong!" Jax shot right back. "You've got to walk up to this girl like you own the place. Make it clear right from the start that *she's* the lucky one to be hanging out with you and not the other way around. Trust me. I've dated a lot of girls and—" Jax stopped, suddenly hearing his own words for the first time. He shook his head, knowing that this very attitude was what had prevented him from having any real relationships. "Look, Mike," he began tiredly, "forget everything I just said." He took a deep breath, feeling suddenly weighed down by his own pride. "Any girl worth having sees right through a guy like me. The truth is, I don't know the first thing about women."

Mike laughed. "Join the club." Then, as quickly as it had come, the lightheartedness left his voice. "But I'll tell you one thing—if we make it out of here, I'm asking Afton out, even though there'll be no doubt who the lucky one will be if she says yes."

Jax placed his battered hand on Mike's shoulder. "I'm not so sure about that, but I do hope you get the chance," he said, his tone likewise sober.

"Me too," Mike murmured.

The two sat in silence for the next few minutes, conserving their energy, but after another series of groans from the steel beams overhead, they both dragged themselves to their feet. After clicking on the flashlight, they decided to work together to try to budge the handle on the jack. Again they pushed, attempting to pry the elevator doors open even a few more inches, but after repositioning their grip and straining every muscle in their bodies, the gap still hadn't widened. Jax finally let go as he stared hopelessly at the doors, knowing that he would never be able to squeeze his broad shoulders through the opening.

"Maybe Lakesha could fit through," Mike said, still struggling for air.

"Then what? How's she going to climb through the top of the elevator and up a shaft with her legs all mangled?" Jax asked, his chest heaving as he struggled for air.

"We could call for help. Maybe there's still someone in the building who would hear us."

Jax nodded, though he guessed that at this point there were probably very few people still in the building and that those who were, were likely in no condition to help. Still, it was an option, and they were running dangerously thin on those. Without exerting the effort to respond, Jax stuck his head through the gap and began to yell for help. Mike was right beside him, pounding on the elevator door in an attempt to get someone on the floors above to hear them. Jax shouted and screamed for the next thirty minutes until his voice was nothing more than a raspy whisper, but all he heard when he stopped was his own strained voice echoing back to him.

"There's no use. We're going to slowly starve to death—if the building doesn't take us out sooner," Jax gasped as he leaned his back up against the doors and drew in several long breaths, which he instantly regretted as dust filled his lungs.

"I better go check on Lakesha," Mike said, his own face crestfallen as he reached for the flashlight.

As Mike started toward the minivan, glancing briefly at the SUV as he passed by, he suddenly froze.

"What's wrong?" Jax asked, seeing his reaction.

Mike didn't answer; instead, he yanked open the door to the SUV and quickly reached inside. A moment later, he was on his way back to Jax with a duffel bag in his hands.

Jax's jaw fell slack. "I thought you lost that thing in the elevator shaft."

Mike was shaking his head. "I thought I did too. Everything happened so fast. I must have tossed it into the SUV just before you dragged me through the window and that elevator crashed to the bottom of the shaft. Then we spotted Hunter after that and went to help him and—" Mike stopped; there were tears streaming down his face.

Jax understood. He stood and grabbed Mike around the neck. "It's okay, man." Then he pulled back, wiping at his own face. "At least we won't starve to death," he said, remembering with relief the bottled water and pastries he had found in the coffee shop just before they had descended the shaft to come looking for Hunter.

Mike shook his head as if Jax were missing the whole picture, but instead of telling him what he had overlooked, Mike reached into the duffel bag and pulled out the first-aid kit.

"I don't understand," Jax said, still not seeing where Mike was going with this. Sure they could bandage up Lakesha's legs and even their own battered hands, but for what? Just so they could die a short time later?

Mike flipped open the first-aid kit, his hands shaking so badly he almost dropped it. Then he began to rummage through it, his eyes lighting up when he found what he was looking for. Jax's curiosity was piqued, though he still had no idea what Mike could possibly have found that would make any difference. Mike lifted his eyes to Jax as he held up the item.

"Petroleum jelly?" Jax said, not even attempting to hide his disappointment. Mike, however, was now beside himself with excitement.

"Don't you see?" Mike exclaimed, gesturing toward Jax with the small tube of jelly. "If we put this on, we might be able to slip through the gap!"

"It could work," Jax said slowly, a broad smile spreading across his face.

Mike nodded, and then the two embraced each other in a firm bear hug, both shouting and crying at the same time.

CHAPTER SIXTEEN

8:50 P.M. / Downtown Los Angeles

James scanned the faces in the crowd as he made his way down the streets of downtown Los Angeles, his heart sinking with each passing mile. The closer he got to Lincoln Tower, the worse the destruction became. He also noted with growing alarm the fires that were popping up everywhere. James berated himself for not getting there earlier, though he knew there was nothing he could have done differently. It had taken fifteen minutes for a nurse to finally make it over to check out Stacy's injuries and to give her something for the pain. Though James felt bad about leaving her, he was relieved to finally be on his way to Lincoln Tower—and McKenna.

James glanced to his right as he passed through the same intersection where he had found Stacy. There was a roadblock about a quarter mile down the road. The National Guard had begun to arrive in droves and was attempting to establish some order. Word on the street was that they had also imposed a curfew, which meant that if James didn't get inside Lincoln Tower soon, he might not get the chance. James quickly turned off the headlights on his four-wheeler and slowed down, hoping that the soldiers, who were busy helping many of the displaced and injured still wandering the streets, wouldn't notice him. Once he was through the intersection, he immediately flicked the lights back on and stepped on the gas.

A few minutes later, James slowed the four-wheeler to a crawl, his eyes riveted on the building before him, his chest suddenly tight. The aerial view of Lincoln Tower that James had seen earlier had been shocking, but seeing the destruction firsthand—and knowing that someone he loved was inside—was overwhelming.

"Hey, you! What are you doing?"

James jerked around to face a soldier off to his left carrying a rifle and coming right toward him. Making the decision without thinking, James gunned the engine and headed for a side street. From behind him James could hear the man shouting for him to stop, but that only propelled James forward. He was over a quarter mile away before he finally slowed, pulled down an alley, and parked next to an overturned dumpster. If he wanted to get anywhere near Lincoln Tower unnoticed, he would have to ditch the four-wheeler. He climbed off it, stuffed the keys into his pocket, then walked around and retrieved his backpack from the trailer. After removing a flashlight and a protein bar, James slung the backpack across his shoulders. Then, taking one last glance at the four-wheeler, he started back down the alley. He had only made it about halfway back to the main road when he spotted a dark form coming toward him. James plastered himself against one of the buildings that lined the alley, hoping that the approaching man wouldn't see him, but the man continued to walk straight for him. James shot a quick glance toward the opposite end of the alley, then took a deep breath and began to run.

"Stop!" the man shouted, his voice echoing off the nearby buildings.

James continued to run, praying that the soldier wouldn't chase him, knowing that each wasted moment meant time he could be looking for McKenna.

"James!" the man screamed. "It's me—Lawrence!"

When the words registered, James immediately stopped and whirled around, his chest rising and falling sharply as he turned on his flashlight. "Lawrence!" James exclaimed, shaking his head in disbelief.

Lawrence continued toward him, his breathing ragged. "What took you so long?" he snapped, though his face was flooded with relief.

"Did you find McKenna?" James asked, ignoring the man's question altogether.

Lawrence shook his head in disgust. "They won't let me in the building," he said as he struggled to catch his breath. "They said it's too dangerous, that they're only allowing trained personnel in—but I haven't seen anyone go in yet. They've blocked off the entrance."

James shook his head as he glanced back toward Lincoln Tower. "There's got to be another way in."

"There's not! I've been all around the building searching for one, but the only way in is through the front doors."

"Then we'll have to go through the front doors," James said.

Lawrence snorted derisively. "Good luck. I even offered one of the soldiers a thousand dollars cash if he'd let me in, but he just threatened to arrest me for my own protection."

James didn't comment; instead, he started down the alley, his mind working swiftly as he tried to formulate a plan.

"If you had stayed with me, we might have gotten in before those weekend soldiers got here and set up shop."

James could feel his face burning, but he held his tongue.

"If McKenna dies because of you, I'll—"

James suddenly felt as if he were about to explode. He stopped, his eyes searing through the man before him. "Because of *me*? You're the one who sent her here in the first place. She wouldn't have even *been* here if it weren't for you."

Lawrence took a step back, clearly surprised, though his eyes quickly flashed anger. "She was here on business," Lawrence hissed. "Unlike you," he shot back sarcastically, "McKenna has a career."

James laughed. "*Yeah*. A career you've shoved down her throat since she was a kid. McKenna hates what she does, and if you took the time to really get to know your daughter, you'd see that."

Even in the dim light, James could see the reddish hue rising in Lawrence Bradford's face, but to James's surprise, instead of blasting him, Lawrence took a shaky breath to calm himself, then turned and walked away. James immediately felt guilt wash over him. Though he hadn't said anything that wasn't true, he knew this was probably the worst possible time to bring it up. The man was certainly never going to be awarded father of the year, but there was no doubt in James's mind that Lawrence loved McKenna and would do anything in his power to help her, even if the effort was misdirected.

"Maybe she got out already," Lawrence said, obviously unwilling to waste any more time arguing.

"Maybe," James said as the two approached the building. James instantly felt his heart drop as he allowed his eyes to climb the face of the battered structure. "What's holding it up?" he mumbled, shaking his head as he stopped in the middle of the alley, his eyes scanning what was left of Lincoln Tower.

Lawrence was silent, which was far more disconcerting than the man's usual condescending comments. James continued to eye the destruction, knowing without a doubt that hundreds of people had probably already died in the building and that many more likely would before the night was over. The question that sent a sickly shiver through his entire body was whether or not McKenna would be one of them. James glanced at Lawrence, and from the look on his face, he guessed that Lawrence was probably thinking the same thing.

"She's alive," James finally whispered, though he wasn't certain if he really felt it or if he was just trying to convince himself and Lawrence.

"I meant what I said about the money," Lawrence began. "I know what you said earlier, but if you get her out of there, you can name your price."

James looked at Lawrence before slowly exhaling, feeling drained by the man's whole demeanor. "Mr. Bradford, why are you here?"

"What do you mean, *why am I here?*" Lawrence snapped, his cheeks still a deep shade of scarlet. "Because I love my daughter."

James nodded. "So do I."

Lawrence seemed taken aback by the sincerity in James's tone. "My daughter's too good for you," he finally said, though his voice lacked the edge it had just seconds earlier.

James nodded again, only this time he added a sad smile. "I know," he said honestly.

It was the one thing that had kept him from telling McKenna how he felt all these years. She was everything that he was not—successful, articulate, and affluent—and Lawrence reminded him of just that at every turn. James knew he didn't stand a chance with McKenna, but that didn't change how he felt. He loved her. That fact was no more clear to him now as he stood willing to risk his life to find her than it had been when he was safely back in his studio apartment in New York. He knew that there was a social gap between them as vast as the San Andreas Fault, and that nothing was going to change that, but try as he might, he couldn't change his heart.

"I love your daughter, Mr. Bradford," James said, looking the man straight in the eyes. "And that has nothing to do with money, or status, or *you.*"

Lawrence stiffened, though he no longer seemed as intimidating. "Let's just find my daughter," he said tightly.

James nodded, knowing that he had just wasted his breath. He glanced out from the security of the dark alleyway to the main road. Three National Guardsmen were across the street next to a Humvee. One was shining a spotlight back and forth across the road while the other two were preparing to move the injured.

James suddenly had an idea. "What would you say to a little blemish on your pristine permanent record?" James whispered, unsuccessfully attempting to suppress a grin.

"What are you talking about?" Lawrence snapped.

"Well, if there's only one way into the building, we need a little diversion, and since you've already made such a nice impression . . ."

Lawrence's jaw tightened, but he didn't say a word; instead, he gave James a searching glance, shook his head in exasperation, then stepped out from the cover of the alleyway and started toward the soldiers. James pressed himself tightly against the wall of the building and watched. Within a couple of seconds, the soldiers spotted Lawrence and started toward him. James couldn't hear exactly what the men were saying, but after only a second or two, Lawrence began to run, drawing the soldiers away from Lincoln Tower. James sprang from the darkness and ran toward the front doors. Within seconds he was inside what was left of the building, his heart racing. He glanced quickly out the doors, but there was no sign of Lawrence or the soldiers.

James clicked on his flashlight and shined it across the lobby, his attention drawn immediately to a body half buried in the rubble. He looked away, fighting the urge to retch. He started toward the stairs, knowing that McKenna had likely been in the restaurant on the top floor with Nathan Rinehart when the earthquake hit. When he reached the elevators, a strong scent immediately caused him to pause. He leaned into the shaft, where the gasoline vapors were even more prevalent, then shined his flashlight to the bottom. All three elevators were at the bottom of the shaft, though two looked like they had taken a plunge to get there. James then repositioned himself so he could look up the shaft, though with only his flashlight to light it, the view was extremely limited. He was about to pull his upper body from the shaft when he heard a sound. Though it was faint, it was also distinct. Someone was calling out for help.

"Hello!" James shouted down the shaft urgently. "Is someone down there?"

Though it was muffled and he couldn't make out the words, James could hear more shouting.

"Hold on! I'm coming," James called out as he shined his flashlight into the shaft, looking for a ladder.

Though his declaration was intended for whomever was trapped at the base of Lincoln Tower, James couldn't help but silently send the same message up to McKenna, who was likely still forty flights above him.

* * *

McKenna eased herself down into a chair in one of the cubicles of the CPA office she was now in and immediately dialed 911 on the satellite phone she had found in the top drawer. The results were exactly what McKenna had suspected, though she had still felt compelled to try. All service in the Los Angeles area, and probably the entire West Coast, was down—including 911. McKenna dialed the next number automatically. The deep voice she heard next made her heart constrict.

"Hi, this is James. I'm not here right now, but if you'll leave your name and—" McKenna hung up the phone. She was crying too hard to breathe, let alone leave a message. For a few minutes she just sat there in the chair and cried. When she finally had herself halfway back under control, she dialed her father's satellite phone. She expected to hear his prerecorded voice message, but instead, her father answered.

"Dad!" McKenna cried, new tears springing to her eyes.

"McKenna!" Lawrence exclaimed. "McKenna, is that you?"

McKenna nodded her head, as a stream of tears made warm paths down her cheeks.

"*Where are you?*"

McKenna had never heard her father so frantic. "I'm still in Lincoln Tower," she said, struggling to steady the quiver in her voice.

McKenna could hear a quick intake of breath, and then her father asked, "Where?"

"I'm on the thirty-sixth floor in an office across the hall from Nathan's, but I don't think I can make it down. I've hurt my leg."

"McKenna, you've got to get out of there!" Lawrence exclaimed, the intensity in his voice rising sharply. "Nathan murdered Mrs. Dillon."

McKenna wasn't sure how her father had come to this conclusion, but she decided that if she didn't end up making it out of the building alive—which was an increasingly real possibility—she at least wanted to make sure that the wrong man wasn't punished. "It wasn't Nathan. It was Alan Sutherland."

"What are you talking about?"

"Sutherland was extorting money from West Link. When Mrs. Dillon found out about it, Sutherland hired Manning to kill her. Now he's stabbed Nathan and is after me."

"Does Sutherland know where you are?"

"No," McKenna said, her eyes going quickly to the door.

"Alright," Lawrence began, clearly trying to sound like everything was under control. "You're going to be okay. James is in the building."

"James is *here?* In Lincoln Tower?" McKenna exclaimed, suddenly feeling light-headed.

"Yes. But he thinks you're up on the fortieth floor, and I have no way of getting ahold of him to tell him otherwise. You're going to have to get out in the hall so he can see you."

McKenna was nodding her head, but her throat was too tight to speak.

"McKenna, did you hear me?"

"I heard you," she cried, desperately wanting to climb through the phone and cling to her father.

Lawrence was silent a moment, but when he finally spoke, his voice was deeper than normal, as though he were struggling to control his own emotions. "I love you, McKenna," he said, his voice cracking.

The effect of his words was immediate. McKenna began to sob. "I love you too."

"I'm sorry I sent you here," Lawrence continued, the pain in his voice making McKenna's heart ache. "And I'm sorry I pressured you into a career you didn't want."

"It's okay," McKenna said, unable to manage anything else.

"Get out into the hall," Lawrence finally choked out once he regained his voice. "Then wait there, quietly, just in case Sutherland is still looking for you. James will be there soon. And McKenna . . . be careful."

"I will."

McKenna held the phone in her hands once the line went dead, savoring the tender words her father had just spoken. Then, using the cigarette lighter to light the way, she took a deep breath, braced herself against the pain that intensified as she stood, and hobbled awkwardly toward the door leading to the hall. A few minutes later she leaned breathlessly up against one of the walls in the stairwell before carefully lowering herself to one of the stairs to sit. She looked down at the lighter in her hand, knowing that the fluid would only last a short time longer. Praying that James would make it to her soon, McKenna reluctantly clicked off the lighter, the darkness instantly surrounding her. She closed her eyes as if she could somehow pretend she wasn't alone in the dark with a killer stalking her. Instead, she replayed the conversation with her father over in her mind, the inflection of his voice, the words of caution, and finally the words she had waited twenty-eight years to hear. *I love you.* Reveling in the warmth those words invoked, her thoughts turned to James. Though having him in the building brought a measure of relief, it also added to her fear. Now she was not the only one in danger. James was too.

* * *

Justice scanned his thermal-imaging camera around the smoke-filled hotel room, but it didn't detect a heat-sensored image. If someone had been left in the room, Justice was almost certain that they wouldn't be alive and emitting heat anyway. The temperature in the room was quickly intensifying, and Justice was beginning to fear that there would be a flashover. Though he had never actually been in the middle of a flashover—a situation in which the temperature in a room became so hot that everything spontaneously ignited—he had seen the scarring effects of one and knew that the likelihood of survival was virtually nil.

"I don't see anyone," Justice said, speaking into the mic in his air mask as he glanced at Archer, who was standing next to him.

"Good. Let's get out of here," Archer said, agreeing with his captain's assessment.

The two quickly crawled back out of the room, unable to stand upright because of the intense heat. Justice was relieved to find the temperature not quite as severe in the hall.

"I'll check the last room," Justice began. "You head down."

Archer was already shaking his head. "I'm not leaving you."

Justice eyed the young firefighter, an image of the two blond-haired boys who called Archer *Daddy* popping into his mind.

"That's an order, Archer," Justice said, pointing toward the stairwell.

The firefighter shook his head. "You'll have to put me on report then, Captain, because I'm staying."

Before Justice could say another word, Thomas Porterman burst through the door to the stairwell, dragging a firefighter behind him. "He panicked and started hyperventilating, then blacked out," Thomas said in between gasps.

Justice shook his head, not at all surprised that Brian had buckled under pressure. "He probably used up all the air in his air pack," Justice said, quickly bending down next to Brian and feeling for a pulse. "He's alive, but he won't be for long if he doesn't get out of this smoke," Justice said, ripping off his own mask and temporarily putting it over Brian's face.

Though the air packs they used were good for forty-five minutes, if a firefighter was moving around a lot or panicked and began breathing rapidly, the air could be sucked dry in thirty minutes, sometimes less.

"My air's almost gone too," Thomas said reluctantly, his eyes on Justice.

"What about the floor you were working? Did everyone make it out?" Justice asked.

"It's clear. Some firefighters from the 092 found a family and got them out, but the rest of the rooms were empty."

Justice nodded as he choked back the thick smoke that was now filling his own lungs. He turned to Archer. "Help Thomas get Brian down to the staging area."

Justice and the captain from the 092 had set up a staging area on the fifth floor—one floor below the fire—where all the firefighters were to meet once they had checked their assigned areas.

"What about you?" Archer asked.

"I'll check the last room and then I'll be right behind you."

Archer hesitated for a split second, then bent to help Thomas pick Brian up under the arms to drag him down to the staging area. Justice put his mask back on, knowing that if he didn't, he wouldn't make it three feet without putting himself in the same condition as Brian. Then he started down the hall. He had long since given up on stopping the fire—the raging blaze was now clearly out of control—and had quickly shifted his focus to getting all of his men, as well as any survivors, safely out of the building.

Justice reached the door to the last room just as the whistle on his own air pack began to blow, signaling that he only had a fourth of his air left. Trying to ignore the uneasy feeling in the pit of his stomach but very much aware of the dire need to hurry, he aimed his thermal imaging camera at the door to see if there were any heat waves coming from it. The thermal imaging camera helped firefighters to detect survivors by picking up their images in a smoke-filled room and alerting them to heat-sensitive areas. Seeing no indication that there was a fire in the room, Justice kicked the door in, then stepped back, just in case. When there was no backdraft, Justice stepped in, then quickly scanned his camera around to see if there was anyone still in the room. Seeing no image appear on the screen, he ran his hand along the wall, making his way toward the bathroom. He had only made it a third of the way across the room when two walls burst into flame, dramatically intensifying the temperature in the room.

Justice dropped to his belly, unable to stand the heat. He could hear his breathing coming in enormous gulps and knew that he was quickly depleting his air supply, but he couldn't seem to slow his breathing or his increasingly accelerated heart rate. With images of Anna filling his head, he turned and started back for the front door. It was time to get out. But the fire was taking over, the heat mounting until Justice could feel the soles of his boots melting on his feet. He continued to crawl toward the door, but his body seemed to be in slow motion, the heat and the lack of oxygen making his head spin. Then, despite his brain screaming for him to keep going, his body gave out and he crumpled to the floor, the fire just seconds from engulfing him. He was going to die, but all he could think of was Anna and the unborn child he would never get to hold.

* * *

When Justice opened his eyes, instead of seeing a raging inferno, he saw a paramedic bent over him calling out his name. He was outside the building. A gust of wind flurried the paramedic's hair, and Justice could hear a loud swooshing sound filling the air.

"Just hold still. Air Evac is going to fly you to the nearest available hospital," the medic said once he saw that Justice was responsive.

"My men?" Justice gasped, the effort causing a jolt of searing pain deep within his chest.

"Don't try to talk," the medic said. "You've inhaled a lot of smoke."

Incapable of doing much else, Justice begrudgingly complied. His eyes fell on the flames climbing from the hotel before him, his mind trying to pull itself from the fog it was in. He vaguely remembered the walls bursting into flame, then crawling toward the door, his body no longer able to move. But how had he gotten out? Suddenly, every muscle in his body tightened as a new set of images flashed before his eyes.

Archer stood over him, calling his name, but Justice couldn't respond—couldn't breathe. The last of his air was gone, and he was seconds from blacking out. Archer looked down at him, his face suddenly filled with determination, though his eyes were unable to hide the dread.

"No," Justice breathed, remembering what had happened next.

With Justice too lethargic to stop him, Archer pulled his air pack off his back, removed his mask, and quickly put it on Justice.

"Hold on," Archer said, his eyes locked on Justice. "You're going to see your wife again. I promise."

Suddenly pulled back to the present by a commotion a few feet from him, Justice slowly turned toward a group of medics performing CPR on a man who was stretched out on the ground. One of the paramedics was doing chest compressions while the other shook his head, saying the man was already gone. Justice felt a sob rising in his throat as he watched the second medic stand back, giving Justice a clear shot of the young fireman lying lifeless in the parking lot of the hotel.

"No!" Justice cried, a new wave of pain coursing through his battered body.

The medic next to him immediately pulled up Justice's sleeve and inserted a needle into his arm, temporarily alleviating the pain that promised to return as soon as his eyes reopened.

CHAPTER SEVENTEEN

9:25 P.M. / Los Angeles; Lincoln Tower parking garage

"It's your door, Elder," the missionary standing next to Hunter said as he stood back to allow him to knock.

Hunter could feel his pulse quicken. It had happened. He didn't know how, but it had. He was a missionary. Hardly able to contain his excitement, he started forward just as a third elder stepped up to the door, his back now to Hunter. Hunter looked at the young elder in confusion.

"I thought I was taking this door," Hunter said to his companion.

His companion didn't respond, didn't even acknowledge that he had heard him. Instead, the other elder rang the doorbell. A moment later a woman opened the door, and the elders introduced themselves. The woman's face lit up, and she excitedly welcomed them into her house. Hunter was thrilled. He took a step forward and extended his hand to the woman, but she turned and started down the hall. Seconds later the woman was introducing them to her husband and some friends who were visiting. Hunter could feel his smile spreading. He had dreamed of this day since he was twelve years old, and now here it was. If only he could share with this family the love he felt for Jesus Christ, could show them by example how the gospel could completely change their lives. He was so caught up in the moment that he didn't notice the man sitting next to him until he spoke.

"Hello, Hunter."

Hunter turned to look at the man. He was dressed in white.

"Who are you?" Hunter asked in confusion.

"I'm here to bring you home," the man said, his eyes kind.

Hunter stared at the man in confusion. "What are you talking about?"

The man's gaze seemed to penetrate to Hunter's very soul, conveying his meaning in an instant. Hunter slowly turned and glanced around the room. The two missionaries were talking to the family, totally oblivious to Hunter and the man's presence, as if they weren't even there. Hunter turned back to the man, the reality of the situation suddenly washing over him.

"I can't die," Hunter began in desperation. "Not yet. Please! I need more time."

The man's entire countenance radiated warmth, his gentle smile instantly calming Hunter and filling him with an indescribable peace. A part of Hunter wanted to go with him and leave the pain and the struggle behind, but the other part wasn't ready. He needed to serve a mission.

Finally, after what seemed an eternity, the man glanced toward the family in the room. "Because of your missionary efforts, these people will receive the gospel." Then he turned back to Hunter. "You will be given the time necessary."

Hunter felt the joy of the man's words filling his entire soul until he felt he would burst. He looked over at the family, taking in each of their faces, anticipating the moment when he would teach them the gospel. Then he glanced at the two missionaries. It was only then that he noticed that their faces were blurred. He smiled knowingly. One of the elders would be him. He looked closer at the two, but as he did, the image began to fade, and he was thrust back to the present.

The pain that had raged through his body earlier had vanished, leaving in its place a numbing chill that made his entire body tremble. Even his head was foggy, making every thought a concerted effort. He slowly opened his eyes, seeing nothing but darkness surrounding him. He tried to call out, but his voice was so weak that it sounded like a raspy moan. Where were Jax and the guy who had been with him? And the girl they had pulled from the car? Were they okay? Had they made it out? Hunter closed his eyes again and prayed for strength, too tired to do anything else. He had to hold on. Help would come. It had to. And yet, with each passing moment, as much as he tried to stop it, he could feel his life slipping away.

* * *

Jax felt a flood of relief rush through him the second he saw Lakesha's body slip through the narrow gap in the elevator doors and into James's outstretched arms. James, a complete stranger, had heard them call for help just a few minutes before and had climbed down the shaft, lowering himself into the battered elevator.

"Is she okay?" Jax called out as he glanced through the narrow opening to the two people safely inside.

"Yeah, but I'm going to need some help getting her up the shaft," James called back.

Jax turned to Mike and handed him the tube of petroleum jelly before glancing toward an enormous steel beam nearby that was moaning from stress. "You'd better hurry," Jax said quietly.

Mike nodded, his hand shaking a little as he began spreading the jelly over his chest and shoulders.

"You ready?" Jax asked once he was done.

Mike nodded, then quickly stuck his arm through the gap and took hold of James's outstretched hand. Jax hurriedly took a stance behind him, ready to push as soon as Mike gave the signal. Mike exhaled all the air from his lungs, then gave Jax a thumbs-up. With James yanking Mike forward, Jax began pushing with all he had. Mike let out a grunt, his body temporarily wedged between the doors, but after another hard push from Jax, he slipped through the gap and landed in a heap on the floor of the elevator. Jax leaned up against the elevator doors, breathing hard.

"Now it's your turn," James said, reaching his hand through the gap.

Jax looked through the narrow opening in the doors, his eyes going past James to Mike as he shook his head. "I can't. Not yet."

Mike rushed to the door, his face frantic. "Jax, he's dead. There's nothing you can do. You've got to get out of there! This building's coming down!"

Jax was already shaking his head. "I'm sorry."

"What's he doing?" James asked, his voice rising sharply as he looked from Mike back to Jax. "We've got to get up that shaft *now!*"

Knowing that James was right, Jax quickly bent down and picked up the flashlight Mike had left propped on the cinder block, since James already had a flashlight in the elevator, then turned to leave, not wanting them to stay and risk their lives because of him.

"Jax, don't do this!" Mike called out.

Jax stopped, then slowly glanced over his shoulder. "I have to," he said simply.

Mike stood there for a moment, his mouth opening and shutting and his face transformed by a dozen different emotions before softening to a reluctant acceptance. He nodded. "I know," he finally managed.

"You better go," Jax said with a sad smile. Then, not knowing if he would ever see them again, he turned and walked away.

* * *

Jax got down on his stomach and peered through the broken windshield, expecting—and a part of him hoping, for Hunter's sake—to find that his friend was already gone. Instead, as the flashlight illuminated his face, Hunter's brow creased and, after a concentrated effort, his eyes slowly opened.

"*Jax?*" Hunter breathed, his expression confused.

Jax nodded, fighting back the tears. Hunter looked awful. His skin was gray, his lips a sickly shade of blue, and his eyes surrounded by dark circles. "It's me, Hunter. I'm right here."

"The girl?" Hunter asked anxiously.

"Lakesha's fine. You saved her life."

Hunter closed his eyes, relief temporarily softening his features. "Good," he whispered.

Jax couldn't help but think of the irony. Lakesha was alive because of Hunter, and now Hunter was dying because he had saved Lakesha. It all seemed so unfair, and yet Jax was certain that even if Hunter had known the outcome, he still would have done the same thing.

"It's so cold," Hunter mumbled, his blue lips trembling.

Jax reached down and touched the top of Hunter's head. "It'll be over soon," he said, hearing his own voice crack with emotion.

Hunter closed his eyes, obviously drained by the effort of speaking. Then, after a few seconds, he seemed to drift back to the semiconscious state he had been in. Jax stared down at him, thinking of Hunter's parents. They would be devastated. Jax felt his throat constrict. He had always considered himself strong. He had been team captain of his high school football and wrestling teams, and first-string quarterback at the Y, but watching his friend slowly die and knowing that there wasn't one thing he could do to stop it made him want to curl up and sob like a baby. Jax was pulled from his thoughts as Hunter began to cough. It took several seconds for him to finally catch his breath.

"I'm here. I'm right here," Jax said, trying to comfort Hunter, knowing he could do nothing else to alleviate his suffering.

Hunter shut his eyes again and was silent for a moment, his entire body straining as he fought to draw in each shaky breath.

"You've got to go . . . before it's too late," Hunter whispered.

Jax shook his head. "I won't leave you."

Hunter's eyes locked on Jax. "Then you'll die—and I can't let that happen."

Hunter was going to give up; Jax could see it in his face. He watched as Hunter closed his eyes. But before Jax could call out to him, Hunter spoke. "I'm not going to serve a mission," he whispered as he opened his eyes to look at Jax, the pain in his face tearing a gaping hole in Jax's chest.

At that moment, Jax knew that if he could have changed places with Hunter, he would have. Hunter would have made a wonderful missionary; he had been waiting for the day he could put on a white shirt and tie and knock on a few doors since he was a kid. No one wanted it more, and yet here he was, minutes from death, trapped beneath a huge chunk of concrete, his dream just barely out of reach.

"Yes, you will," Jax began, his tears finally falling. "Just not here."

Hunter stared at Jax, his eyes suddenly widening as the implication of Jax's words hit him, instantly lighting the graying tones of his face. His eyes filled with tears. Then he looked past Jax, his expression suddenly lit with an inexplicable joy.

"Grandpa!" he breathed in wonder.

Jax glanced over his shoulder, and though there was no one there, he felt a tingling prickle run through him. He looked back at Hunter.

"But what about that family?" Hunter asked, his brow knit in confusion as he stared over Jax's shoulder into the darkness.

After a moment Hunter's eyes widened again; he smiled, and tears ran down his cheeks. He glanced at Jax, all the pain that had wracked his body seemingly swallowed up in an indescribable peace radiating from him. Then, almost as suddenly as it had come, the expression on Hunter's face faded, and his raspy breathing stopped. It was over. Hunter was gone. It was then that Jax pulled his knees to his chest and sobbed until he could barely breathe.

* * *

Jax sat next to Hunter for several minutes, but when the building began to protest its duress, he reluctantly stood and looked down at his friend for the last time in mortality.

"Good-bye, Hunter," he said, knowing that this moment would forever be etched in his mind.

He said a silent prayer, thanking his Heavenly Father for allowing him to be apart of the miracle that had just occurred. Then, wiping his tears from his dirty face, he turned and started toward the elevator. When he finally got there, he found it empty. Though he hadn't expected anyone to wait for him, he suddenly felt a sense of loneliness and despair he had never before experienced. As he looked around the dark parking garage feeling the anguish of losing one of his best friends, new tears surfaced. He fought them back, trying unsuccessfully to remember the feelings that he had just experienced. When they didn't return, he picked up the discarded tube of petroleum jelly and began applying it to his body. Then he reached his hands and head through the gap in the doors and, following Mike's example, exhaled and pushed. Though he made it farther through the gap than he had before when they had tried without the jelly, his thick chest was soon stuck. Jax tried again, desperate to make it through the narrow opening, but again his efforts failed.

"Please, Father," he begged, knowing that he would never be able to do this on his own. "Please, help me!"

Within seconds, Jax saw the light of a flashlight reflect off the walls of the elevator, followed immediately by a thud as someone jumped down onto the metal roof.

"You need some help?" Mike called as he lowered himself through the opening in the roof of the elevator.

Jax exhaled, a surge of relief rushing through him.

As soon as Mike had reached the floor of the elevator, he grabbed ahold of Jax's arm and began to pull. Though it took several minutes,

Jax was finally able to slip through the gap. He collapsed on the floor, his chest rising and falling rapidly as he took in deep gulps of air.

Mike reached down and offered him a hand up. "I'm sorry about Hunter," he said, once he and Jax were eye to eye.

Jax nodded, the wound too fresh to talk about.

Mike placed his hand on Jax's shoulder. "Come on. Let's get out of here."

As soon as Jax walked out the front doors of Lincoln Tower, his eyes fell on James, the man who had helped them get through the gap in the elevator. He was directing a medic over toward Lakesha, who was lying in the center of the road next to several others in need of medical attention. Jax quickly scanned the survivors, hoping to see Payson, Gwen, and Tristin, but there was no sign of any of them. Knowing that they would never willingly leave the area if they thought that he and Hunter were still trapped inside the building, Jax turned his attention to a paramedic standing nearby.

"I'm looking for some friends," Jax said, following the medic as he made his way to Lakesha. "How do I find out if they've been taken to a hospital?"

"You'll have to go look. We haven't had time to compile a list yet," the medic said as he examined Lakesha's mangled legs.

"There's a hospital not too far from here," Mike offered as he came to stand by Jax's side.

Jax didn't answer; instead, he stood back, looking at what was left of the building before him. From behind him, he could hear a bulky soldier shouting for everyone to get back in case the structure came down. Jax felt his breath catch, not wanting to believe even for a second that his three friends were still trapped inside. Yet at the same time, he knew at least one of his friends would never leave.

"Hey, you can't go in there!"

Jax glanced over to see a soldier approaching James, who seemed to be on his way back into the building.

"Look, I've got to get back in there," James insisted.

"I'm sorry, sir, but I'm not letting anyone in that building."

James was just about to protest when another man came running up beside him. "Where's McKenna?" the man asked, looking around frantically.

"I haven't found her yet."

The man looked as if his knees were about to give way. "James, she's in there. She just called me on my satellite phone."

"You talked to her?"

The man was beside himself now. "Sutherland is after her. If he finds her, he'll kill her."

James turned back to the soldier, his jaw tight and his face filled with determination. "I've got to get in there!"

The soldier stepped between James and the front door, his tone stern. "Sir, I'm sorry, but for your own safety, that's not going to happen."

Jax looked away, feeling guilty that James had taken the time to rescue them and was now unable to get back into the building to help the person he had come there to find—someone he apparently cared about deeply. Saying a silent prayer that whomever James was looking for would somehow be protected, Jax turned and walked to the center of the street, moving out of the way of falling debris.

"Jax!"

Instantly recognizing the voice, Jax frantically scanned the dark street before him. Tristin, who had been sitting on a curb a safe distance away, was now standing and waving her arms wildly. Jax felt a surge of relief the second he spotted her, though it was short-lived when he saw that she was alone.

Tristin shook her head as she approached, the look on her face all the answer he needed. "They're still in the building. They went to help some people stranded in an elevator, but they should have come out by now."

Jax felt nauseated as his mind flashed back to the wreckage of the two elevators sitting at the bottom of Lincoln Tower.

"What's wrong?" Tristin asked, seeing his reaction.

Jax shook his head. "Nothing," he said, trying to sound convincing, though his knees suddenly felt weak and he had to take a seat on the curb to keep from falling. "I'm sure they're fine."

Then Tristin's eyes widened. "Where's Hunter?" she asked, sitting down next to him and taking him firmly by the arm.

Jax's eyes climbed the high-rise he had just escaped before slowly turning back to Tristin. "Tristin . . . Hunter didn't make it."

She stared at Jax, the words not seeming to register. "No," she finally breathed as she shook her head slowly back and forth, tears welling in her eyes.

Jax reached out and wrapped his arms around her while she buried her face in his chest. After several minutes she pulled back, her green eyes glassy with tears. "What about Gwen and Payson?"

Jax looked back at Lincoln Tower, the building now a dark silhouette. "I don't know," he said, praying with everything in him that they hadn't been in one of the elevators that had plunged to the base of the high-rise. "But we can't give up hope—not yet. If there's any way out, Payson and Gwen will find it."

* * *

Payson watched as Chad prepared Kimberly to be lowered down into the shaft. Then, knowing that he would be going down too, he made his way over to Anna to check on her one last time.

"How are you feeling?" he asked, taking a seat on the floor next to her, then glancing down at the baby snuggled in her arms.

"Surprisingly, I feel pretty good," Anna said, her eyes going back to the baby.

"He's beautiful. Have you picked out a name?"

Anna shook her head. "Not yet." Then she turned to look at Payson, touching his arm. "Thanks again for delivering him. Sorry it was kind of . . . intense."

Payson rolled up his sleeves to reveal several fingernail marks. "Kind of?" he asked, though a big smile was already spreading across his face. "So tell me, how did you and your husband hear about the Church?"

Anna glanced down at the baby. "A couple of missionaries knocked on our door. I was interested, and Justice . . ." She shook her head before looking back at Payson. "I guess he's just not ready yet."

Payson nodded. He didn't want to pry, but he felt a kinship to this woman and her family. He reached down and touched the baby. "You never know what the Lord has in store. Sometimes we just have to have faith and be patient."

"You're right, sometimes we do have to be patient, and . . ." Anna stopped, her eyes on Gwen. "And sometimes we have to turn our faith into action."

Payson sighed, understanding the innuendo all too well. "You're probably right," he said as he squeezed Anna's arm. "I'll see you at the bottom." He stood, making his way over to Gwen.

"Can we talk?" Payson asked.

Gwen looked up from her spot on the floor next to Sam, who quickly looked at her. "Just get it over with," he said.

Payson could feel his jaw pull taut at Sam's comment, but he held his tongue instead, keeping his eyes on Gwen as she finally nodded, then stood. Payson started down the hall, wanting to have at least some degree of privacy. When he was certain they were out of earshot, but not so far away that they couldn't see the light from Chad's flashlight, he stopped, then turned to face her. Though he knew what he wanted to say, he suddenly didn't know how to begin. She was standing so close to him, her blue eyes looking back at him expectantly. How could he say good-bye when his heart ached at the very thought?

"Can we sit?" Gwen finally asked, breaking the silence.

Payson's eyes moved across her face, and he once again noticed how tired she looked. He quickly walked into a nearby room and, by the small amount of light coming in through the windows, found a chair and brought it back for her.

"Thank you," she said as she sat down, unable to hide her fatigue.

"Gwen, what's wrong?" Payson asked, no longer willing to accept the excuses she had given.

"Nothing's wrong. I told you, I—"

"Gwen, don't lie to me; I can tell you don't feel well," Payson said with mounting concern. "Maybe you have some internal injuries. That would explain the vomiting and the nausea. Did you fall in the elevator, or did anyone slam into you during the earthquake? You might not have even realized that the blow was severe enough to do any real damage. I had a cousin once who—"

"Payson, I have cancer," Gwen said, the words tumbling out in a rush.

For a minute, Payson felt as though the rotation of the earth had suddenly and violently been stopped, throwing his entire world off its axis. "Cancer?" he breathed, the word siphoning the air right out of him.

Gwen shook her head, apparently berating herself for telling him. "That's why I came here. Sam's family recommended Doctor Sing. He's one of the foremost physicians in the country for the type of cancer I have. I'd just had a round of chemotherapy when I ran into you outside the elevator."

Payson had to reach out to brace himself with the wall. "Why didn't you—"

"Because I knew you'd stay with me if I told you, and I didn't want that."

Payson gaped at her, everything suddenly making perfect sense. "Of course I'd have stayed with you—not because you're sick, but because I love you."

"Payson, I could die," Gwen said bluntly. "The doctor said that more likely than not I'll lose my hair and that there's even a possibility that I'll never be able to have children."

"Hair grows back," Payson offered. "And even if it doesn't, you'll still be beautiful. And we could adopt. It doesn't matter to me if our children have our DNA. They'd probably be grateful to know they weren't biologically connected to my Uncle Leonard anyway."

"Payson, there's a thirty-five percent chance I won't make it to Christmas."

Payson flinched, feeling as though he had just slammed into a cement wall at high speed, though he quickly tried to recover his reaction for her sake. "We might never make it out of this building," he replied. "Or even if we do, I could have some kind of accident and die tomorrow. Life doesn't give us a guarantee." Then his voice caught and he had to lower it to a whisper. "But God does. If we're married in the temple, even death can't separate us . . . not for long anyway."

Gwen's eyes were blurry with tears now, the overflow making streams down her dimpled cheeks. Payson immediately dropped to one knee, his eyes never leaving hers. "I want to marry you, Gwen. I've never wanted anything so much in my life."

Gwen was crying now, but Payson just enfolded her in his arms, wishing he could somehow take her pain away. "I love you," he whispered.

"I love you too," she said, her thin shoulders rising and falling.

Payson glanced in Sam's direction, suddenly remembering the obstacle that still stood between them. "What about him?"

Gwen reluctantly pulled back, following his gaze. "Payson, I love Sam," she began. "And I always will. But I'm not *in love* with him. I met and taught him and his family on my mission."

Payson slowly began to nod in understanding.

"Sam decided to transfer to the Y, and when he came up to check out campus, he ran into me. When I told him about the cancer, he called his dad, who is also a physician, and he told me about Doctor Sing."

Payson glanced over at Sam. "I feel like such an idiot. He was only trying to help you, and I was so jealous I couldn't see straight."

"Don't feel too bad. I knew what you thought, but I let you think it anyway because I didn't want you to feel obligated to stay with me."

Payson eyes locked on hers. "Don't you ever think that. I'd rather have one day with you than a lifetime with anyone else." Then he pulled her into his arms again and held her.

"I guess she told you?"

Payson and Gwen pulled back, their eyes on Sam, who had come up beside Payson and now stood there smiling.

"So, do you still want to punch me?" Sam asked, his cheeks splitting into a grin.

Payson smiled as he stuck his hand out to shake the man's hand. "I never said anything about punching you."

"No, but you wanted to," Sam said with a laugh. "Hey, I don't blame you. I'd put up a fight for Gwen too if she loved me half as much as she loves you."

Payson squeezed Gwen's hand before glancing up at Chad, who was looking their way.

"You ready?" Chad called out to Payson.

Gwen looked at Chad, then at Payson in confusion. "What's going on?"

"Chad asked me to rappel down first so I can be at the bottom to help Kimberly," Payson said.

"But there's no light," Gwen said, her eyes showing her concern. "Shouldn't we wait until morning?"

"We can't wait," Sam interjected. "This building won't make it through the night."

"Sam's right," Payson agreed. "We've got to get out now."

* * *

Payson stood at the edge of the elevator shaft, ready to descend into the darkness.

"Be careful of the cables," Chad said, clearly trying to sound casual, though from the look on Gwen's face he didn't succeeded.

"I'll be okay," Payson assured them both.

Gwen didn't look convinced, but she went to him and kissed him lightly on the lips anyway. "I love you," she whispered, making his whole body tingle.

Payson smiled. "Yeah, but will you say that after we're married and I'm watching a football game when you want me to take out the garbage?"

"Maybe I'll just watch the football game with you," Gwen said with a grin.

"Okay, now I *am* fighting for her," Sam teased, a giant smile lighting his face.

"Me too," Chad added. "Any girl who likes football is worth a little roughing up."

Payson smiled, though his expression grew serious as he turned back to Gwen. "I'll see you soon."

Gwen swiped at a tear. "You better."

Without another word, Payson stepped off into the darkness with Sam and Chad holding the other end of the rope. At first Payson could see the light from the small flashlight Gwen was holding, but as he descended deeper into the shaft, the light gradually faded until he could barely see anything. It was then that the earthquake hit. It started with a rumble that gradually grew until the sound seemed to consume everything. With a force that took his breath away, Payson slammed hard into the side of the elevator shaft, only to swing back and plow into the opposite wall with an even greater force. Payson could feel himself screaming, but he couldn't hear it over the shrill pitch of metal twisting and bending. Protecting his head as best he could, he slammed into the sides of the shaft several more times. Then, as quickly as it had started, the earthquake stopped. Payson's breathing came in gasps as he continued to swing slowly back and forth in the darkness.

"Payson!" Gwen screamed, the sound echoing down the shaft.

"I'm still here," Payson called back, though his entire body was trembling and pain was beginning to shoot across different parts of his body.

"Are you hurt?" Chad shouted.

"Not too bad," Payson called back.

"Hold on. We'll lower you down."

Payson felt them begin to lower him, but at the same time he felt friction on the rope, as if it were twisted around something.

"Stop!" Payson shouted, realizing in an instant what had happened. "The rope's twisted around one of the cables. I can hear it fraying."

For a minute no one called back. Payson's heart pulsed violently as he waited to see if the rope would snap. "Hey! Did you hear me?" he shouted.

"We heard you," Chad called out. "Just try not to panic. Can you swing yourself to the wall and grab ahold of the ladder?"

"I don't know. I'm not sure how far up the rope is tangled," Payson said, reaching his hand out and following the rope up as far as he could.

"If you can't make it to the wall, I'll send Sam down to help you," Chad called out.

Knowing that the rope might sever at any moment, Payson swallowed hard, then began to swing his body back and forth, hearing the rope fray further with each swing. "The rope's going to snap!" Payson called out.

"Okay. Hold still. Sam's on his way down," Chad yelled.

Payson looked up the shaft, but there was nothing but darkness. He closed his eyes, trying to calm himself, though the next few minutes promised to be the longest of his life.

CHAPTER EIGHTEEN

McKenna held tight to the handrail as she stood, ready to make her way carefully down the stairs in the dark. Fear coursed through her, making her entire body tremble. Another earthquake had hit just moments earlier, making the upper floors sway until McKenna feared that the massive structure would finally collapse. By the time it had stopped, McKenna had made her decision. There was no way she was going to just sit there and wait for James to find her. Regardless of the pain or the impenetrable darkness, she was heading down. She had only made it down a couple of stairs when the satellite phone in her pocket rang, startling her. Holding tight to the railing in order to steady her trembling legs, she answered the phone. The second she heard her father's voice, she knew something was wrong.

"McKenna, you've got to get out of the building. They won't let James back in."

"Who won't?" McKenna asked, trying to remain calm herself, though her hands were shaking so severely that she almost dropped the phone. "What happened?"

"It doesn't matter," Lawrence began, clearly fighting to remain calm. "You've just got to get out of there. James is going to try to find another way in, but you can't wait for him. There might not be time."

McKenna could hear the desperation in her father's voice. She leaned against the wall, fearing that her legs would give out.

"McKenna, did you hear me?" Lawrence shouted, his calm courtroom persona replaced by panic.

"I heard you," McKenna said, her own voice beginning to strain as the reality of the situation began to sink in.

"Start down now, and hurry, but be careful just in case that lunatic is still in there."

"I don't know if I can," McKenna mumbled, feeling tears begin to fall.

"You've got to!" Lawrence shouted. "You don't have a choice, McKenna. Your life depends on it." He fell silent for a moment, but when he finally spoke, his tone was more subdued, almost gentle. "When your mother died, a part of me wanted to curl up and die with her. She was everything to me. But then I saw you. When the doctor placed you in my arms for the first time and I looked down at your little face, so fragile and helpless, I felt my heart begin to beat again. I was stronger than I knew . . . and so are you."

McKenna couldn't speak, could barely breathe.

"I'm proud of you, of the woman you've become," Lawrence finally said, his words releasing the tears that McKenna had stubbornly been attempting to fight back.

She nodded, her throat tight. "Thanks, Dad," she whispered.

"I'll see you soon," Lawrence said.

"You too," McKenna said, unable to say anything else as she clicked off the phone and put it in her pocket.

For a moment she just stood there in the dark, feeling more alone than she had ever felt in her life. Her father, who had always seemed so sure of himself, was now crumbling like the building around her. And James, who had always been her emotional support as well as her best friend, would not be coming to rescue her this time. She was on her own. McKenna was pulled from her thoughts by a faint, though familiar smell. Her eyes widened when she realized what it was—cigarette smoke. Someone was in the stairwell with her. McKenna sucked her breath in, her eyes racing across the dark expanse for the glimmer of a lit cigarette. At the same time, she heard footsteps coming from the stairs below her, just on the other side of the bend in the stairwell. It was Sutherland. It had to be. Who else would be coming up when the building was on the brink of coming down?

Shooting a glance toward the door to the next level, though it was too dark in the stairwell to see it, she began to move, knowing that Sutherland would have heard her talking on the phone. Temporarily forgetting the pain, she threw open the door and slipped inside, hearing Sutherland click on his flashlight and quicken his pace behind her. She slid her hand across the wall, feeling her way since she couldn't see. She knew she was next to the elevators and needed to get farther down the hall to one of the rooms so she could hide, but she was out of time. At any moment, Sutherland would be opening the door she had just come through, and then he would have her.

It was then that McKenna remembered seeing that one of the elevator doors on that floor had been pried open. She had noticed it earlier when she and Nathan had gone to his office with Sutherland. The woman she had met in the hall had told her that some of the men trapped on the upper floors had come down through the shaft to this floor because the stairs for the two stories above had been taken out.

Feeling a familiar knot form in her stomach at the thought of heights, but out of options, McKenna threw the crutch down the hall, knowing that she would never be able to keep her grip and hold on to the crutch at the same time. She felt for the opening in the wall and then the ladder. Finding it, she swung herself into the shaft. Biting down on her lip against the pain, she held tight to the metal bars, the stress on her knee causing her entire leg to throb. It was then that she heard the door to the floor she was on swing open and slam hard against the wall. McKenna squeezed her eyes shut, though she couldn't see anyway. She held her breath and listened as Sutherland started down the hall, going in the direction she had guessed he would look. Only then did she release the air in her lungs. She had to get out of there, but she would have to wait until he left, thinking that she had sneaked past him and doubled back to the stairs. She couldn't take the chance of him hearing her as she climbed out of the shaft.

Tightening her grip, she waited, hearing him go from room to room until he finally headed back toward the stairs and the adjacent elevators. McKenna held her breath again, expecting at any moment to hear the swoosh of the door opening, but there was only silence. Then, after a moment, he was there, standing next to the shaft and holding the paddle that she had been using as a crutch. He threw it down the shaft, then took a long drag on the cigarette in his mouth.

McKenna could see the tip of his cigarette glowing red as he stood right next to the drop-off. When he exhaled, he was so close that the smoke swirled around her face. McKenna didn't breathe, didn't move a muscle. Instead, she watched silently, expecting death to come at any moment as Sutherland inhaled the smoke one more time, then flicked the butt into the shaft, its glow swallowed up almost instantly as it disappeared into the darkness. The sound that McKenna heard moments later was like the roar of a lion magnified a thousand times over as an enormous fireball erupted at the bottom of the shaft, causing the entire building to tremble. McKenna clung to the metal stairs, unable to do anything but watch in horror as the fire rose several floors in a matter of seconds, lighting up everything in the shaft and promising to consume anything in its path. She tightened her grip on the rungs and then glanced at Sutherland, who stood gaping down at the swirling flames, his jaw falling slack. McKenna quickly closed her eyes, praying that he would step back from the shaft before he spotted her, but he didn't. When McKenna opened her eyes, Sutherland was staring right at her, his features momentarily twisted in disbelief, though his expression was all too quickly replaced by a hate-filled smirk.

"So there you are," he said, his eyes like dark marbles, lifeless and devoid of sympathy.

McKenna's palms were slick with sweat, and her limbs were trembling so severely that she was sure she would slip and fall into the raging fire below.

Sutherland glanced down at the fire, then back at her, his face flooding with a sick satisfaction. "It won't be long before that ladder is too hot to hold on to."

McKenna looked down at the glowing inferno, then quickly back at Sutherland. "Don't do this," she begged.

"Give me the satellite phone, and I'll help you out," he said calmly, extending his hand.

Desperate to get out of the shaft, she clung to the ladder with one hand and then reached for the phone in her pocket with the other. Then, having no other choice, she extended it to him.

"Now the disk," Sutherland said.

McKenna hesitated. He was lying; she could see it in his face. Sutherland had no intention of helping her. In that moment her fear turned to rage. She began to shake her head defiantly. "Liar! You'll just leave me here to die."

A slow smile spread across his face. "I guess when you put it that way, there's really no need for me to get the disk anyway. It'll just be destroyed—along with you."

His words seemed to steal her breath, but she couldn't resist striking a blow herself. "I might die in here, but you'll die right along with me. You just severed the only way out."

McKenna expected her words to instantly wipe the smirk from his ugly lips, but instead his smile broadened. "That might have been the case before you handed me this phone, but not now." With that he began to dial. A few moments later he clicked off the phone, having confirmed that his private helicopter was preparing to air-vac him off the roof. His eyes scanned over her. "It's too bad that someone as beautiful as you has to die."

"You're disgusting," McKenna snapped, her eyes searing through him, her body trembling.

He feigned offense, placing one hand over his heart as if her words had hurt him, then his smile broadened. "I'd love to stay and chat, but I've got to get up to the top through the vent shafts and you've got to . . . die," he said indifferently.

McKenna wanted to beg him to take her with him, but she knew he would never let her live, so instead she held his gaze, her jaw tight, until he finally turned and walked away. It was then that the tears came. Sutherland was right. In a very short time the fire below would heat the metal stairs until they would be impossible to hold on to. If she wanted to live, she needed to get up to the roof. Fighting to regain control of her emotions, she reached for the next bar, biting her lip against the pain that erupted the second she bent her knee. She climbed several rungs, willing her body forward, knowing that if she didn't keep going she would die. She thought of James and her father, who were both down at the base of Lincoln Tower watching helplessly as the building was consumed by fire. That thought alone pushed her forward, helping her to bear the pain and quicken her pace as she made her way to the top of the forty-story building.

* * *

"Help me!" Payson screamed, the fire just a few floors below him.

"I'm coming," Sam called out as he hurried down the metal stairs in the shaft a few yards away from Payson.

"I can't wait!" Payson cried, feeling the heat singeing his clothes.

"Swing toward the wall," Sam called out, his eyes on the cable where Payson's rope was tangled. "I'll cut the rope."

The heat was building, the entire shaft illuminated by the fire, and for a moment, Payson couldn't take his eyes from the twisting flames below him.

"Payson! Look at me," Sam yelled.

Payson slowly turned to look at him, though his body felt immobilized by fear. Sam's forehead was beaded with sweat, and he was struggling to breathe in the extreme heat.

"Swing toward me," Sam repeated as he made his way down the last few rungs so that he was parallel to Payson.

Payson's eyes flashed back to the fire as it began to climb even higher.

"Look at me!" Sam demanded, his face flushed and his shirt soaked with sweat.

Payson slowly pulled his eyes from the flames. "I'm going to die," he breathed, feeling every muscle in his body tighten with terror.

"No, you're not!" Sam shouted back, rotating his hands on the hot metal rungs. "You're going to help me get Gwen and the rest of them out of here."

Payson shook his head, Gwen's name pulling him from the state of panic that was quickly paralyzing him. He swallowed hard, forcing himself to look at Sam and not the flames which continued to build.

"Swing toward me," Sam said as he pulled a Swiss army knife from his pocket. "I'll grab ahold of you and cut the rope."

Payson bobbed his head. "Okay."

He glanced up at the rope that had frayed considerably as it had rubbed up against the cable. Knowing that any movement could snap it but also fully aware that if he didn't move, the fire would reach him in minutes, he began to swing toward Sam. It took several attempts, but Sam finally caught hold of his outstretched arm and pulled him toward the stairs. Then, with the blue tips of the flames less than two floors below them, Sam severed the rope with his knife, and the two scrambled up the metal rungs. By the time they reached the others, Payson was exhausted. He crumpled to the ground while Gwen bent down next to him, her cheeks damp and her eyes filled with tears. She didn't say a word, but instead wrapped her arms around him and cried.

"We've got to find another way out of here," Chad said as he scanned the little group around him.

"How?" Anna cried as she clutched her baby tightly in her arms.

"I'm not sure what happened, but I think the fire started in the elevator shaft. If we hurry, we can climb down to the next floor through the shaft, then open the doors to that level and take the stairs before the fire spreads to the rest of the building."

"And if we can't?" Sam asked, his chest rising and falling.

Chad took a deep breath but didn't answer the question. He continued on. "I saw a trash slide on the third floor. If we can make it down that far, we can use the slide."

With Gwen's help, Payson was already getting to his feet.

Chad turned to Sam. "You take the baby, and I'll get Kimberly."

Sam glanced over at Kimberly, who looked as though she were slipping further into a state of shock. Then he turned back to Chad, his eyes going to the ribs Chad had been favoring. "There's no way you're going to be able to carry her down that shaft. You'll both end up dead. Just strap her to my back."

Chad gave Sam a hard look before shaking his head slowly. "Are you sure?"

Sam let his breath out. "We don't have a choice."

Chad hesitated for just a moment, but with smoke already wafting up through the shaft and across their feet, he quickly complied. A few minutes later, Sam made his way to the opening in the shaft with Kimberly on his back. The woman protested at first, screaming and crying hysterically, but after a few minutes, she passed out, her body dead weight on Sam's back and shoulders. Sam, Chad, and Payson had already agreed that Payson would go down first so he could open the shaft door one floor below them with the metal bar he had placed in his back pocket. He walked to the drop-off, then glanced back at Gwen. She quickly stepped to him and kissed him, the intensity stealing his breath. When she finally stepped back, the tears that had been in her eyes ran in streams down her cheeks.

"Be careful," she whispered.

He nodded, his throat too tight to speak. Then, with everyone anxiously watching, he reached in and grabbed ahold of the ladder, grateful that the rungs at this height had not yet heated up, though he was certain that wouldn't last for long. He had only made it down a few feet when Sam swung himself onto the ladder with Kimberly strapped to his back. Payson held his breath, wondering if Sam would be able to keep his grip with the extra weight or if he would fall and drag Kimberly and Payson down with him into the fire. Fortunately for them all, Sam maintained his grip and started the strenuous journey down. Payson tried to widen the gap between them so he could have the shaft doors open before Sam made it to him, but he couldn't help glancing up just to make sure that Gwen and the others were also on their way down. Once he spotted Gwen descending the shaft, he quickened his pace.

"You okay?" Payson called out to Sam.

"I'm okay," Sam said, his breathing labored.

Payson shook his head, knowing that it was taking all of Sam's strength just to maintain his grip as he descended the vertical shaft.

"I'm here," Payson called out once he reached the shaft doors to the next level. "I'll have it open in a minute."

Sam said something, but it came out as more of a grunt. Payson wiped at the sweat dripping from his forehead and then pulled the metal bar from his back pocket and pried it between the closed doors, holding on as best he could.

"You've got to hurry," Sam groaned. "I can't hold on much longer."

"I've almost got it," Payson said as he leaned forward in an attempt to pry the doors apart.

"I'm not going to make it," Sam said, his words sounding more like a resignation than a declaration.

"Yes, you will!" Payson shouted as he slid the doors apart.

A minute later, Payson was standing on the other side of the open elevator doors, his hand stretched out toward Sam. "Give me your hand," he demanded.

"I can't," Sam said, his arms trembling uncontrollably as he gripped the metal rungs that were already heating up.

Payson could see the strain on his face, could hear it in his voice. Knowing that even if he grabbed hold of Sam, he wouldn't be able to support both his and Kimberly's weight, Payson began to pray. The desperate plea for help had no sooner crossed his lips, when Sam leaned over and placed one of his feet in the opening between the doors, then reached one of his hands out and grasped ahold of Payson's. With both of them exerting every ounce of strength they had, and receiving a measure that Payson knew exceeded their own, Payson pulled Sam and Kimberly through the opening, the three of them falling in a heap.

"Is everyone okay?" Chad called out from within the shaft.

Payson looked at Sam and shook his head, still in a state of awe over what had just happened. "We're fine," he finally called back as he got to his feet, knowing he would need to help the others.

A few minutes later, they were all out of the shaft and making their way down the stairs. Payson had Kimberly cradled in his arms while Chad helped Anna and the baby. Sam clutched Gwen's hand, though after his stint in the elevator shaft, it looked like she was the one helping him.

The smoke thickened the lower they got. "We've got to pick up the pace," Chad yelled. "We've got to make it to the third floor before the fire does."

"Are you sure we can get out through there?" Sam asked as he shined the flashlight down the stairwell.

Chad clutched his ribs but didn't answer. "Just hurry!"

Payson tried to keep pace with everyone else, but he was having a hard time keeping his footing with Kimberly in his arms, and he stumbled several times. Chad gave the baby to Anna and moved back to help him, but there was little he could do besides hold on to Payson's belt loop to steady him.

"How much farther?" Payson asked. Sweat ran into his eyes, making it almost impossible to see, especially with only one flashlight.

"Not much," Chad said, coughing against the thick, billowing smoke. "But we're getting close to the fire."

"Take them on ahead," Payson began, knowing that he was slowing them all down. "I'll be right behind you."

Payson paused and struggled to catch his breath.

"If you wait for me," he continued, "that baby won't make it. The smoke is getting too thick."

"We don't have another flashlight—you'll be going in the dark," Chad warned.

"I'll follow the railing down. Prop the door to the third floor open and send someone back for us as soon as all of you get out."

Chad glanced farther down the stairwell to Anna, who was clutching the backpack that held her newborn son. He looked past her to the bend in the stairwell where the others had just passed, then turned back to Payson, a determined look in his eyes. "Keep going, and don't stop. I'll be back for you as soon as I get them out."

Payson nodded, though his arms were burning from exertion and the cut on his head was beginning to drain, the slow drip of blood mingling with his sweat. "I will," he mumbled, trying to sound confident, though his resolve was already weakening.

Chad gave him one more hesitant glance, and then, with a discouraged shake of his head, started down the stairs. Within seconds Payson was standing in the dark stairwell alone. He felt the gloom, the utter despair seeping deep within his soul. He felt the weight of the woman lying unconscious in his arms and the overwhelming responsibility of getting her out alive. Then his mind turned to Gwen, who was hopefully on her way to safety. He thought of Tristin and felt certain she had made it out, though he knew she was probably watching the building burn and worrying for her friends, who were still trapped inside. Then he thought of Jax and Hunter, his two best friends. Where were they? Were they still in the building, or was it already too late? Not liking the emotions these thoughts inspired, Payson lifted Kimberly higher in his arms and quickened his pace.

CHAPTER NINETEEN

"We've got to go back for him!" Gwen cried, fighting to break free of Chad's grip.

Chad held her tight but could feel the strain on his ribs and knew that he wouldn't be able to hold her much longer.

"I'll go back," Chad promised, looking her straight in the eyes.

Gwen was shaking her head, tears staining her cheeks, but Sam had also stepped to her side now. "Gwen, come on. You've got to get on the slide."

The five of them, Chad, Sam, Gwen, Anna, and the baby, had made it to the third floor, where an entire section had been taped off for remodeling. A trash slide that emptied into a metal dumpster in the parking lot below was attached to one of the window frames, providing them with a viable way out, though Chad knew that if they waited too much longer, even that would be consumed by fire.

"I can't," she cried, though her protest was already dissolving into tears.

"Gwen, Chad's a firefighter. He knows what he's doing. He'll find Payson," Sam said, taking her by the arm.

She looked up at him, her blue eyes pained, then slowly turned to Chad, her face showing her resignation. "I can't lose him."

Chad nodded and then watched as Sam led her over to the slide, where Anna and the baby had just disappeared. "You won't," he promised.

A moment later, Gwen was on her way down to the base of Lincoln Tower.

"You're next," Chad said, his eyes on Sam.

"You're going to need some help."

Chad opened his mouth to refuse, but Sam was already heading out of the room with their only flashlight. Having no alternative, Chad hurried after him. The smoke in the stairwell was thick, making it difficult to see.

"Stay close," Chad said, reaching out and taking the flashlight from Sam.

Sam pulled the front of his shirt over his mouth to help filter out the smoke, then nodded, allowing Chad to take the lead. Then the two started up the stairs. They had only made it up one flight when they spotted two dark forms sprawled out on the stairs, neither of them moving. Sam rushed to Payson while Chad bent down next to Kimberly and felt for a pulse. After a quick shake of his head, he glanced over at Sam.

"She's gone," he said. As Chad took in the look of death on Kimberly's face mingled with the pungent smell of smoke in the air, long-buried memories threatened to surface. He shook his head, forcing the thoughts from his mind as he watched Sam lift Payson into his arms.

"Is he alive?"

"Just barely," Sam said.

Without another word, the two of them started back. Chad felt his lungs and eyes burning, so he yanked off his shirt and wrapped it around his mouth, tying it at the back so that his hands were still free to hold tight to the railing. Sam was having a hard time keeping his balance with Payson in his arms, but he still managed to make it to the third floor, though as soon as he was out of the stairwell, his knees buckled and he fell. Chad was at his side in an instant, already grabbing ahold of Payson's arms so he could drag him.

"Come on," Chad shouted to Sam, though the words were muffled through the material wrapped around his mouth.

"I'm sorry," Sam mumbled, slowly getting to his feet, though even his own weight seemed an enormous burden.

Chad coughed on the thick smoke that now filled every inch of airspace as he extended the flashlight to Sam. "It's okay. Come on."

Chad watched as Sam forced himself forward, then his attention shifted to the raging pain in his side as he dragged Payson toward the slide. He tried to push the pain out of his mind and concentrate on the task, but it was too intense.

Just a little farther, he told himself as he continued down the hall. He brushed his shoulder up against the wall so he could feel his way, since the light from the flashlight Sam was holding didn't penetrate far through the smoke.

Though each step was agony, he eventually made it into the room and felt his way toward the slide in the dim evening light coming through the windows. The pain that he had experienced while dragging Payson was nothing compared to the pain that exploded as he attempted to lift him. Chad cried out. He could feel his peripheral vision begin to blur, but he fought it, willing his mind to focus. He lifted Payson's body one last time, positioning him on the slide, then let go. With a surge of relief, he watched as Payson's dark form disappeared into the night. Chad hurried to the window, quickly spotting the shadowed dumpster below. Knowing that they were running dangerously low on time, Chad turned around to help Sam, but there was no sign of him or the flashlight he had been holding.

"Sam!" Chad called out as he started toward the door.

The ventilation around the slide helped to filter out the smoke in the room, making seeing and breathing considerably easier, but the smoke in the hallway was still as dark and dense as pitch.

"Sam!" Chad called out again, feeling his head spin as he started down the smoke-filled corridor.

He searched the darkness, strained his ears for any sound, but there was nothing. Then, not far from where Sam had fallen the first time, he found him, crumpled on the floor. He hurried to him, then bent down and shook him, knowing that there was no way he was going to be able to carry him. Sam began to stir.

"Come on!" Chad shouted, grabbing his arms. "We're almost there."

Sam staggered to his feet, then leaned against Chad for support.

"Where's the flashlight?" Chad asked as he began to choke on the smoke.

Sam groaned. "I don't know."

Chad glanced around the floor, but it was too dark to see anything. He finally shook his head, knowing that they would have to find their way without it. He stood motionless for a moment, trying to remember which was the way to the stairwell and which was the way to the room, but he couldn't tell. His bearings were too jumbled. It was in that instant that the panic began. He could feel his heart rate accelerating, could feel his breathing coming in bursts. Then, from the corner of his eye, he saw a firefighter in full gear, including a light strapped to his helmet, coming toward them. Chad felt his body flood with relief.

"I lost my way," Chad said as he looked up into the man's face, his features distorted through his face mask.

The firefighter pointed down the hall, then headed in that direction, motioning for Chad and Sam to follow. Both men followed him, and within a few minutes were standing in front of the room with the slide. The firefighter stepped to the side to let them enter. Overwhelmed with gratitude and relief, Chad glanced back at him.

"Thanks. I don't think we would have made it out of there without you," Chad acknowledged.

"Don't feel bad. You did everything you could," the firefighter said.

Chad nodded and then glanced over at Sam. When he turned back to the firefighter, there was no sign of him. Chad looked out the door and into the hall, but the smoke covered any sign of him. Chad began to call out, but then stopped, the firefighter's words jumping out at him. *Don't feel bad. You did everything you could.* Chad's eyes opened wide.

"Dad!" he breathed, the realization causing him to lurch forward.

"Chad, hurry," Sam called out, choking on his words.

Chad scanned the darkness in front of him for the firefighter, but there was no sign of him.

"It's hot!" Sam exclaimed.

Pulled from the moment, Chad turned toward Sam, his brow still wrinkled in disbelief.

"The slide. It's hot," Sam repeated.

Chad glanced one more time at the darkness in the hall, not completely sure what had just happened but having no time to sort it out. He turned back to the room, quickly making his way to the full-length window positioned just to the left of the slide. What he saw next instantly snatched the sense of peace he had just felt. Flames that hadn't been there just moments ago were now shooting out from the floors below them, completely engulfing an entire section of the slide.

"There's no way out!" Sam cried, his eyes on Chad. "We're going to die!"

Chad looked from Sam back to the flames, his mind spinning. Somehow he had to get this man out of the building, but how? Their only way out was in flames. Then, as if someone had just whispered the answer in his ear, his eyes fell on the backpack he had given to Anna to use as a carrier for the baby. It was on the floor next to the slide. Apparently, Anna had taken her baby out of the backpack so she could hold him in her arms as she slid down.

Grateful the smoke wasn't thick enough to hide the backpack from view, Chad rushed over to it and unzipped one of the side compartments. At the very bottom, he found two small packages, each no bigger than a wallet. When a firefighter knew that he was not going to make it out of a fire, as a last resort he would take out his heat-resistant tarp and pull it over him like a tent. The liner was designed to withstand extremely high temperatures, but even so, many firefighters still died inside the tents, their lungs fried by the intense heat. Chad handed Sam one of the packages.

"What's this?" Sam asked, holding it up.

"A fireproof liner. Open it!" Chad urged. "We'll cover ourselves with them and slide down the shoot. It might get hot, but hopefully they'll keep us alive."

"This is crazy," Sam barked.

"Just do it," Chad demanded.

Sam looked terrified, but he pulled the liner from its package and began to wrap it around himself. Then, doing as Chad directed, he climbed cautiously up onto the slide. "I don't think I can do this."

"Yes, you can," Chad said. "Now cover your head and don't pull the liner off no matter how hot it gets."

Sam looked doubtful, but he obeyed. Then, before Sam could change his mind, Chad gave him a push. The last thing he heard was Sam's scream disappearing into the night. Chad rushed to the window but couldn't see anything at the base of the building except for flames and thick, dark smoke. Not wanting the fire to get any worse, Chad wrapped his own liner around himself and climbed up onto the slide. Feeling every muscle in his body contract, he let go. A second later, he too was screaming down the slide, his body wrapped in the thin liner.

The second he hit the section of the slide that was surrounded by fire, he felt the heat, the burning in his lungs. He held tight to the liner, knowing that the thin barrier was all that stood between himself and death. Then, in a split second, he was through it, his body slamming hard into the debris in the large dumpster. Slightly dazed, he slowly pushed the liner off his head and looked up at the building that towered above him. Flames were everywhere, climbing higher and higher into the night sky, threatening to destroy everything they touched. Somewhere off to his left he could hear Sam calling out his name. Chad mumbled something about being okay, but his mind was elsewhere, his thoughts flying back to the firefighter who had just saved their lives. He could hear his voice, the words speaking to his soul. *Don't feel bad. You did everything you could.* For the first time in almost a year, Chad felt an immense weight lifted from his shoulders. He glanced at the third-story window, the flames now rising to that level. Then he lifted his eyes beyond that to the sky, even though it was dark with smoke. It was then that he felt the first raindrop fall on his face. He shook his head in wonder as the drops steadily increased until they became a downpour, causing steam to rise up from the building next to him, slowly extinguishing the flames that were shooting out from shattered windows everywhere. With the rain now mingled with his tears, Chad smiled.

"Thank you," he whispered, somehow knowing that his father was smiling down at him. "Thank you."

CHAPTER TWENTY

10:30 P.M. / Los Angeles; The base of Lincoln Tower

James stood still, staring at the smoke billowing from the bottom floors of the high-rise. The inside of the building was still on fire despite the rain. National Guardsmen were scrambling to get the injured a safe distance back while Lawrence was on the phone trying desperately to reach McKenna. All James could do was stare up at the building before him, knowing that the woman he loved was trapped inside. She was alone and terrified and cut off from her only way out. It was then that James saw the helicopter veer toward the top of the skyscraper, then hover just overhead. His heart began to thunder inside his chest while a surge of adrenaline flooded his limbs.

"I'm going up!"

Lawrence glanced at him as he held the phone in his hand. "The lobby's on fire. There's no way in."

"I'm not going through the front door," James said, pulling his rappelling gear from his duffel bag.

"What are you talking about?" Lawrence said, his eyes widening as they fell on the equipment in James's hands.

James was already pulling on his gear. "Just keep trying to get ahold of McKenna. Tell her not to go down but to go to the roof. I'll meet her there and help her onto that chopper."

Lawrence quickly looked up to see the helicopter hovering overhead. He had been so focused on getting ahold of McKenna that he hadn't even seen it. He turned back to James, his eyes searching his face. "Can you really climb forty stories, straight up, *in the rain?*"

James glanced at the white rock that made up the face of the structure. "I will, or I'll die trying."

"And what if I'm not able to get ahold of her to tell her to go to the roof?"

"Then I'll go find her."

Lawrence shielded his face from the rain with one hand as he allowed his eyes to climb the building. "You really do love her," he said, his eyes reflecting a newfound respect mixed with a measure of regret and guilt.

"You have no idea," James said, clicking on the small flashlight in the center of his headband and then starting toward the building.

A moment later he had his first handhold and was on his way up, the climb promising to be the most challenging of his life. Lawrence stood back, watching him for a moment before he turned back to the phone to do as he had been instructed.

"What's he doing?" James heard a woman cry.

"Get down from there!" a soldier shouted. "You're going to get yourself killed."

James continued to climb, his mind tuning out everything but the next rock. He was four stories up before the insanity of what he was doing fully registered. Though he had spent extensive time mountain climbing, mostly so he could paint the stunning views the climbs offered, he had never scaled forty completely vertical stories. He pushed that thought aside, forcing his mind to think only of the rocks and the clamps, filtering out the screams below and the smoke and heat that seemed to be intensifying. He dug his toes into the gaps, stretching and grasping for the next handhold, climbing higher and higher, using clamps only when it was absolutely necessary so he could climb faster. He knew the risks. There could be another earthquake, or the building could finally give way and collapse, or he could simply lose his grip and fall, but he couldn't let himself think of any of that. He had to get to the top and get McKenna on that chopper. It was her only chance.

Finding another handhold, he pulled himself up, his arms and thighs feeling the burn, though he guessed he was still a good twenty-five stories from the top. There were cracks everywhere in the face of the structure, and rocks that had once been firmly cemented in place were now breaking off and falling when he tested them. He was grateful that the National Guard had widened the perimeter around the base of the building so he wouldn't have to worry about anyone getting struck by one of the falling rocks. He continued to climb, every muscle burning with exertion. At some point he began to hear the shattering of glass as the fire inside the building expanded, licking the sills of multiple windows on the bottom floors despite the rain slowing its progress.

James looked above him, straining to see through the pelting rain. The distance left to the roof still seemed like an endless expanse, and his muscles felt as if they were on the verge of collapsing. Taking a deep breath, he pushed forward, willing his body beyond what he had ever deemed possible. He placed another clamp and reached for another handhold, careful not to lose his grip on the slick rocks. When he was a little over halfway up, he stopped to catch his breath, his clothing now completely saturated and his hair clinging to his face. The wind was also starting to pick up, and the combination was quickly dropping the temperature, causing his limbs to shake. He looked up above him again, searching for any sign of the helicopter, but though he could hear the swoosh of the blades, he could see nothing. Knowing that the chopper could leave at any moment, he took another deep breath, then placed a clamp and reached for a rock just to his right, but as he did, the rock gave way, causing him to lose his balance. He began to fall, his limbs swinging wildly in search of the rocks that were just out of reach. Then the safety rope that was secured by the clamp he had just placed snapped, jerking his body to a stop. The force knocked the wind out of him, but he was alive.

As soon as he had regained his wits, he swung himself toward the building and caught hold of the closest rock, planting his feet firmly in a fissure below. His entire body tingled with a rush of relief and adrenaline. He had just cheated death, and he wondered if death itself would retaliate, determined to reclaim its victim. He glanced up at the top of the building, still many floors above him. He repositioned his handhold and, having no time to recover, began to climb.

* * *

McKenna could see a small amount of light just above her in the elevator shaft and guessed that she wasn't far from the opening to the top floor. The View, the restaurant she had been in when the first earthquake hit, took up the entire fortieth floor, and fortunately for her—ironically enough—it was almost entirely framed by large, full-length windows that now seemed to be filtering in a portion of the evening light, though even that was extremely limited. McKenna's arms were shaking violently, but she continued to climb higher, the end finally in sight.

"There's nowhere to go, McKenna."

McKenna screamed, nearly losing her grip.

Sutherland laughed. "The vent shaft's blocked, so I guess I'll just have to take your way up."

Fighting to control her trembling limbs, McKenna quickly grasped another rung on the ladder, trying to speed her pace, though her knee was so swollen it would barely bend.

"You might even make it to the top. But what then?" he asked, taunting her. "This building's coming down."

McKenna tried to ignore him, instead concentrating on her footing so she wouldn't slip and fall, but she could hear him behind her, cutting the distance between them. It was then that she remembered the compact she had in her pocket. She stopped climbing for just a moment, pulled the item out, and then glanced over her shoulder at Sutherland. Realizing with alarm that he was closer than she suspected, she threw the compact at him, striking him in the right hand. He cried out and let go of the ladder with that hand, though he continued to keep his grasp with the other. He began to scream at her, his words vile and threatening. McKenna quickly reached for the next rung on the ladder, hoping that it would take Sutherland a moment to recover, but instead his anger seemed to propel him forward. McKenna looked up at the light that was just a few feet from her now. But Sutherland was right behind her, his breathing coming in angry gasps.

McKenna tried to hurry, but each movement was agony. When she finally reached the fortieth floor and began to pull herself through the opening, Sutherland's hand brushed the ankle of her bad leg. McKenna screamed, then, despite excruciating pain, she kicked at Sutherland with the foot he had tried to grab. One kick found its mark, hitting him squarely in the head. McKenna scrambled through the opening, finding herself sprawled out on the floor. She turned and stared at the dark shaft, but there was no sign of him. Too afraid to walk back to the edge to see if he was still on the stairs, she slowly got to her feet and started toward the stairwell leading to the roof. She climbed the stairs in the dark, fear and adrenaline dulling some of the pain, though her leg continued to throb. She wanted to look over her shoulder, but Sutherland could have been right behind her in the darkness, and she wouldn't have seen him anyway.

Just when she thought she couldn't go another step, she was at the door. Pushing it open, she walked out onto the roof of Lincoln Tower, rain pelting her in the face while the wind from the sharp blades of the helicopter hovering above her swirled her long auburn hair.

She began to wave her arms frantically. "Help!" she screamed, blinking rapidly as she looked up at the belly of the chopper. "Help me!"

The pilot quickly began lowering a metal basket. She hobbled toward it, her heart racing as the wind from the blades continued to swirl the air around her, making it difficult to see. She kept her eyes trained on the basket as it swung dangerously back and forth in the wind. When it finally reached the roof, McKenna hurried to it, feeling a rush of relief sweep through her body. She placed her bad leg in the basket first and was about to put the other one in when she felt someone grab her from behind. The next thing she knew, she was on the ground and Sutherland was hurrying past her. He was heading toward the basket that was now being dragged across the roof of the building as the pilot fought to keep control of the craft with the wind building in intensity.

McKenna slowly got to her feet, her eyes locked on the basket. She started forward just as the helicopter began to lift into the air, the pilot no longer able to hold it steady. Sutherland leaped for the basket, catching hold of one of the sides and causing it to rock precariously. McKenna watched in horror, knowing that she was going to be left behind—that after all of this, Sutherland was going to live and she was going to die. Then, from the corner of her eye, she saw movement near the ledge of the building. She glanced in that direction just as a man climbed over the side. McKenna gasped, not fully comprehending what she was seeing. It was James. He had come for her. James glanced over at her briefly before turning his attention to Sutherland. Getting quickly to his feet, James started toward Sutherland. McKenna stood back and watched the scene unfold, her heart beating wildly.

Sutherland was already three feet off the roof, his feet dangling as he clung to the basket, but in a rush of movement, James dove for him, grabbing him mid-thigh. For a moment, Sutherland maintained his grip on the basket, but as the helicopter began to climb, he slipped, and the two men crashed onto the wet roof with a dull thud. Sutherland was on his feet in seconds, his face wild with rage. He swung at James, catching him squarely in the jaw. James, who had not yet gotten to his feet, went flying backward, his body smacking hard into the roof. McKenna screamed and limped toward them, but there was nothing she could do. Both men were rolling on the ground now, each fighting for his life. McKenna glanced up at the helicopter as a jagged flash of lightning momentarily lit the entire sky. She could see the pilot watching from his vantage point, but the wind was mounting by the second, and she could tell by the way the chopper was rocking that the pilot wasn't going to be able to hold his position much longer.

"Get in!" James screamed, glancing toward McKenna before turning back to Sutherland.

McKenna looked up at the helicopter, then slowly turned her eyes back to James. When he had first climbed over the ledge, he had clearly been miles past exhaustion, but now, with blood spilling from his lip and his right eye dark and swollen, it looked like he was having a hard time just holding his head upright. McKenna shook her head, knowing that she would never be able to leave him. She glanced up at the pilot one last time and then started toward James, hearing the sound of the blades cut through the wind as the helicopter broke away, disappearing into the night. Knowing that she had just sealed her own fate, McKenna hobbled over to help James. Sutherland was striking him repeatedly, cursing and screaming at James for causing him to miss his only chance of rescue. James lifted his head to McKenna, his eyes barely able to focus before he fell back, his body limp. Sutherland staggered to his feet and turned to McKenna. She recoiled at the look in his eyes. She had never seen such raw enmity. He started toward her, his fists clutching at his side and his face so twisted in rage that he no longer even remotely resembled the man she had met at lunch earlier that day. McKenna stepped back, desperate for any escape—even the building's collapse. Instead, she felt her back brush up against the door to the roof. It was over. There was nowhere else to go. McKenna closed her eyes, hoping that death would at least come quickly. Then she heard it: a solid thud followed by the sound of a body crumpling to the ground. She opened her eyes to see James standing before her holding a rappelling clamp, his chest rising and falling and his eyes on Sutherland, who lay unconscious at his feet. McKenna rushed forward, falling into James's outstretched arms.

"You shouldn't have come for me," McKenna cried as she buried her face in his chest, shaking as she sobbed.

"I had to," he whispered.

McKenna pulled back and looked at him, her eyes rushing over the familiar features of his face. "I love you," she said, saying out loud what she had known deep down for a long time.

Relief filled his eyes. He reached out and wiped at her damp cheeks, then pulled her back into his arms. "I love you too."

"I'm scared," McKenna said quietly, flinching as a threatening clap of thunder shook the ground beneath them.

"I know," James soothed, pulling her closer, as if he could protect her from the inevitable.

At that moment the helicopter rose up from behind the side of the building, the blades swiping boldly through the air. McKenna and James stood back and stared at the chopper in disbelief.

"Come on," James shouted over the swish of the blades. "We don't have much time."

He grabbed her hand, and the two of them started across the roof, rain slapping them both in the face. The helicopter stopped just to their right and began to drop the basket. James leaped up and grabbed the bottom, pulling it down toward them.

"Get in!" he yelled, grabbing one of McKenna's arms to help her.

Once she was inside, she reached her hand out to him. He moved to grab it, but then turned around, his eyes on the man still lying on the roof of the building. He turned back to her.

"I'll be right back," he said hastily.

"*No!*" McKenna screamed, though the sound of the blades drowned out the sound of her voice. "There's no time!"

But James was already running back toward the still form. He reached down, but in his weakened condition, he wasn't able to lift Sutherland. Instead, he grabbed hold of the man's arms and began to drag him toward the helicopter. Again, the basket began to slide across the roof as the pilot fought the storm.

"Run!" McKenna screamed as the basket dragged her away from him. James stumbled and fell, smacking hard onto the roof.

"Get up!" McKenna shouted as the basket finally came to a stop just a few feet from the edge of the building.

James staggered to his feet, then reached down and, straining with the effort, lifted Sutherland into his arms, his limbs trembling as he stumbled toward the basket. Once he reached it, McKenna helped pull Sutherland into it before reaching her hand out to James. He took it, and then began to lift his leg over the side. At that moment, the ground began to shake. James lost his balance and fell back onto the roof. McKenna looked at him, wild-eyed as the noise that was now roaring all around them continued to mount until it seemed to permeate everything.

"It's going down!" McKenna screamed, knowing that they were all a split second from death.

James scrambled to his feet, but the rumbling was increasing, and the base of the building was already giving way. James's eyes locked on McKenna just seconds before the ground beneath him buckled and plummeted. He jumped, grabbing hold of the side of the basket, causing it to swing so sharply that it almost tipped McKenna out. At the same time, the helicopter began to lift away from the building. McKenna stared down in shock as what was left of Lincoln Tower folded in on top of itself and crumbled to the ground, a large cloud of dust billowing up from the mountain of destruction. Then her eyes flew to James, who was struggling to maintain his grip on the side of the basket. She hurried over to him, grabbing him by the wrists, though she knew she would never be able to pull him over the side in the condition she was in and with the helicopter maneuvering around the other skyscrapers that dotted downtown Los Angeles.

"Hold on!" she cried.

James closed his eyes and grimaced. "I don't know if I can."

McKenna knew that his body had been pushed far past its breaking point and that he was likely only holding on by sheer will. Her eyes raced over the basket for something to help him, but there was nothing. Then her eyes flew back to James, her attention drawn to the rappelling gear still strapped to his body. She got down on her belly, reached out, and grabbed hold of a short rope dangling from his waist that had a clasp at the end, then quickly pulled it up.

"Hurry," James begged, his fingers already slipping.

McKenna threaded the rope through the bars of the basket, then reached out and hooked the clasp to one of the metal loops hanging from the rappelling gear strapped to his waist. She had no sooner hooked the clasp in place when James lost his grip and fell. The basket immediately jerked to the side once the slack pulled taut, but the clasp held. McKenna leaned over the basket.

"Are you okay?" she shouted, shuddering at the thought of how close he had come to falling.

He nodded his head and gave her a small smile.

McKenna slumped to the bottom of the basket, only then feeling the pain in her own body resurface. She glanced down through the open metal basket at the city below. Steam was rising from fires that were scattered everywhere, while a steady rain continued to pour down on them. Then she glanced at James, still dangling below her. He had come for her, had risked his own life to save her. The feeling that flooded through her was powerful, almost taking her breath away. He loved her—he always had. And it had been her fear of losing that love—that friendship—that had stopped her from admitting how she really felt about him, even to herself. She looked down at him, the tears now streaming down her face mingling with the rain that continued to fall.

"I love you," she whispered, the words a release as she allowed herself to feel for the first time what she knew he had felt all along.

EPILOGUE

Three months later / New York City

McKenna glanced across the room at James, who was surrounded by a large semicircle of elegantly dressed people. One woman, a tall, slender brunette, kept touching his arm and laughing, hanging on his every word.

"Could she be any more obvious?" Tatum said to McKenna, rolling her eyes as she looked over at the woman.

McKenna just smiled and shook her head.

"Maybe you should rescue him," Tatum said.

Just then James looked over his shoulder and spotted McKenna. He at once began waving her over, his expression bordering on desperation. Tatum smiled. "The man has absolutely no idea how to handle his newfound fame or money."

"He'll figure it out," McKenna said.

"Until then, you better help him, before that brunette gets her acrylic nails into him."

McKenna handed Tatum her ginger ale. "I'll be back."

"Hurry, before she invites him out for a day of Botox and Slim-Fast shakes," Tatum said, tilting her head and looking at McKenna knowingly.

McKenna shook her head, though she couldn't help smirking as she started toward James, who reached his hand out to pull her next to him, his expression filled with relief. He bent and kissed her cheek.

"Thank you," he whispered, his breath sending a warm shiver through her. Then he turned back to his admirers. "I'd like you all to meet my fiancé."

McKenna felt her heart race as he gazed at her. The tall brunette looked like she had just lost a beauty pageant. She immediately made an excuse to leave and hurried over to another artist who also had his work on display.

"Will you excuse me?" James said to the group as he took McKenna by the arm and escorted her down the hall. "This is crazy," he said once they were out of earshot.

"You'd better get used to it," McKenna said, squeezing his arm.

"Hey, I've spent my entire adult life as a starving artist. This is way out of my comfort zone."

"If it will make you feel any better," McKenna began as they approached one of the pieces of art he had on exhibit, "I'll fix you ramen noodles once a month after we're married, just so you don't have withdrawals."

James laughed; then, taking her by surprise, he bent and kissed her, his touch once again taking her breath away. When he pulled back, his expression instantly sobered. "Are you worried about the trial tomorrow?"

McKenna shrugged, though just thinking about coming face-to-face with Alan Sutherland again made her skin crawl. "I just want to get it over with."

"How's Nathan doing?"

"I talked to Judge Rinehart this morning, and he said Nathan is recovering more quickly than his doctors anticipated."

"I'm glad to hear that," James said as they both turned toward the canvas next to them. McKenna shook her head, still in awe over the change that had taken place in James's art over the past few months. The transformation was incredible. The passion that his work had lacked before was now evident in every stroke.

"It's beautiful," McKenna said, taking in the rich colors and subtle intricacies before her eyes finally fell on the small SOLD sign next to it. "It sold!" she exclaimed, turning back to James.

"I know," he said, his eyes showing his pleasure.

"Who bought it?" McKenna asked, excited for James but also a little sad at losing such a beautiful work of art.

"I don't know," James said thoughtfully.

"Well, I do!"

They both turned to the man who had approached unnoticed.

"Dad?" McKenna said, unaware that her father had even been at the exhibit.

"I thought it would look great over the mantel in the study," Lawrence said, eyeing the painting appreciatively before turning his eyes back to his daughter.

"But what about the picture of you and mom you have there now?"

Lawrence smiled. "Not my study, McKenna . . . yours." Then he extended the bill of sale to James.

McKenna let out a squeal, causing a few heads to turn, though neither she nor James—nor even Lawrence—seemed to care. "I love you," she said, throwing her arms around her father's neck.

He laughed but then quickly turned his eyes to James as McKenna stepped back. "The picture's impressive—but not nearly as impressive as the artist. I owe you everything for what you did."

"I don't need anything but your daughter," James said, smiling at McKenna.

Lawrence nodded as he slapped James affectionately on the back. Then he turned to McKenna. "I was also thinking that something else would look really good on your mantel below the painting."

McKenna looked at her father curiously. "What's that?"

Lawrence handed her a thick manila envelope. "Maybe a best seller."

The puzzled look she gave her father as she began to open the envelope changed to disbelief once she had. "How did you get this?"

"I saw the manuscript on your coffee table a month ago and . . . borrowed it," Lawrence began, shrugging sheepishly. "I stayed up most of that night reading it."

McKenna's eyes widened in surprise, though the surprise was quickly replaced by apprehension. *"And?"*

"And . . . it was amazing."

McKenna let her breath out, a giant smile lighting her face.

"Your fiancé was right all along. You're a good attorney, but your heart isn't in it." He pointed at the manuscript. "It's in this . . . in every word."

McKenna felt her eyes welling up, though she couldn't speak. Instead, she looked first at her father and then at James, a thought suddenly striking her. Though the two most important men in her life were vastly different, they were surprisingly very much the same.

* * *

Provo, Utah

Jax got up from his seat on the stand and walked to the podium, feeling every eye in the chapel on him. He placed his new set of leather scriptures on the podium, his eyes going briefly to Hunter's name embossed on the front. Hunter's parents had given them to Jax just before the meeting started, insisting that they knew Hunter would want Jax to have them. Jax felt his throat constrict as he thought of the gesture. He looked out at the congregation. The entire first row was crowded with different girls he had dated in high school and college, each of them smiling brightly, as if to tell him that they would still be there when he got home. Embarrassed, he cleared his throat and looked away, his eyes going to the middle of the room where his friends were seated. Payson was sitting next to Gwen, who had a tasteful scarf wrapped around her head to cover the hair loss after several rounds of chemotherapy. Though she was certainly not out of the woods yet, the doctors were pleased with her progress, and, as of a week ago, they had officially declared that she was in remission. Jax's eyes then fell back on Payson, who was beaming up at him. The only thing that had even remotely compared with the excitement of Gwen's acceptance of Payson's wedding proposal two months ago had been Jax's surprise declaration that he was going on a mission. Even now Jax could vividly remember the look on Payson's face, followed by the crushing bear hug.

Then Jax glanced a little farther down the aisle to Tristin. He smiled at her, surprised once again that he had never noticed how pretty she was. Ever since the earthquake, he and Tristin had spent a lot of time together. In fact, though Jax had made up his mind to keep his focus on his mission rather than girls, she was the one girl he honestly hoped would write to him.

Finally, Jax's gaze fell on Hunter's parents, who were sitting next to his own. Hunter's mom's eyes were red and swollen, but she was smiling at him; Hunter's dad had his arm wrapped protectively around her shoulders. Jax swallowed hard before attempting to speak.

"Good morning, brothers and sisters. I'm going to make this short, mainly because Brother Hanson took up all the time." Everyone chuckled, including Brother Hanson. Jax took a deep breath. "A few months ago, I thought I'd be snorkeling off the coast of Maui instead of leaving on a mission. But I guess the Lord had something else in mind."

Jax felt his throat catch as he thought about Hunter and all the changes that had taken place since the earthquake. He saw Payson nodding his head knowingly, encouraging him on. Jax tightened his grip on the podium and turned his eyes to Hunter's parents.

"One of my best friends passed away a few months ago." Again Jax stopped, fighting to keep control of his emotions. "He had been waiting since he was twelve years old for the day he could leave on his mission. I was with him when he died, and he told me that his one regret was that he wouldn't get to serve. I told him that he *was* going to serve . . . just not here." Jax glanced at Hunter's mom again and could see that her cheeks were wet. "But what he didn't know . . . what *I* didn't know at the time . . . was that he already was serving. I'm going on a mission today because of his example." Jax could feel tears streaming down his face. "Hunter went quietly around doing good, his big, goofy smile pulling you in." Jax could see Payson laugh and several others nod their heads.

"Even Hunter's final hours were spent helping others." For the first time, Jax looked over at Lakesha. She was sitting in the back, looking a little uncomfortable since she wasn't a member. He smiled at her, appreciative that she had come all the way from L.A. at his invitation. "But that was just Hunter. He was so grateful to his Heavenly Father for the gospel that had completely changed his life that he wanted to tell everyone. Hunter knew that God loved him, but, more importantly, Hunter loved God more than anyone. And it was that very love that directed every part of his life. So, instead of snorkeling off the coast of Maui," Jax began, feeling a warmth slowly envelop him as though someone had just placed a hand on his shoulder. "I've decided to trade in my flippers for a couple of black suits. And, with the Lord's help, share the gospel with everyone I can in Los Angeles."

* * *

One year after the earthquake / Los Angeles

Justice smiled as his son stuck his whole hand into his birthday cake and then shoved his cake-filled fist toward his mouth, smearing white and red frosting all over his little face. Anna laughed as she snapped several pictures.

"Look at him! The kid eats just like his dad."

Justice glanced from Anna to Chad, who was smiling from ear to ear, though Justice wasn't certain if it was because of the teasing he was dishing out or because of Lyssa, the attractive dental hygienist wrapped affectionately in his arms. The two of them had been dating for just over six months, and from the constant grin that always seemed to be on both their faces these days, they were obviously in love.

"I can't believe Payson's a year old already," Anna said as she walked toward the sink to get a washcloth.

The smile that had been on Justice's face slowly began to fade as he reluctantly allowed his thoughts to drift to the very thing he had tried for days to forget. Today was not just his son's birthday, but it was also the one-year anniversary of the L.A. earthquake. Justice felt his chest tighten, a myriad of different emotions assaulting him at once. He quickly slipped into the family room and sat down in his recliner, not wanting to spoil the mood that the others were enjoying.

"You're thinking about Archer, aren't you?"

Justice looked up to see Chad enter the room, the lighthearted expression that had been on his face also gone. Justice shook his head before letting the trapped air out of his lungs. "I'm spending the day with my family, and Archer's not—and he never will again." Justice could feel the familiar pang in the pit of his stomach, the one he felt every time he thought about Archer's two young, fatherless boys.

"How are they doing?"

Justice shrugged. "It's been a tough year for them. For the first few months, they kept expecting their dad to come back—like he was just out of town or something." Justice's throat constricted. "Then when they realized that he wasn't coming back . . ." He shook his head, the emotions that were rising threatening to choke him.

"Justice, it wasn't your fault. Archer knew what he was doing when he gave you his mask."

Justice nodded. "I know, and even though I don't like it, I can live with that part. It's those boys never seeing their dad again that gets me."

They both looked up as Anna and Lyssa entered the room, the two of them laughing about something. Chad shot Justice a glance that said they would talk later, though Justice was already regretting saying anything at all. Rehashing everything just reopened old wounds, and he didn't want that—not today. Justice was plotting how he was going to end the evening early when the doorbell rang. Anna, who had just placed little Payson on the floor next to the toy fire truck that Chad and Lyssa had given him for his birthday, quickly headed for the entryway. A moment later Justice heard her excitedly greeting someone at the door. He turned around in his seat just in time to see Anna escorting two young men in suits into the family room.

"Justice," Anna began, her whole face aglow, "this is Elder Hampton . . . Payson's friend . . . and his companion, Elder Wells."

Justice stood and extended his hand to both men, though his eyes quickly returned to Elder Hampton. "It's nice to meet you. Anna mentioned that you were serving here."

Elder Hampton nodded. "I've been in California for several months now, but I just got transferred to L.A. a few days ago and thought I'd stop in and say hello." Then Elder Hampton's eyes went to the little boy playing contentedly on the floor. "This little guy must be Payson."

Anna walked over and scooped up her son, who squirmed in her arms and let out a squeal. "He's past his cuddly stage," she said as she placed Payson back on the floor and then gestured for the elders to take a seat on the couch.

Chad stood and retrieved a couple of chairs from the kitchen for himself and Lyssa. Then all of them sat down in the family room. For a few minutes they talked about Payson and Gwen, since Chad was just as anxious to hear about them as Anna was. Then their conversation meandered to the earthquake and the recovery effort going on in L.A., along with the entire Pacific coast. When there was a lull in the conversation, Elder Hampton turned and looked at Justice, his eyes seeming to go right through him.

"Mr. Stevens, would you mind if we shared a message with you?"

Justice had been fully prepared to tactfully decline, but, instead, he held the elder's gaze. The guy was so young, and yet there seemed to be a depth to him that intrigued Justice. The Church had certainly made an impact in Anna's life. Maybe the kid did have something worth listening to.

Elder Hampton picked up his scriptures and began thumbing through them, though he didn't seem to be looking for any scripture in particular. A moment later, he stopped. Then, after clearing his throat, he began to read. "John 15:13. 'Greater love hath no man than this, that a man lay down his life for his friends.'"

After he had read the verse, he closed the Bible and lifted his eyes to Justice, who suddenly felt as though he couldn't breathe. Justice glanced over at Anna and could see that she had tears in her eyes.

"Mr. Stevens," Elder Hampton continued, his own eyes wet, "I feel impressed to tell you about a friend of mine who gave his life for me . . . and for you. His name is Jesus Christ."

ABOUT THE AUTHOR

Sonia O'Brien was born in Germany and raised in Utah, although she has spent much of her adult life in the South. She has been married to her husband for seventeen years and has six children, whom she adores. Readers who appreciate her work will also enjoy *The Raging Sea* and *Perfect Shot*. Anyone interested in writing to Sonia can send an e-mail to obrien.eric@sbcglobal.net.